MY LORD RAVEN

KNIGHTS OF THE ROYAL HOUSEHOLD

JAN SCARBROUGH

SADDLE HORSE PRESS, LLC

My Lord Raven

First published in 2017. This edition published in 2023.
Copyright © 2017 by Jan Scarbrough

Digital ISBN: 978-0-9971920-0-1
Print ISBN: 978-0-9971919-9-8

Edited By: Karen Block
Cover Design By: The Killion Group, Inc.

This edition is published by agreement with Saddle Horse Press LLC, PO Box 221543, Louisville, KY 40252.

❀ Created with Vellum

INTRODUCTION

To protect what little family she has left, Lady Catrin Fitzalan switches places with her cousin when King Edward orders the pious girl to wed his royal champion, a vicious knight called the King's Raven. Rumors abound that this savage is responsible for the deaths of Lady Catrin's father and brother. How can she allow her sweet cousin to wed a murderer?

Bran ap Madog, bastard son of a Welsh prince, has devoted his life to serving the English king. His badge is the raven, a creature that feeds off rotting spoils, just as Bran feeds off the spoils of war. Now he wants a reward for his service: a wealthy wife and the land and power she can bring him.

But there's another side to the rapacious black birds Bran has chosen for his badge. Social and family-oriented, ravens mate for life. Which gives them something Bran never had— a family, a sense of belonging, and a rightful place in the world. Bran has fought for everything he's ever had. But his last battle, with his new wife, may cost him the one thing he isn't prepared to lose: his heart.

DEDICATION

For Karen Block,
Thanks for your support, your faith, and your sharp red pen.

CHAPTER ONE

The King's Tournament, near Shrewsbury
October 1283

"Let me pass!"

Lady Catrin Fitzalan, chest heaving from her haste, glared at the tall, imposing knight who barred her way. How dare he block the path? Her brother Gilbert waited for her at his tent where he made ready for the king's forthcoming mêlée.

Yet, the knight said nothing, just stood in her way, his mail-clad legs spread in a determined stance.

The back of her neck prickled with unease. Before her stood a fearsome creature in full battle armor, broad of shoulder and chest. He wore no crest upon his great helm or coat of arms upon his black surcoat. Why did he glower at her through the sights of his visor?

Drawing an angry breath, she made a fist. "If I were a man, I'd force you out of my way!"

The brute raised his leather gauntlet and pointed at the

red silk scarf she gripped in her other hand. "If you were a man," he mocked her in a carefree voice, "I would not find myself seeking your favor."

Her chin came up. She clutched the scarf. Did he think she'd part with her precious favor on the day of her brother's first tournament? She and her cousin Olwen had spent hours on its creation, each embroidering a Rothmore golden lion rampant on opposite ends of the silk stole for Gilbert to tie on his sleeve this special day.

"Stand aside," she ordered. "You will gain no favor from me."

"Then you will not pass this way." His words hissed through the breathing holes in his face guard. "I will have your favor."

Catrin swayed, frustration simmering into fury. "You presume too much, knave!"

"My lady, you dishonor me." He bowed slightly. "I am the king's servant, but I'm no unscrupulous boy."

He leisurely removed the helm from his head, revealing harsh and rugged features. Black eyebrows drew into a frown above the bridge of his straight, hawkish nose. As custom, his upper lip was clean-shaven. She could see no more of him, for he wore a mail coif with a ventail wrapped under his chin.

Yet, she could not tear her gaze from his glittering and wickedly beautiful eyes. He had a wild-blooded look about him that stole her breath away. For an instant, she thought him threatening. What else must account for the strange flutter in her chest?

"As God is my witness, I mean you no harm." His eyes sparkled and a smile now tilted one corner of his mouth. "I only ask for part of your favor, a simple silken token to carry with me into the lists, for I have no maiden fair. Will you honor me, my lady?"

Dare she believe the sincerity of his request? His flattery? Catrin bit her lip, looking for a way to escape. She'd no more time for banter. The tournament would soon start, and she must deliver the scarf to Gilbert.

She glanced at the knight again. The amused light in his eyes darkened.

"Oh, very well," she said, abruptly making up her mind to cover the surprising tingle of attraction. "My brother waits. I have no time for your foolish game."

"I insist, my lady."

"You may not have it all." Catrin held the scarf between her outstretched hands.

Her tormentor smiled slightly, lifted his sword, and deftly sliced the scarf in two.

Catching her breath, she thrust her right hand forward. "Take this if you must."

Bowing as any chivalrous warrior might, he accepted the jagged piece of silk without a thank you and stepped aside with a courteous bow. "You may pass, my lady."

Catrin picked up her skirts and bolted from him, sprinting as fast as she'd run during childhood days in the fields near Clun Castle.

"GILBERT, STAND STILL!" Catrin clapped her hands impatient with her brother's shifting from foot to foot.

Dressed and ready for the tournament, Gilbert wore a red surcoat emblazoned with the Rothmore coat of arms—a golden lion standing on one hind foot with a foreleg raised above the other and the head in profile. He cradled his great helm under an arm.

Gilbert's squire stood beside him, holding the reins of his spirited destrier in one hand and the tourney lance in another.

"You will be proud of me this day, sweet sister."

"I always am proud of you, my lord," she said, her heart filled with love.

He winked. "Get on with it then, sister, for I have important men's work to do."

"Hush, you ungrateful boy," Catrin said in a playful tone.

As long as she could remember, she'd cared for Gilbert. Their mother had died in childbirth with him. Being two years older, she'd taken on the role of mother. Gilbert had always been such a capricious child. Yet, now he was a man full grown, recently knighted, and since the murder of their father, a powerful earl in his own right.

She tied the torn scarf around his mail-clad arm. Lifting up on tiptoes, she kissed his cheek. *Dear God, I love him.*

In her eyes, Gilbert was yet a boy, playing at being a man. One day he'd compete with the best knights in the land. God willing, he'd return from the lists in one piece today.

"Be safe, my lord brother."

He laughed, impatient with her. "Aye, Catrin, you need not fear."

She gave him a quick hug for luck before he turned from her.

A SHORT TIME LATER, Catrin elbowed her way through the crush of bodies assembled on the edge of the lists, a level and cleared field the king's men had fenced to make ready for the mock combat to come. Trumpets blared and a hush of anticipation settled over the crowd.

'Twas a sunny, autumn day with a chill in the air. Everyone was in high spirits, because of King Edward's triumph over the rebellious Welsh. Tomorrow the king would execute Daffyd, the traitorous Prince of Wales, but today Edward licensed this tournament "for pleasure" so his barons might celebrate.

For the first time since the death of her father on Lammas Day, a twinge of hope filled Catrin. How could it not? Gilbert was so anxious to prove himself.

A yeoman guard at the foot of the steps let her pass, and Catrin climbed to the temporary scaffold facing the list. Inching forward through the highborn throng of finely clad and perfumed ladies, she claimed a spot at the railing.

Warriors mounted on specially trained destriers dotted the field below. King Edward's household knights formed a line on the right, and on the left stood the ranks of competing barons. Vivid pennants of vermilion, blue, and white fluttered in the wind. Lances painted every color caught the afternoon sunlight, flashing bold and bright.

Catrin's pulse raced. She leaned against the rough railing, attempting to catch a view of her brother, but even with identifying crests and personal coats of arms, she found it impossible to locate him.

Knights held their straining horses and couched their lances. Suddenly, the herald sounded a trumpet and a man cut the long cord separating the opposing forces. The free-for-all started with a thunderous charge and shrill cries of "Huzzah!"

"Where is your cousin Olwen?" the Countess of Rothmore asked over the din of cracking lances and shouts of men.

Catrin tensed at the sound of her stepmother's voice and gripped the railing. Long held resentment settled hard against her heart. Before she spoke, she prayed for Christian charity, hoping to temper the unholy dislike for Isadora, the woman who'd come to live at Clun Castle as a sixteen-year-old bride eleven years earlier.

"She chose to remain at the pavilion," Catrin answered as evenly as possible, not looking at the older woman who stood behind her.

"More than likely closeted with her prayer beads," Isadora snorted.

Catrin turned to glare at her stepmother and bit her lower lip to hold back harsh words. The former Isadora Mortimer, young second wife of her father Earl Rothmore, John Fitzalan, was of high birth and carried herself erect and with grace as if she were Queen Eleanor herself.

"You know she fears for Gilbert's safety," Catrin said. "Olwen cannot bear to see him hurt and so is saying prayers for his well-being."

Isadora shook her head. "'Twould be better if she were more concerned about her own welfare. She needs a husband, else Edward will choose one for her."

"He will do that no matter, my lady. We are royal wards," Catrin reminded her and rudely turned back to the battle.

Left and right, riders tumbled from lathered horses. Knights who remained astride drew swords, calling for those downed to accept surrender. Others rushed to their comrades' defense. Yet she didn't spy Gilbert. Concern weighed upon her. Then the herald sounded retreat, thus ending the rough-and-tumble mêlée. King Edward's men had won the day.

The spectacle was not over. But not for long.

From the end of the list, a lone knight, garbed all in black galloped to the middle of the field and reined his big, black destrier in circles, challenging one and all. An unknown knight riding alone into the lists 'twas not uncommon.

However, a buzz of curiosity erupted from the crowd, for the black knight bore neither crest nor distinction upon his person. Tipping his lance to the stands where King Edward and Queen Eleanor watched, he acknowledged them. The crowd cheered.

Catrin stiffened her back. Her heart skipped once, twice. When no one accepted his challenge, the knight spurred his horse around the edge of the stockade, the great animal's head bobbing with each prancing step. Billowing with every jarring motion was her silky scarf, now tied to the anonymous knight's right arm.

Catrin touched her lips with cold fingers. *'Tis the black knight who blocked my path.* She sucked in a sharp breath. Why did her pulse suddenly beat with such fierce passion? Was she secretly flattered by the man's rude attention?

Lady Rothmore spat the name like a curse. "The King's Raven."

Catrin glanced at her stepmother. "He wears no badge. How do you know it's the King's Raven?"

"'Twas disclosed the black knight would compete today as king's champion."

Her stepmother's words sank in, and a slow dread crawled through Catrin's stomach. The King's Raven was reputed to murder in cold blood, ravish women, and then plunder his victims' possessions for his own gain. To think she'd given her favor to this black-hearted beast, the very man many people accused of murdering her father.

"How can you be certain 'tis he?" Catrin asked.

"Lord Leighton told me the black knight would ride."

Guy de Hastings, Lord Leighton. Catrin disliked the family's pompous neighbor who coveted their land. The baron had brought her father's body home to Clun Castle that dreadful day several months earlier. Claiming to have witnessed the murder, Lord Leighton was oddly too far away to have prevented it. His failure hadn't stopped him from blaming the king's champion of doing the deed, yet he presented no proof, nothing but his word, which was oft maligned. From that accusation, word had spread, indicting the knight of the royal household.

Many wondered aloud if Leighton had committed the crime instead. Others said a murderer would not have so boldly brought the earl's body home.

With no further witnesses and no proof, King Edward believed his favorite, not the feckless baron. Thus, the king had dismissed Leighton's indictment and the matter was dropped.

Except by Catrin.

She clamped her teeth together, fighting frustration and a simmering anger. Justice had not been served. Her father's murderer went unpunished.

At that moment, a stir among the spectators grew into a cheer. Catrin's attention shifted to the far end of the lists. Another lone knight entered the field, signaling acceptance of the challenge.

Catrin held her breath.

The Rothmore coat of arms.

"What does Gilbert do?" Isadora demanded.

Always Catrin had defended her brother and now would be no exception. She stiffened, setting her jaw. 'Twould not do for Isadora to see her sudden fear. "Gilbert vowed to make me proud today," she said softly. "Mayhap he believes Leighton's accusation and seeks revenge."

Trumpets blared again. The challenge was now met. Almost directly in front of her, the black knight settled his destrier, controlling the horse with one hand and holding him back as he readied the steed to run the course. Then he lowered his lance over the left side of the horse's neck and tucked the butt end of the weapon under his arm. At the far end of the field, Gilbert did the same.

"He's no match for a seasoned knight." A cruel smirk curled Isadora's lip. "The foolish lad will be unseated."

Catrin held her tongue. She feared the same and even worse but refused to acknowledge her concern. Her pulse quickened. Would that she held Gilbert in her hands right now, for she wanted to box his ears.

The spectators murmured in expectation. Then silence fell. Catrin only had eyes for her younger brother. Gilbert leaned forward in the saddle, tucked his chin and raised his shield. He pushed his feet forward in his stirrups and charged. The crowd screamed their encouragement.

Catrin's gaze darted to the black knight who had urged his horse forward. She swallowed fast and hard, sickened by the power of the rushing steed. Gilbert stood no chance. His opponent rode with more experience and confidence. Even at a distance, the disparity was evident.

"Wait…Wait…" she muttered, straining forward as if to will her brother patience.

At the last second, the seasoned knight moved first, thrust forward, rising in his stirrups, and struck Gilbert's shield, the full weight of man and horse behind his single blow. The force jerked her brother's lance upward and knocked the boy backward off the horse. He landed in the dirt. The crowd cheered for the king's champion.

Catrin's fingers bit into the wood of the railing. She couldn't go to Gilbert, although every fiber in her being urged her to run across the field to his defense. She would not dishonor her brother. Nay, he had accepted the challenge. Now let him suffer the consequences.

Nonetheless, she held her breath until Gilbert struggled to his feet.

A hue and cry arose. "Look! The Earl of Rothmore uses no coronel!" someone shouted. "His lance is not blunted!"

"The young earl fights unfairly!" another exclaimed.

"Heavenly Father," Isadora murmured, "the crowd speaks truth."

The implications of Gilbert's actions chilled Catrin. She lifted her hand once more to her lips, knowing full well her brother's actions dishonored the whole family. By fighting with an improperly fitted tourney lance, Gilbert intention had not been sport. He had tried to kill the royal champion.

Thus, he had struck a symbolic blow against King Edward himself.

The black knight rode forward calling for her brother's surrender, but Gilbert stood his ground, not backing away from the challenge. The crowd cried out when Gilbert drew his sword, the mighty, razor-sharp sword of the Rothmore earldom.

God save him! What was her foolish brother thinking? Revenge was not worth his death.

The black knight slid from his horse. In a slow and deliberate move, he turned his back, a sign of great disrespect, and drew his tourney sword from the sheath on his saddle. When he faced Gilbert, her brother charged. Squires and tournament judges rushed forward to stop the fight. Spectators gasped.

'Twas no contest. With one swift motion, the champion disarmed Gilbert, sending the Rothmore war sword sailing high into the air.

The family's disgrace was complete. Yet Gilbert lived. The King's Raven had spared the life of the brother she held most dear.

Catrin shut her eyes for a moment and gave thanks for the black knight's forbearance. She had lost too many of her family. How could she bear to lose another?

CHAPTER TWO

"Remove my helm, Rhys!" Sir Bran ap Madog shouted to his sergeant-at-arms as he approached his encampment. He'd taken a blow to the head during the second mêlée of the afternoon. Now his great helm was stuck, molded to his head by the glancing blow of an opponent.

Rhys scowled at the King's Champion and pointed to a spot of hard ground before an anvil. Uttering a guttural sound, Bran lowered himself on one knee and turned his head, feeling the firm hands of his sergeant shoving his great helm onto the iron block.

Accustomed to the smaller man's familiar manner, for they had been companions for over ten years, Bran didn't mind his sergeant's brusqueness. He simply wanted the constricting headpiece removed. 'Twas hot and his breath stale. He tasted the salt of his own sweat.

With the first strike of the hammer ringing in his ears, Bran steeled himself against the further shock of more blows. He much preferred the freer Celtic way of fighting, unimpeded by mail and helm. True death came swifter and surer, but there were always trade-offs in life. That's what made it interesting.

Strangely, he was no longer afraid to die. Too many battles fought and too much death seen had taught him not to fear.

Of late, however, he regretted his dissipated lifestyle. For he wanted more out of life. His own land. A helpmate. A son to rightfully carry his name.

Sadly, his name was all he owned.

On the sands of the Holy Lands, King Edward had knighted him and then dubbed him the "King's Raven."

"Cultivate a ruthless reputation," the king had ordered. "Go out and spy for the crown."

The hammer crashed once again upon metal. The muscles in Bran's jaws locked his mouth into a grimace but his thoughts focused elsewhere.

Over the years, Bran had won much by living the life of a knight-errant and serving the king. But he had paid a heavy price. Now, weariness settled like bad mead into the pit of his stomach. He was tired of the deception he fostered in the king's name. He was tired of fighting.

"Try it now." The sergeant's voice sounded far away.

Bran raised his head and put his hands on both sides of the pitted helm. How many times had Rhys beaten out such dents? Hundreds perchance? How many times had Bran faced an imposing challenger and come away the victor?

Turning his neck, Bran lifted the helm and freed himself from its burden. A rush of brisk air greeted him. He could breathe again. Rhys took the headpiece, and Bran slowly stood, inhaling deeply.

Trreeck! The deep, throaty call sound of a raven pierced the air. Bran spied his bird Mair perched outside his tent.

His mood lifted. "Hush, you greedy bird. Rhys will feed you soon enough."

The sleek, stately raven, slightly larger than a peregrine falcon, cocked her head and fixed a bright eye on her master. Where other knights kept hawks or hunting birds, according to their station, Bran kept a raven. He and the creature shared a certain kinship. Not only did his own name mean "crow" or "raven," but like the raven, he made his living feeding off the spoils of war.

These rapacious black birds held a certain nobility that appealed to Bran. Further, these creatures were social and family-oriented. They picked a mate for life. Because of this, a raven possessed something Bran had never had—a family, a sense of belonging, and a rightful place in the scope of society, unlike Bran ap Madog, bastard by birth and traitor to his Welsh countrymen by choice.

"Sir?"

Bran turned toward Rhys. He allowed the smaller man to unbuckle and unwrap the ventail from his chin and loosen his mail coif. Bran pulled the skullcap from his head, and Rhys took it.

"She was a beautiful lady," Rhys murmured, as if reading what was on his master's mind.

Bran smiled. Always with an eye for the ladies, Rhys had not forgotten the noblewoman on the path and neither had his master. As he unknotted the sword belt around his waist and handed it to his sergeant, Bran smiled. The lady represented everything he desired in a wife.

Swathed in a gown the color of a green apple, the lady's elaborate headdress banded her chin and a silver net crespine confined her hair. Her garments concealed her from head to foot—all, that is, but for her gracefully slim hands and the fair oval of her face. She had a straight nose, rosy lips, and sapphire eyes that had glared at him with anger.

What a comely visage.

The woman symbolized what he needed in order to gain wealth, position, and acceptance. Yet too many women of high birth were put off by his landlessness and afraid of him because of his reputation for cruelty. He remained a bachelor, much to his chagrin.

"I envy the noblewoman's true love," he said to Rhys, unafraid to sigh in front of his trusted servant. "When I stopped her, she was on her way to bestow her favor on her lover."

The other man grunted and rolled his eyes.

Bran laughed at his man's response then glanced at his sleeve. The piece of torn red silk was gone. "Have you seen the favor the lady gave me?"

"The one you took, you mean?" Rhys motioned and Bran raised his arm. The sergeant grunted again and unlaced the sides of his master's dark surcoat. "You must have lost it during the last mêlée."

Bran nodded. "A shame."

As Rhys removed the surcoat, Bran pondered his image of the noblewoman. Her faithfulness intrigued him. He had never inspired such love from another, let alone a beautiful and noble lady.

"My guess is she'll not welcome your attention," Rhys volunteered. "She is much above your station. The favor bore the Rothmore crest."

"Rothmore." Bran tasted the name of the great Marcher earldom on his lips. The challenge now made sense. The new earl, just a boy, had fought him believing the vicious rumors told by Lord Leighton. Fie on Guy de Hastings, his enemy from days when they had competed against each other in tourneys and marched with Edward to the Holy Land.

"Edward will pardon young Rothmore for fighting unfairly," Bran predicted. "The king will take the lad's youth into account."

"Considering no harm was done," Rhys agreed.

Bran turned from his sergeant's ministrations. He pushed his heavy padded hacketon from his head. A cool wind stirred a lock of his black hair, lifting it from his gritty forehead. He wanted a bath and food.

He wanted a measure of peace.

Bran evaluated the scene around him with the indifference of one who had compromised much in his life. Ranks of colorful tents stood warrior-like in rows, their banners of red and yellow, stark contrast against the cool blue sky. They belonged to knights who, like him, had gathered in the field for the victory celebration.

Of a sudden, shouts carried among the rows of tents like the discordant screeches of angry fishwives. Bran jerked up his head as the frantic words reached his ears and drew a harsh breath.

"Murder most foul! The young Earl Rothmore is dead!"

CATRIN KNELT at the head of her fallen brother, her open palm on the still pulse point of his neck. Her brother's breastbone had been severed, ripped apart by a slayer's sword. Blood seeped from the ragged gash and soaked the fabric of his scarlet surcoat as well as the hem of Catrin's skirt. She trembled at the ghastly sight, breathing in the stench of fresh blood.

Touching her brother's clean sword, the mighty sword of the Rothmore earldom, Catrin slowly lifted her eyes to search the faces of the yeomen and squires gathering around Gilbert's body. He had fallen where he had been struck down outside the family's pavilion.

Her mind reeled from shock and grief. "Did no one witness this deed?" she cried out.

Waves of heat washed across her skin and face, followed by slices of icy cold. Dropping her gaze, Catrin fought the tears choking her throat and burning her eyes. She gritted her teeth, refusing to succumb to her anguish.

"What happened?" a shrill voice hollered.

"The King's man killed him," another said. "Just as he killed the boy's father."

Nay! Catrin reeled at the accusation. The black knight had shown Gilbert mercy on the tourney field. Why would he slay her brother after the fact and in such a dishonorable way?

"Fie on the young earl," an old woman camp follower spat. "He disgraced himself today."

"And brought shame to his family."

"'Tis fitting vengeance for defaming his family on the field," a man muttered.

What were these people saying? Catrin longed to cover her ears. Instead, sitting back on her heels, she loosened the red scarf on her brother's arm. Her hands were clammy and her fingers refused to work quickly. She removed the silk, holding it to her breast, clutching it as if the tiny piece of rent fabric continued to bind her to her beloved brother.

"My lady." Gilbert's squire extended his hand proffering

a scrap of red cloth. "I found this near my lord's helm." He lowered his eyes as if embarrassed that he'd failed to protect his master. He was but a boy himself—so much like Gilbert.

With shaky hands, Catrin accepted the other half of the silk scarf with the Rothmore arms, knowing well from whence it came.

The King's Raven!

So the allegations *were* true. The black knight, who'd taken her favor, had also taken her brother's life. This fragment of red scarf proved it. She curled her fingers around both pieces of silk. Her nails bit into the palm of her hand, pricking her flesh and mixing her blood with that on the silk.

Who would give her justice? The king had pardoned his favorite when Lord Leighton had spoken against him. Would the sovereign believe these new charges?

Would her proof be enough? Who'd believe a mere woman? Treachery oft occurred during a tournament. Not after. And this time her beloved brother bore the brunt of such treachery.

Catrin opened her fingers and stared at the pieces of fabric. Shards of ice sealed her heart. In that moment, a steady determination gripped her.

Somehow. Some way. She would avenge her brother's death.

CHAPTER THREE

Catrin backed away from the shrouded remains of her brother, already prepared for burial and lying in a corner of the Rothmore pavilion. Holy candles surrounded the body, pinpricks of light casting an eerie aura in the closely confined tent.

"Why?" She balled her fists, craving answers.

Gilbert's squire looked up from where he buffed his fallen lord's shield, burnishing it so the steel gleamed like a mirror. He ducked his head as if unwilling to meet her gaze.

Catrin exhaled a deep breath and turned away from him toward the sound of quiet sobbing. Olwen huddled by the brazier. Her cousin's pale hands busily worked her prayer beads.

Catrin's soul ached for Olwen. The two young women held a special bond, being close in age and so much alike in appearance. An only child, Olwen had truly loved young Gilbert as if he were her own brother.

And now Gilbert lay dead.

"Why?" Catrin whispered again, her voice holding a plaintive, hollow sound.

She circled the quiet tent and stopped to glance down at her maid Gwendolyn. The woman turned her head away as if afraid to confront Catrin's grief. Her questions.

Only Olwen had courage enough to meet Catrin's eyes.

"Before the tourney, Gilbert confided in me of the black knight's treachery. Guy de Hastings reminded him of it last night." Her cousin's soft voice was uneven but strangely tranquil. It halted Catrin's pacing. "Lord Leighton said the black knight meant to ride out as the king's champion. That's why Gilbert accepted the challenge today. 'Twas for revenge."

Catrin's temple throbbed. She unclenched her fists and bent to pick up her brother's iron coif, fingering its cold, metal rings. How like Gilbert to be impetuous and rash.

Yet Olwen's explanation failed to satisfy her, for Gilbert had been no ignoble lad. He was a Fitzalan. Proud of his noble heritage. Proud of his new lordship. Why would he dishonor his family?

The weight of the coif lay in her hand like an anchor. She studied it, unable to deny the truth. Gilbert *had* fought unfairly.

With a sharp intake of breath, Catrin dropped the coif beside the diligent squire. She wanted revenge. Her desire for it sucked at her lifeblood like a barber's leech. She didn't fight the biting emotion, but added it to her already overwhelming sorrow.

Olwen looked up from her beads, misery in her red-rimmed eyes. "You must forgive the person who murdered Gilbert," she said as if reading Catrin's mind. "God will punish him."

Of a sudden, Catrin hated Olwen's Christian piety. She had never had strong faith, and now she'd no patience for it. If she were a man, she'd take revenge in a direct and honorable way. She would challenge the black knight openly as Gilbert had done.

Yet an open challenge was not meant to be. The confines of society meant all she could do was fall back on her womanly wiles.

Catrin sucked in a breath, making up her mind. "Come with me, Gwendolyn."

Grabbing her cloak, she pulled back the tent flap to find the way barred by her stepmother.

"I am glad to find you here," Lady Rothmore said. "I must speak with you."

Catrin recoiled. She stepped aside to let the older woman enter the pavilion. Isadora's lady companion followed her inside.

Processing slowly around the hushed enclosure, her chin held high, Isadora acknowledged Olwen with an indifferent nod of her head as if the noble lady was a common servant.

"His Grace is furious." Isadora kept her face carefully composed when she spoke. "Gilbert was an important vassal, and King Edward is unhappy to have his victory celebration marred."

"His celebration marred?" Catrin fisted her hands on her hips. "Gilbert's life was stamped out like a foul beetle! Some say by the king's own champion!"

Isadora dismissed Catrin's charge with an impatient wave of her hand. "Edward is unlikely to believe this new rumor about a favorite, the knight-errant who once saved Edward's life."

Catrin faced her stepmother. "King Edward must listen to the charges." She fought the rise of hysteria in her voice.

"There is no evidence, only wild rumor."

Nay! There *was* evidence. Did she dare reveal it? Were two scraps of red cloth enough? 'Twould only be her word against the black knight's.

Catrin glared at Isadora and changed tactics. Her step-mother might have answers, for she was aware of court gossip. "What do you know about this knight? This Welshman?"

Isadora appeared anxious to talk, lowering her voice. "His given Welsh name fits his wicked reputation. Women love and fear him."

Catrin's jaw clenched. "The king must trust him."

Isadora nodded and lifted a haughty eyebrow. She thumbed a red apple lying in a wooden bowl. "He is a bastard, you know, the son of the Welsh prince Madog Vychan."

"Do you believe he killed my father as Lord Leighton says?" Contempt rose in Catrin's voice. Of recent days, the neighboring lord oft consoled Isadora in her widow's grief. Catrin felt his attention improper given her father's recent murder.

Lady Rothmore lowered her lashes and continued to wander the tent, restless as if she was loath to answer Catrin directly. Finally, she paused and looked up. "Be careful, Catrin. You are as rash as Gilbert. All these years, I have worried about you both, fearing the Welsh blood running in your veins."

Catrin hated mention of a heritage she didn't acknowl-edge. "Our Welsh mother had no influence upon our upbringing. Gilbert and I were raised by our English father and by *you*, my lady, if you so recall."

Catrin battled the animosity she felt for her stepmother. 'Twas a childish hatred, she knew, bred of sadness and loneliness because of her mother's untimely death. "Don't worry," she said with derision. "You are now well rid of one of your stepchildren."

Olwen's horrified gaze flew up in reproach. "Catrin! Shame on you!"

"You accuse me of not doing my duty." Isadora squared her shoulders. "I have treated you as I treat my own son."

Catrin drew a shaky breath. "So you would have had my father believe, but I know you never cared for Gilbert and me. Father is gone, my lady. Let us not trifle with one another. We have no need to play games."

"You have always been a contentious child."

"I may be contentious, my lady, but I am no longer a child."

Isadora clutched the great Rothmore ring, the ring once belonging to Catrin's mother, and twisted it on her finger. "Mayhap 'tis reason for the king to find you a husband."

Catrin glowered. Her stepmother was right. Custom dictated daughters leave their homes. Only one mistress ran a household. Theirs had grown too crowded.

While her father had been alive, Catrin had avoided marriage. She'd been his only daughter, a favorite, and when she'd turned eighteen, the earl had been loath to force her to do what she disliked, marry not for love. Gilbert had been of the same mind. They'd indulged her, postponing the inevitable.

Catrin's future and that of Olwen had been left undecided for months while the war with the Welsh raged. Now

King Edward would arrange her marriage, motivated only by political consideration.

For the first time in her life, Catrin had no adult male relative to protect her.

"I shall request an audience with Edward," Isadora said, pointing a slender finger at Catrin. "I must remind him you are of marriageable age."

"Then I, too, will see the king." Catrin renewed her resolve. "I will ask permission to take Gilbert's body back to Clun Castle for a proper burial."

"I forbid it." Isadora's expression turned hard. "There's time enough. You will stay here until the king settles your marriage. Yon squire shall return the body to Clun."

Catrin hid her fists in the folds of her gown. Her brother's death left her with no control. Because of it, her ten-year-old, half-brother Richard was now earl. Isadora would allow no challenge to her newfound power as his mother.

Catrin lowered her eyes to conceal her contempt. Let her father's widow believe she'd won. Better to challenge her in a different way.

Isadora rested a hand upon her shoulder. "You know I seek only your best interest, do you not?"

"Aye, my lady."

"Change your ruined gown and come with me to the king's banquet."

Catrin refused to look up. She stared at her green gown stained with her brother's blood. "'Twould be unseemly given the circumstances."

Isadora squeezed Catrin's shoulder as if meaning to console her, but the grip of her fingers was like that of a hunting hawk. The widow drew a quick breath reacting to

Catrin's silence and quickly left the tent followed by her companion

Catrin moved her shoulder in an effort to release tension. Her emotions left her feeling exposed like the craggy outcrops and hills of the Striperstones. She turned to meet her maid's sympathetic gaze. Gwendolyn understood.

Her maid understood the impotence that welled within her soul like a dark storm forged of rage and grief.

ALONE, dressed now in Olwen's second gown, Catrin circled the outskirts of the dark encampment, remaining in the shadows and avoiding the campfires. Night had fallen and 'twas not wise for a woman to wander out, especially with battle-tested knights and the riffraff that followed Edward's army nearby.

Most of the men were still celebrating the king's victory by feasting and drinking. Mayhap no one would notice a lone woman strolling along the rows of tents.

She had felt as penned up as a chicken in a coop and unable to kneel with Olwen in prayer as was proper.

Guilt tweaked her, shooting sharp twinges across her already throbbing forehead, but she knew herself not to be as pious as her cousin. Not tonight. Not with sinful thoughts of revenge on her mind.

Father. Now Gilbert. Why had God taken so many of her loved ones from her?

Catrin gamely fought the tears burning her eyes. Pulling her woolen cloak over her head, she clutched the edges of the fine fabric with icy fingers. The garment barely protected her against the chill wind, but it concealed her identity well. Passersby would not know her, which suited her well this night.

Isadora considered her wild and blamed her Welsh parentage, but Catrin knew 'twas something else that caused her restlessness. She'd never been like other women. She wanted more from life than just mindlessly tending a hearth, locked in a loveless marriage dictated by parent or king.

Dear Lord, she was more than chattel. She wanted respect from a husband. She wanted to be treated as an equal. E'en more than that, she wished to choose the man she married because she loved him in a heartfelt way—the way described in the chivalrous tales of King Arthur.

Catrin sucked in a quick breath of the night air. It smelled of burning peat and roasting meat from the countless campfires outside the staked pavilions. Wind stirred again, carrying the scent of horses and sweet fodder, and the stench of manure and outdoor latrines.

Trreeck!

A raven foretelling death. A scavenger that picked the flesh of rotting animals.

She jammed a fist into her mouth, stifling a gasp. The black bird startled from a perch near a tent, its wings flapping wildly. Tethered, it was unable to escape. He couldn't hurt her. Still her throat constricted as she stared at the creature, knowing whose camp she'd found.

The King's Raven! Who else pitched a tent of expensive and uncommon black fabric? Who else owned a string of ebony horses, including the mighty destrier she recognized from the tourney? Who else kept a raven on a perch?

Catrin steadied herself. A nice touch. So much black. Did it conceal an equally dark heart?

She slipped her right hand inside the folds of her cloak

and into the sheath that hung from her belt, touching the sharp edge of the dagger she'd taken from Gilbert's belongings. 'Twas her way of remembering the lad who once used the small knife. Careful not to cut herself, she slid her thumb along the slick blade and over the carved bone hilt.

Given the chance, would she have the courage to use the knife on her brother's murderer?

A twig snapped behind her. Catrin gasped, but before she could turn and run, an arm snaked around her, pulling her against a wall of hard muscle. A leather glove clamped her mouth and nose.

"Who are you?" an angry voice growled in her ear. "What do you want near my encampment?"

Terror sliced through her body, weakening her limbs. Confined by the cruel grasp, she jerked her head side-to-side, twisting, trying to break free. Catrin found herself as helpless as the bird tied to its perch. Could she unfetter her right arm and the hand holding the knife?

"Why do you prowl near my horses?"

She thrashed now just for air. Her body tensed in reaction to his strength and his very maleness. Her senses filled with the sound of his rough breathing and the faint hint of wood smoke on his clothing.

The arm that bound her chest slipped downward, crushing her breasts. "A woman!"

The darkness and the similarity between male and female outer garments had protected her identity—until now. Catrin's chest heaved against his burly forearm.

He dropped his gloved hand from her mouth, and Catrin gulped a welcoming breath. "Of course I am a woman!"

"To what purpose do you come? Are you a spy or simply a whore?"

"Take your hands off me!"

"Answer me." He jerked her back, pressing her even closer to his long length. She felt the muscles of his hard chest, the firmness of his thighs.

"I am a serving maid, walking after supper," she said. "I lost my way."

"You walk alone in the dark?"

It sounded implausible even to her ears. Catrin nodded, not daring to speak again.

"So be it, serving wench." He suddenly released her.

She stumbled forward, trying to regain her balance and pricked her thumb on the small knife in her hand. "Ouch!"

"Did I hurt you?"

Catrin pulled her hand from her purse where she'd been fingering the knife and popped the bleeding finger into her mouth, tasting her own blood. Still with her back to him, she shook her head.

"Who are you?"

Catrin swallowed, trying to contain her fear. With a shred of control, she lifted both hands and pulled the hood of her cape more securely over her head so it covered her veil and shrouded her face. Then she turned slowly. Keeping her eyes cast down, she hoped the shadows concealed her identity.

"You do not know me," she said. Catrin heard his grunt of disbelief.

"Very well, let me see your hand."

She curled her fingers close and kept her head lowered, like the demur maid she claimed to be. He paused only a second. Stepping forward, towering above her, he grasped her hand.

His black leather gloves were cold and abrasive against

her fist. Stronger by far, he pried open her fingers one by one. Awareness of him, of his rough masculinity, slithered through her body from her fingertips down to her toes.

Then he rubbed his thumb over her tiny wound.

"'Tis a simple knife cut," he said. "Did you come to murder me and steal my horses?"

Catrin caught her breath. "Of course not!"

"You protest much."

Catrin snatched back her hand, feeling his masculine presence, just as she'd sensed it on the pathway. She dared not show her face, although she yearned for a better view of him, more than the folds of his black cloak and the tips of his leather boots.

He extended his hand, this time as a gentleman would to a lady. "I will take you back to your tent."

"Nay!" Catrin picked up her skirts and fled from him.

She never looked back, running once more from the black-clad brute, the man she believed had killed her brother. The man's touch stirred something strange within her. Something she'd never before felt.

While she ran, blood pounding in her ears with every step, Catrin let fear and heartache turn to anger—cutting, hard anger. She had behaved like a spineless woman. Not like the warrior she longed to be.

But of this, she was certain. No longer could she depend on the king's justice or trust an uncaring God who had allowed all those she loved to be taken from her.

She must take matters into her hands and seek her own vengeance. The next time she must not fail.

CHAPTER FOUR

Dawn broke just as baying hounds routed ducks from the rushes of the riverbank. As the birds rose into the air, the long-winged gerfalcon swooped to strike its prey. Bran's pulse quickened.

"Huzzah!" King Edward shouted. The falconer lured the hawk back to the king's gloved hand while a pack of retrievers hurled themselves into the cold water after the fallen mallard.

Bran wheeled his stallion in a circle. "Well done, sire."

Edward covered the bird's head with a tiny, belled leather hood. "A good hunt is the mark of a good handler," he said.

The falconer preened himself like one of his charges. It seemed the king was feeling magnanimous this morning. Bran studied his mentor and sometimes friend. Imposing, very much with the deportment of his noble rank, Edward was tall, even taller than Bran. Fair-skinned and blue-eyed with a fine head of short-cropped, golden hair, Edward's finely chiseled features showed strength of purpose. Only the slight droop of one eyelid bespoke his humanity.

Quick to anger, often vindictive, Edward of England could be a loyal friend to one who served him well. Bran had depended upon on that loyalty since, as a fourteen-year-old lad, he left his English foster family and went into royal service, forsaking forever his Welsh homeland.

Most recently, Bran had served Edward in France where, in the guise of seeking his fortune, he had spied for England and acted, at times, as envoy for his adopted sovereign. He'd gone to Gascony to recruit crossbowmen for the army and recently, because he spoke the language, gathered information for Edward in Wales during the conquest of the rebellious princes.

Bran's jaw tightened with anticipation. The mere pressure of his hand on the reins caused his spirited stallion to snort and twirl. He sat deep in the saddle and relaxed, settling the horse.

"I shall buy that black steed from you!" Edward said and kicked his horse into a gallop.

Caught off guard, Bran spurred the steed under question and raced after his liege. Like yesterday, the October day was crisp and cool. High wisps of clouds raked across the bright blue sky. Bran's spirits rose. He followed Edward into the wood, dodging the stately growth of larch and ash.

He sensed something of import about to happen. God willing. Mayhap today was the day he'd worked and waited for. Bran's spirit soared.

Edward paused in a small clearing to allow him to catch up. Other retainers stayed their distance. Bran's hand tightened once more on his reins, and he halted before the mighty King of England.

Edward's cheeks were flushed from the ride, and his eyes lit from exertion. He carried the hawk on his outstretched wrist, handling his own horse with one hand.

"What say you, Welshman? Do you sell me that black destrier?"

"Nay, sire." Bran answered, knowing when to deny a request. "The stallion is not for sale. A poor knight, such as I, may not be able to buy another worthy steed."

"Ha! Poor indeed. More than likely, you won that animal beneath you." Edward lowered his voice and winked. "You are rich in reputation, as well as horseflesh. Would that I had such luck in the tourney fields of France *and* with the ladies!"

"I fear, sire, you exaggerate. Ladies are frightened of me. My reputation as the black knight precedes me."

Edward laughed. "You've cultivated your reputation well, as I requested." He grew serious and leveled a direct gaze. "Sir Bran, you have served me faithfully as the black knight."

Bran lowered his eyes in affirmation of the king's words. Hope surging through his veins, he waited patiently astride his restive horse.

Edward shook his head in mock dismay. "Mayhap keeping that noisy raven is carrying the ruse too far."

"A nice touch, think you not?" Bran looked up and grinned. "I have come to respect those winged scavengers."

"Just as I have respected your work and loyalty." Edward's words sounded carefully measured. "'Tis time I rewarded your service."

Bran bowed his head once more. "You do me honor."

"I cannot offer you what I know you have always wanted —your father's keep, the fortress of Dinas Bran." He paused before adding, "Because of your birth."

Bran tensed and now fastened his gaze on Edward's. "You know me well, sire."

"I gave Castell Dinas Bran and the lordship of Yale and Bromfield to John de Warenne."

"The Earl of Surrey," Bran murmured in acknowledgment, hoping to hide his disappointment. "Of course."

Edward nodded. "And to Roger Mortimer, I gave your father's lands south of Llangollen."

The king's words were like ashes left from a fire, gray and gritty. He had feared this. Over the years, Bran had learned Edward believed bastards should never share inheritance.

Bitter bile rose in Bran's throat. For once, he wished for the Welsh custom that divided the land equally among all sons. His father had died at English hands and so had his two half-brothers. Although illegitimate, he *was* Madog Vychan's son. Was he fool to think Edward would deal differently with him even after his years of faithful service?

"I shall reward you another way," Edward said with a sly wink. "I have several marriages to arrange, wards of the state. One lady brings a wealthy, border castle where I need a strong hand. The other one offers a bigger dowry but a smaller property near Shrewsbury."

Fighting his disappointment, Bran mentally gathered himself as if he approached a knight in battle. The king was speaking of valuable property and a hand in marriage. Dinas Bran, his father's castle, was lost to him. Just like everything of import had been lost to him—his mother who'd died when he was young, his grandmother, and the randy nobleman he never knew, the prince who'd spread his fertile seed throughout the Welsh countryside.

His ultimate goal thwarted, Bran still might have a wife,

property, and eventually children. He could settle down. Become respectable. Shed the reputation of the black knight. He was a man used to compromise, after all.

"One is old Rothmore's daughter, Lady Catrin Fitzalan." Edward measured him thoughtfully. "Quite an independent miss. In fact, you rode against her brother yesterday."

"Fitzalan?" Bran returned the king's look with a calmness he didn't feel.

He shook his head, rejecting the king's suggestion. The lady would not bring him the peace he sought. Now was the time for practicality. Unlike yesterday on the path with the unknown woman he'd met, he could no longer afford a simple dalliance. "Rumor links me to the death of her father and brother," Bran said quietly.

"Ah, a bad business." Edward dropped the reins and rubbed his chin. "'Tis fortunate for you, Sir Raven, that I know you were in Wales on my business when the elder Fitzalan was slain. Yesterday's actions are another matter. I know you well, but others don't. That is why I have ordered an investigation."

"Thank you, your grace." Bran fisted his gloved hand, knowing himself fortunate indeed. Yet his luck could change as quickly as the king's trust in him.

Edward shrugged. "Verily, 'tis the de Belleme heiress for you then, a more demure lady, and with her hand, you receive her father's castle at Northbridge where there is no male heir."

A castle of his own. A wife. Bran lifted his eyes to the king. "Sire, I cannot begin to thank you."

"Nor I, Welshman. I remember that stormy eve in Acre."

Their gazes connected, the powerful English king and

the lowly knight, bound together by sacrifice and loyalty and a strange respect.

Catrin's anger festered all night, a welcome replacement for the grief and shock of her brother's cruel and unexpected death. She pushed her sorrow aside, preferring to allow the hot fires of wrath consume her. Nothing else mattered. Setting her jaw, Catrin approached the great hall with Olwen by her side.

Compact, portable, and transient, the royal court never stayed long in one place, the king always needing to see and be seen by his subjects. For the duration of Parliament, the royal household had set up housekeeping at Acton Burnell, the manor home of Chancellor Robert Burnell, the king's closest confidante.

"I am unsure of this," Olwen murmured, dragging her steps.

Catrin felt Olwen tense. Her cousin had always possessed a timid disposition. In her years fostering at Olwen's home, Catrin had been the prod, encouraging her fair and beautiful cousin to stretch herself beyond her limits. But her efforts had been futile. 'Twas not in Olwen's disposition to be other than sweet, serene, and pious.

Catrin took her cousin's chilled hand. "What is wrong?"

"I am afraid."

"I know, but you agreed with me earlier," Catrin said. "You even bade me to replace my blood-stained gown with your second one so that I wouldn't disgrace myself."

"Isadora forbade us to approach the king," Olwen reminded, short of breath.

"But she failed to mention the queen," Catrin said coyly.

"Why do you constantly provoke your stepmother, Catrin? She means you no harm."

Catrin remained inflexible. "I have always disliked her."

"'Tis a habit, certainly," Olwen reflected, "stemming from your disagreements during childhood. Something you can correct, with God's grace."

Catrin swallowed her impatience and dismissed the comment with a wave of her hand. She wanted nothing to do with God's grace. God had no time for her. Hadn't the actions of the previous day proven that?

She stopped and turned to Olwen. "I must concentrate on giving my brother a proper burial, Olwen. I need your support—for the love you bore Gilbert."

Olwen measured her with a steady gaze. "Aye," she said with a sigh. "And for the sake of his soul."

Relief flushed through Catrin. She squeezed Olwen's hand and gave it a tug.

Together they quickened their steps, pushing their way into the crowded great hall where they were jostled by a myriad of royal servants who prepared for the midday meal.

Catrin paused at the chaotic sight, memory of her year at court flooding her. The hectic traveling and lack of privacy, confined as she'd been with the queen's women, had played havoc with her freedom-loving spirit. All the while, she'd longed for the wild Marcher lands of her home. After her father's death, she'd been allowed to withdraw.

Steeling herself against the bitterness of her brother's death and the inevitable changes in her life to come, Catrin pressed Olwen's hand and signaled with the other to catch Hamon's attention. The sergeant of the chamber approached, sweeping them a flourishing bow, a huge grin on his boyish face.

"Ah, the two most beautiful women in the kingdom return to court," he said, merriment twinkling in his shrewd eyes. No wonder he was Queen Eleanor's favorite.

"You mustn't let the queen overhear your flattery, Hamon," Catrin warned, able to play his courtly game even with a heavy heart. "She may remove your slovenly head."

"'Tis no joking matter," he parried, gripping his throat with a fine hand. "For what I hear of the Welsh Prince Daffyd's coming demise, I fear he would welcome a simple beheading."

Although she'd heard Edward had devised a new kind of grisly death—something called hanging, drawing and quartering—Catrin hadn't come to talk politics. "I care not about the traitor. I hope to see the queen."

Hamon cocked his head and waited.

Catrin caught the meaning behind his hesitation. "You know I have nothing to bribe you with," she said with a smile. "Just a swift kick in your backside if you do not arrange my audience."

Olwen's grip on her hand tightened at her audacity. After all, this was the queen's man, and one had to be careful.

"Always persuasive." He grinned, obviously not offended. "And always a favorite of Her Grace, or else I should never contemplate such a request."

"You were ever the gentleman, Hamon." Catrin dipped her eyelashes, feigning the guise of a perfectly demure lady.

"And you were always the charlatan. Wait here. I will see what I can do."

'Twas not long before Hamon ushered them through the crowded hall. He pushed aside a tapestry at the end of the room and showed them into the presence of Eleanor of Castile, wife of King Edward.

Catrin and Olwen entered and bobbed a curtsey at the door. Then they crossed a short distance and dropped once more to their right knees.

Queen Eleanor and her closest ladies were much as Catrin remembered from her time with them. Sitting in a private solar, dim except for the faint glow from several beeswax candles, they were quiet but for a matron's steady reciting of Eleanor's beloved Arthurian romances. As was her custom at every resting place, the queen had ordered the rushes swept clean and replaced with luxurious carpets from her warm homeland of Castile.

The Queen motioned them forward. "Ah, Catrin." Eleanor extended a hand. The familiar, light scent of roses wafted in the air.

"Your Grace." Catrin kept her gaze respectfully on her sovereign as she approached. "Thank you for allowing us an audience. Do you remember my cousin, Lady Olwen?"

"The Northbridge heiress." Eleanor acknowledged with a nod. "I have oft commented on how much the two of you resemble each other."

Catrin met the queen's smile and smiled herself. The queen's high forehead, straight brow, and firm chin were framed by her barbette, delineating her exotic foreign beauty. A gold net crespine encrusted with jewels hid her black hair. As courteous as she was beautiful, 'twas no wonder Eleanor had captivated her royal lord for so many years.

"I am so sorry for your recent loss. Trouble has come twice to the family of Rothmore in such a short time."

Eleanor folded her slim fingers over Catrin's hand. "Please sit, my ladies."

Catrin and Olwen sat on small stools at the feet of the queen. "We have come to ask permission to remove Gilbert's body to Clun, to allow him to be given a proper, Christian burial," Catrin stated quickly, her voice hushed.

"Of course, and I shall provide prayers for his soul."

So simple, the granting of the boon. Catrin's spirits soared with relief. Now to leave Acton Burnell before Isadora discovered her defiance.

"Such a tragedy." The queen shook her head. "Your brother was unwise to take up Sir Bran ap Madog's challenge."

Catrin nodded. What more could she do but concede the truth? "I believe he held a grudge against yon knight."

"Aye," Olwen spoke up quickly. "Gilbert wanted to avenge the death of his father."

"So I have heard the rumors." Eleanor shook her head again. "Yet, there are other, honest ways to seek justice—for example, he could have requested a royal ruling."

"My brother was rash." Catrin felt the need to somehow smooth over Gilbert's growing ill repute. By removing the protection on his blade, he was thought to have fought unfairly in the game. "He was impertinent and quick to anger."

"Revenge. Hatred. All are sins against God," Eleanor said softly. "We need to pray for his soul."

Olwen began to cry. Catrin eyed her uneasily. Having gained her wish, the audience was fast slipping out of Catrin's control.

"My brother was murdered, your grace, soon after the tourney." She drew a deep breath, surprised at her growing bravery. "I want justice for him." She lifted her chin, unwilling to reveal she knew about a torn piece of scarf dropped beside Gilbert's body. "I would know more about this black knight, this King's Raven."

"Court gossip is oft counterfeit." Eleanor's sympathetic gaze settled on Catrin's face, and she shook her head in warning. "Yet Edward tells me Sir Bran *was* in Wales at the time of your father's death acting as a spy. He serves the king, not the Welsh princes, and so would have no reason to kill your father, a tenant of the crown."

Eleanor reached out and clasped Catrin's hand. "My lady, rest assured, if Sir Bran had wanted to kill your brother, he would have certainly done so during the tourney. 'Twould be like calling off a gyrfalcon from its kill if he desired to avenge the dishonor done to him on the field."

"I do not understand why everyone defends this knight," Catrin said with anger.

Eleanor held Catrin with her steady regard. "I understand you are grieving. Yet, know this. Bran ap Madog is a knight of the household, trained by Edward during the crusade, knighted on the battlefield, a loyal diplomat, and a faithful servant to my lord. In Acre, he drew the poison from Edward's wound, saving his life. My lord trusts him completely."

Catrin faltered under Eleanor's scrutiny. The intense ache of loss was replaced once more by anger as sharp as shards of winter ice. This was the truth of her position. No one would take up her cause against this knight. No one believed the rumors, and now the king gave his Welsh ally an alibi for her father's death. She could very well put herself and Olwen at risk if she continued to question his honor or revealed the evidence of the pieces of red fabric in her possession.

Justice would be served, but left to her own devices, like so much in her life had been left up to her own wiles, her strength. She accepted it, much as she accepted her ultimate marriage for dynastic reasons.

"I understand," Catrin replied, dropping her gaze.

"Still yourself against the fires of hatred, my lady. Let my Edward seek justice for your brother."

Catrin's eyes widened at the queen's keen insight into her feigned submission.

"You have other matters to consider." The queen's blue-black eyes sparkled. "Edward plans to find you a husband."

Catrin knew Eleanor thought about their many disputes on the subject of arranged marriage. Disagreements Catrin had always lost. Eleanor had thought her father foolish for not settling the matter of his daughter's future.

"My fate was written in the stars yesterday with the death of my brother," Catrin conceded quietly.

Eleanor patted Catrin's hand again, and then withdrew it, placing her palm on the flat of her stomach. "I see myself in you. Although I was married to Edward when I was ten, and I knew my duty to my father, my country, and my God, I was frightened at first."

The queen's eyes grew misty. Catrin held her breath at the honor of her lady's confidence.

"I was attracted to my lord immediately and quickly grew to love him, as you will grow to love the husband Edward chooses for you." Eleanor lowered her gaze to her pale hand. "And just like me, you will find yourself blessed by your lord's children, both living and dead."

"Your grace?" Catrin caught Eleanor's meaning. The queen was again with child.

Eleanor looked up and smiled. "This will be my sixteenth confinement."

"Oh, God bless you," Olwen exclaimed.

A wave of humility washed over Catrin. She took Eleanor's now outstretched hand and kissed it, her throat closing with emotion. The love between king and queen was stuff of romances. Catrin longed for such love but held no illusion that any arranged for her would be successful. Dreams had a way of not coming true.

"Go, my dears," Eleanor said, "and remember to open your heart to your future husbands. Be good helpmates to them." She extended her regards to Olwen. "I shall see that Edward chooses wisely for both of you."

"Thank you, your grace. We can ask for nothing more." Catrin climbed to her feet and helped Olwen to hers. They withdrew with a bow, leaving the presence of the most gracious woman in Edward's kingdom.

CHAPTER FIVE

Catrin and Olwen stepped from the solar and were met by Hamon, who drew them aside. "The King's Raven comes to the great hall," he whispered, his eyes alight with mischief.

Surprise rendered Catrin speechless. Sharp memories of his gritty glove upon her mouth and his body pressed firmly against her back and thighs sent waves of anger and fear skittering through her.

Hamon puffed himself up like a bird preening its feathers. "He seeks Mistress Olwen! Our king has bestowed to him her hand in marriage."

Catrin's stomach plummeted, and she glanced fleetingly at her pale cousin, who gasped and clutched her prayer beads. She shifted her gaze back to Hamon. "Our queen mentioned marriage, but we did not know of this."

"The arrangement has just been struck," he said, exchanging gossip. "During the morning hunt."

There was no need to question Hamon's veracity. 'Twas his business to know what happened at court.

Olwen plucked at Catrin's sleeve. "I cannot."

Her cousin's plaintive cry struck Catrin's soul. "Hush, dear cuz. You must be brave."

For what more can a mere woman do?

Tears spilled down Olwen's cheeks. "What with Gilbert's death, I cannot bear this."

Catrin shot a look at Hamon, who observed Olwen's reaction with keen interest. If he reported the girl's reluctance, Olwen would be in danger—from the king *and* from the beast the king had pledged her to wed.

Catrin forced a smile upon her lips. "You see my cousin's distress at the sudden news. Olwen is sensitive. She wants to look her best for her bridegroom. Mayhap you know a private place for them to meet for the first time?"

Hamon's brow cleared. "Of course! Follow me."

The sergeant of the chamber led them outside the busy hall and around the back to the manor's kitchen garden. A woven wattle fence enclosed side-by-side beds, one fallow from the growing season and another still green with early winter crops of leeks, kale, and garlic. Savory, marjoram, sage, and thyme looked gray and uninteresting next to the aromatic mint that consumed much of the herb plot.

"With the household at dinner, no one will disturb you here. I will tell Sir Bran where to find his bride and her chaperone." Hamon left them with a saucy wink and a casual wave.

Olwen sank onto a rustic bench and buried her face in her hands. Catrin's stomach knotted with anxiety. How could she help her dear cousin? Encouraging forbearance would prove useless. Catrin doubted Olwen capable of the courage to make the best of this appalling situation.

How could her cousin be expected to cope? Olwen had loved Gilbert. Now within twenty-four hours of his death, she was to be betrothed to the man rumored to have killed him. Where was justice?

Olwen's wan eyes lifted to meet Catrin's. "I cannot wed."

"Shh, sweeting. You must follow the command of the king."

"No! I will take vows. This I will tell to Sir Bran when he comes."

Catrin's fingers clenched. She knew her cousin well. Though pious and quiet spoken, Olwen possessed a streak of stubbornness. This trait boded ill for her and for the good folk at Northbridge.

Curse Edward for putting political interests ahead of human ones.

Catrin's eyelashes drifted over her eyes. She stood silently, refusing to pray, hardly able to think.

'Twould not be wise for this wicked knight to see his betrothed in tears, nor wise for Olwen to speak her true heart to him. Catrin had been unable to save her father or brother. Could she save her cousin?

She pressed her lips together. What if she had been chosen as the bride of the King's Raven instead of Olwen? What would she have done?

She would have used the opportunity for revenge.

Catrin splayed her fingers wide and flexed them. "Olwen, you are not in a condition to meet your betrothed. You must collect yourself, dry your tears."

Confusion clouded Olwen's eyes. "Why? Once he hears my vow to God, he will be content to let me leave. You need not worry."

Catrin frowned at Olwen's naiveté. "I doubt he will agree to let you take vows. Yet once you're under the protection of the church, your betrothed will have no say.

We must buy time. Then get you to a convent before he can wed you."

A knight-errant with the reputation as a fierce lover and fighter, the King's Raven always won. For him, Olwen and Northbridge Castle were worthy prizes. What would prevent him from kidnapping her cousin from the sanctuary of the Lord's Holy Church? She would not mention her fears to her fearful cousin.

Olwen seemed to consider Catrin's words as she clutched her beads. Looking up, she said, "Mayhap you are right."

"I pray so." Catrin took a deep breath. "The knight must not see you crying. Go inside. Ask for water and wash the tears from your eyes. Gather your courage and come back here. I will wait for you."

"Thank you, sweet cuz."

An insidious knot tightened in Catrin's stomach. "Hurry. Go now! I will make sure there is no problem if he comes."

No problem—except for the stark image of a black-helmed Welsh knight.

KNEELING, Bran kissed the slim, pale hand of Queen Eleanor, her dark eyes alight with amusement.

"Welcome, Sir Raven," Eleanor said. "You have cultivated quite a gallant way during your absence."

"Aye, your grace. I fear the French have influenced me, and for the better, I hope," Bran replied, smiling.

"Come, sit." Eleanor patted the stool beside her. "Do you yet fight like the warrior I remember?"

Bran straddled the stool. "Of late, I seem to regret my skill with the sword and my frequent days at war." He shrugged and favored the queen with a smile. "Perchance I am growing old."

"I have found a certain peace in my later years." Eleanor nodded, returning his smile.

Bran gazed at the flickering light of the candles. "A peace I have yet to find."

"'Tis time for you to settle down. A good wife will help you."

He lowered his head as a sign of respect. "You are wise, your grace."

"And you are still a charmer, but I am afraid it shall be wasted on your new bride."

Eleanor's comment piqued his interest. He looked up. "Know you of my coming nuptials?"

"Aye, Edward spoke of them." Eleanor's expression darkened. "'Tis the reason I wanted to see you before you are introduced to the heiress Lady Northbridge."

"I long to meet her." Bran thought of the woman whose hand would provide him the wealth and land he'd always lacked. Would she give him the peace he sought? "I am honored his grace found me worthy of the lass."

"Oh, Edward has his greater purposes." Eleanor picked up her stitching. "Even now he needs a strong hand near the borders."

"To keep the Welsh away," Bran said tongue-in-cheek.

"Aye, scoundrel. To keep your kinsmen from ravishing our countryside." The soft gleam of the candle illuminated the humor in Eleanor's eyes.

"My kinsmen, your grace, have been suitably subdued by Edward's army."

"And so it seems." Eleanor grew quiet and plied her needle.

Bran waited, curious about her real purpose for the audience.

In a moment, she spoke softly, "You must be patient with your new bride."

Now he understood. His reputation; however, counterfeit. "Your grace, I'm afraid my name oft does me discredit. I assure you, I am not the randy rake where women are concerned. To the contrary, I am oft as chaste as a priest."

Eleanor kept her attention on her needlework. "I have known many a disgraceful churchman to forsake his vows of celibacy."

What was the reason for her concern? "You know of my parentage," he said. She glanced up. "Except for a few indiscretions during my youth, I have kept myself whole for marriage. I would not wish a child of mine to be called *bastard*."

Bran turned his restive gaze away from the queen. This was the first time he had revealed the secrets of his soul to another human being.

Eleanor leaned forward and took his hand. He found hers cool, but firm, with quiet authority and wise compassion.

"I'm not making myself clear, and for that I apologize." The inflection in her voice was kind. Bran raised a baffled gaze. "My concern is with your reaction to your bride," Eleanor explained. "Olwen de Belleme is a sweet girl. Quiet and childlike. Nonetheless, I fear she is better suited for a nunnery than for a marriage bed."

The queen's confession startled Bran. Etched in his memory were the fiery eyes and the defiant chin of the woman in the apple green gown, a woman whose spirit was match for his own. To know his future wife was his exact opposite caused a tremor of trepidation. Could he deal with such a lady?

Eleanor squeezed his hand. "'Tis why I counsel forbearance. I'm sure you will grow to love her. Do not spoil your chances to have what you have always wanted and what my Edward gives you through marriage."

Bran nodded, understanding. "You honor me with your insight."

Eleanor drew back. "You have been of interest to me since that day in Acre when you saved the life of my husband."

A simple repayment, but Bran sensed there was more to it. When Edward brought home a wife from the hot lands of Castile, he had also brought home an earthly saint.

"Now, tell me about these ugly rumors. Why do people implicate you in young Fitzalan's death?"

Was even Eleanor given to believe the rumors? "I know my word is questioned, but I had nothing to do with the lord's death."

"Still the gossip persists." Eleanor turned to her stitching again.

"Aye, my name continues to be sullied."

"A bad business. How can you prove your innocence?"

"My sergeant-at-arms can vouch for me."

Eleanor nodded and then leveled her gaze at him. "I know Edward seeks the truth. I pray, sir, you do as well."

Bran knew full well he'd been given more wise advice. His word had been accepted solely because he was the king's man. He would do well to find the murderer if he wanted to dispel the scandal.

"Might the purpose of the gossip be to defame me?" Bran speculated. "The lad could have been an unwitting victim in someone's scheme."

Eleanor considered, tilting her head. "That, too, bears investigating. Look to your enemies."

A clamor arose outside, and King Edward swept into the quiet solar, cursing. "Lady! You worry me like a pesky gnat."

A retinue of the king's attendants paused at the curtain, but a noble woman followed him. She did not kneel out of respect. Her audacity was as large as the ring that sparkled on her finger.

"Your grace, I am a widow trying to settle the circumstances of my household," the noble woman insisted.

"My lady, I will take your concerns under advisement."

Eleanor's eyes widened. "My lord, what is wrong?"

Edward glanced at his wife, and then shifted his gaze toward Bran, acknowledging him with a brief nod. He tossed down his gloves on a side table. "Lady Rothmore is petitioning me to give the wardship of her son Richard to Guy de Hastings, Lord Leighton," he said to his wife. Edward whirled and leveled his royal gaze at the intruder. "Some say Leighton is her lover."

Lady Rothmore drew in a shocked breath. "Your grace, you wrong me! My own husband is but newly deceased. Lord Leighton is merely a family friend and neighbor. His lands are near the Rothmore holdings. I would keep my only son close."

Bran felt the gentle touch of Eleanor's hand upon his as if she willed him to be quiet. He understood her counsel. He'd best not speak.

"You seem to have everything carefully thought out," Edward said with cold disdain.

The woman puffed herself like a peacock, looking more regal than the quiet and demur queen. "Sire, the wardship of my only son wasn't in question until his brother's unfortunate demise yesterday. My son, the new Rothmore earl, is a sickly lad. I want what is best for him, which is a position at Lord Leighton's household where his infirmities are understood."

"And for you, my lady?" Edward's wrath was evident in his manner. He measured her with another probing look.

Bran thought the lady would also be wise to be silent. Instead, the Queen intervened.

"My lord, Lady Rothmore speaks as any mother," Eleanor said gently.

Edward paused. He smiled at his wife, relenting a little, his anger suddenly controlled. "I have dealt with many a well-meaning mother, and from experience, I've learned not to trust them," he said so all might hear. "Too often they have stolen their precious children away, hiding them from the king's grace or they have married them against the will of the Crown." He wagged his forefinger to emphasize his point. "This I will not have, for Rothmore holds castles vital to the Crown. The matter is too important for a woman's whim."

Eleanor's gaze connected with her husband's, and Bran saw a knowing look pass between them. He wondered about it, amazed that they could communicate by a mere look. Had Eleanor's comment been meant to defuse her husband's wrath? In the deep recesses of his core, he marveled at such a wife, a wife of understanding and love.

Lady Rothmore seemed fittingly subdued. "I submit to your wishes, your grace." Her gaze was lowered, but Bran noticed a slight movement of rebellion in the clench of her jaw.

"Good! I shall take your son's position under advisement." Edward motioned for a servant to bring a cup of wine.

"And my stepdaughter, your grace? What shall become of Catrin, Lady Fitzalan?"

Catrin. The woman in the apple green gown was named Catrin. Bran's heart missed a beat at the knowledge, even as he considered her stepmother's conduct impudent. Didn't the brazen woman know when she was dismissed?

Edward glanced once more at his queen. A look of amusement flared briefly in his regal eyes. He turned toward Lady Rothmore.

"Her position is also under advisement as well. I will send you word when we find a suitable husband."

"I thank you, your grace." She curtsied briefly and left the solar.

Eleanor shook her head and hid a smile. "Patience, my lord," she counseled.

The king's hand curled into a fist. "Bran, be thankful you are not a king and have to suffer such well-meaning widows!"

Bran grimaced in fitting agreement. "Sire, I believe you have my sympathies."

Edward nodded. Offering a hand to his wife, he said, "Come, my lady, let us all take our noonday meal."

CHAPTER SIX

Her fingers trembling, Catrin stuck her hands into the folds of the gown she'd borrowed from Olwen. She was anxious to depart for home to deliver Gilbert's body to Clun Castle.

As she gazed over the garden, her thoughts spiraled in a thousand directions. The muscles in her shoulders grew tense and her throat dry. Would Olwen be able to manage the savage black knight? Even briefly for their first meeting? Her cousin's only hope was to escape to a nunnery. That was clear after hearing her foolish plan to tell the truth.

Footsteps crunched on the gravel path. It was a heavy sound, not light like Olwen's. Catrin's lower lip quivered.

"My lady, Hamon told me where to find you," a deep voice said. "I am surprised, but gratified to find you alone."

Slowly, Catrin turned to face the man she suspected of murder. He was taller than she remembered. Well-built, he stood before her like a frozen specter with his black, wool surcoat falling in folds from his broad shoulders. Not as fierce-looking as when he had stood before her encased from head to foot in mail and helm, the Welshman still presented a frightening sight. With shoulder-length, unfashionably long, ebony hair, his dark brows framed eyes as black as his raven namesake.

She felt heat in her cheeks. What was wrong with her? This was the man who'd clutched her breasts with an iron grip. His very presence both terrified and excited her. A feeling of vulnerability oozed through her veins like honey. If he had this effect on her, what would he do to Olwen? She lifted a hand to her lips.

He took one step forward, then stopped. "Have I frightened you?"

"Nay!"

He searched her face with a questioning gaze. A thin, self-deprecating smile curved his lips, lightening his countenance and making him almost handsome. Deep in his gray eyes, a light burned. "I'm not as dreadful as my reputation, my lady."

Confusion stilled her tongue.

"You mustn't be afraid of me, Lady Northbridge," he said gently extending his hand toward her.

She averted her gaze. Did he think her Olwen? Quick! Just this once she could protect one of her own. She could pretend to be Olwen and save her cousin from the torture of this meeting.

Yet would he know her identity?

When he saw her on the path, she wore a green gown and like now, she'd been covered from head to toe, except for her face. Now she wore Olwen's second-best gown, so surely he wouldn't recognize her from her clothing. And last night in the dark, she'd been careful not to show her face.

"Olwen is a lovely name. May I call you that?" He took

another step. "Please use my given name, since we are to marry. You may call me Bran."

Deliberately she lifted her head and stared at his unwavering gray gaze with its strange spark of light. She pressed her lips together.

How could her sweet cousin deal with such a devil—a man with a steady gaze that burned into a woman's soul? Her instinctive need to protect her family thudded hard against her chest.

He cocked his head. "You look familiar to me."

Catrin quickly lowered her eyes like the shy maiden she pretended to be and found her tongue. "Perchance I look familiar because you have seen my cousin Catrin, Lady Fitzalan. We are oft called sisters because of our resemblance."

"You and Lady Fitzalan are cousins?"

"Aye, my mother was twin sister to Catrin's father, Earl Rothmore. That is why we have a similar appearance," she whispered, finding this part of the story easy to tell for 'twas the truth.

He nodded, watching her intently. "You already know the king's decision?"

"Aye, news—both good and bad—travels fast." Unblinking, her breathing shallow, she lifted her eyes and regarded him.

"You consent?"

She raised her chin. "I am the king's ward. I must do as I am told, as is custom."

"Custom also says you have the right of refusal."

"Duty bids me to wed. What matter to whom?"

"I am glad you will do your duty, my lady," he said. "Yet I hope our marriage will be something more than an obligation. If not love, perchance a pleasant tolerance will grow between us."

Catrin had not anticipated the genuine fervor in his eyes or the appealing tilt of his head. Nor had she expected to be touched by his words. She fought back with her finest haughty manner, reserved for recalcitrant servants or dealings with Isadora.

"Love? You have lofty expectations, my lord."

Humor lit his eyes. "Aye, and oftentimes my expectations have been met."

"You presume much."

He lifted a black eyebrow. "Presumptions oft have a way of becoming reality."

His air of easy confidence shattered her annoyance. She felt herself succumbing as she had last night, when his hands had roused a tingling in her breasts and farther down in the place she kept private.

Straightening her spine, Catrin battled her wayward body. Granted, the king may not believe this knight a murderer, but others accused him. Further, she had proof— the torn piece of scarf—and she needed only to hold onto that knowledge.

"Then you do not know me well, sir," she said, using her cold anger to combat the odd weakness in her knees. "I am not easily swayed."

"And you know me not at all, my lady, for I delight in picking up a gauntlet once thrown down. I believe we will do well together."

His gaze stopped the breath in her throat.

Whoremonger. Bastard. Murderer.

How dare he unclothe her with his look?

How dare he?

He had every right as Olwen's betrothed.

An inner voice quieted Catrin's thudding heart. This wasn't real, only a game of the moment—a ruse to prevent the black knight from harming Olwen before her cousin might flee to the convent. She bit her tongue, her fingers curling into her palms.

His dark eyes sparkled. "What, no more challenges, my lady?"

Had she made matters worse by not acting enough like Olwen?

"Our king spoke of your beauty." He stepped nearer. "I find His Grace speaks truth."

The fearsome knight towered above her. Catrin's pulse quickened. The scent of wood smoke and horses drifted to her. 'Twas a manly smell that clung to his clothes, the scent of one who spent time outdoors. There was a faint vanilla-like whiff of woodruff as well.

"Blue eyes the color of the Welsh sky." He reached out to stroke her forehead just beneath her barbette. Tracing the outline of her face framed by her concealing headdress, he whispered, "Faith, what color is your hair?"

His touch held her hostage. No man had ever taken such liberty. Yet as her betrothed he had the right. Nay! He was Olwen's man. She'd do well to remember.

She failed to speak. He lifted a fingertip and touched her lips. A drugging lethargy spread through Catrin's limbs at the very nearness of him. The knight's contact strangely soothed her, mesmerizing her by his soft caress.

"Your hair, my lady?"

"Flaxen," Catrin forced herself to say.

What was the matter with her? With him? He wasn't behaving like the hideous black knight but as a lover. His smile cleared his countenance and chased away the dark aspect of his being. What of his heart? Was it still black and deceptive? She knew not. She only knew his closeness clouded her reason and her thoughts. Her eyebrows drew together.

"Do not frown, *cariad*," he said.

The intimate endearment rattled Catrin to her very core. An unfamiliar fire ignited deep within, destroying what was left of her common sense.

Cariad. Sweetheart. With difficulty, trance-like, she raised her chin, but she could not pull away from his warm fingertips.

"A kiss to seal our bargain before I come for you at Northbridge?"

She dared not protest. She must play the part of Olwen. Her cousin would not think to object to a simple betrothal kiss.

He favored her with a look of compassion as if he understood the affect he had on her. "I will be ever gentle, *cariad*, and never harm you."

Before Catrin could question his promise, the knight's lips were upon hers. Tentative at first. Questing, as if her mouth were the Holy Grail.

He cupped her face tenderly with his hands, and with a gentle roughness his mouth began to request, and then demand more from her. His tongue sought entrance and once inside, took the soft flesh of her mouth with wicked thrusts. Instead of being repulsed, Catrin responded. His growing excitement stimulated and empowered hers.

The fire in her belly spread, igniting her until her whole body was an unholy blaze of desire. He pressed the length of his hard bulk against her, the bulging presence in the folds of his surcoat obvious. She should have been horrified, appalled by his audacity. Instead, Catrin burned with a need she had never before felt.

As his mouth devoured her own, taking her breath away, a niggling inner voice sounded warning. Why did her body betray her? This knight was her sworn enemy.

Fear—as hot as her lust—ripped into her gut.

Catrin's neglected hands became her only defense. She placed her palms against his chest and shoved against him with all her might, her breath choking in her throat.

"No!" She twisted from him and backed away.

"My lady?"

Panting, Catrin glared at him. His desire-filled eyes narrowed in bewilderment.

"I meant only a chaste, betrothal kiss." He lowered his head. "Forgive me."

Frightened because of her mysterious response to his mouth and body, Catrin's hands knotted.

"You bastard!" The words left her mouth quickly.

Puzzlement flickered in his dark eyes, turning immediately into black, stormy anger. He seized her shoulders with a grip of iron, pulling her to him. His breath was hot on her face.

"Bastard I may be, but you, my wife, shall never call me that."

Mustering all her courage, Catrin tipped her head back and glared at him. "Then do not play the part."

His hard gaze traveled over her face, branding her. "Our lady queen called you a demure maiden and counseled caution so that I not frighten you. She was wrong. You are no timid miss."

His words sounded in her ears. What had she done? If

her cousin failed to escape to the nunnery, what would this man do when he learned of their deception? She had wanted to protect Olwen. Instead, she had made matters worse.

"Take your hands from me," Catrin ordered in a soft, tight voice. "You will never force yourself upon me again."

"What, never kiss you, my wife? Tell me, *cariad*, did I kiss you against your will? I think not. You responded with desire equal to my own."

The truth stung. "I did not!"

Laughter teased his eyes. "So 'tis your game. Well met. I shall play as well, for I love a challenge."

"I do not play," Catrin said stiffly. "Yet I will do my duty."

His face softened. "Duty is oft turned into something more, sometimes love. Beware, *cariad*, for we will have a long life together, God willing."

"I will never grow to love you! You killed Gilbert, my bro..." She caught herself. "My cousin."

His fingers relaxed upon her shoulders. "You do not do well to listen to court gossip."

"I am sorry for the King Edward's decision to ignore the rumors."

He released his grip, and his jaw firmed. "So be it, Lady de Belleme. Believe what you must. You were bred to do your duty, and you shall do it. Of that, I am certain."

His words nettled, but Catrin refused to be goaded further. Shaken, she stepped back, wrapping a cloak of silence around herself for protection.

"Go home and prepare for our wedding," he ordered. "I will come for you in three days."

Turning on his heel, the King's Raven left her standing alone. She could do nothing but look after him, befuddled by her actions and by an aching throb deep within.

CHAPTER SEVEN

When a bank of gray clouds swept across the sun snuffing out the morning's bright sunshine, the air grew chilly. Overhead, the jarring *kraa* of a raven pierced an otherwise complacent noontide around Acton Burnell. Drawing her cloak closely around her, Catrin fought back a sudden premonition of death.

Gilbert's squire and her maid Gwendolyn had prepared for the journey while she and Olwen sought out the queen and later she'd played an impostor to Olwen's betrothed.

Her maid's eyes shifted nervously around the busy campground. "We'd best be on our way, milady."

"Aye." Catrin understood her anxiousness. "Let me wish Olwen farewell."

Catrin approached her cousin, who stood beside Gilbert's shroud-covered body, slung ingloriously across the back of a packhorse—a sad, dishonorable end for her proud brother. Catrin knotted her fists against the pain and choked down the lump in her throat.

She reached out to cup the Olwen's cheek with her right hand. "We must go before Isadora discovers our departure."

Her cousin's eyes filled once more with tears. "Oh, Catrin, my heart shall break."

"No, it shall not break. You must be strong. To honor Gilbert's memory."

"I cannot bear it."

"You must." Her cousin had no choice but to be brave. She was a woman.

Olwen clutched her arm. "Let me go with you."

Catrin shook her head. How could she admit she'd made matters worse for Olwen by her quick tongue? So she'd lied, telling her sweet cousin Bran ap Madog had failed to come to the garden. How could she now tell Olwen he promised to come for her in three days at Northbridge? How could she admit her deception?

With a sigh, Catrin drew Olwen's hands down. "Go home, and then make haste to the nunnery. Do not delay."

"I will go," Olwen said, "for I have no desire to wed. I wish you God's speed, my dear cousin."

Catrin hugged Olwen then broke away. She mounted her palfrey and pulled Gwendolyn up behind her. Gilbert's squire led the string of packhorses, and the small group turned onto the old Roman road. Two Rothmore men-at-arms joined them.

Casting a glance behind her, Catrin lifted her hand in farewell. Olwen stood like a nun at confession, head bowed, eyes lowered, and palms up in supplication.

At the stark image, a chill rippled down Catrin's spine.

Reality was harsh. Throughout her life, loss had been her constant companion. Catrin had never known her mother, and now all her immediate family had been taken from her

—all but for a half-brother, a mere boy of ten. 'Twas hard now to invest oneself in a relationship of any kind, knowing all affiliation was transient, fleeting—like white wisps of morning clouds fleeing on the wind.

Yet part of her dreamed of the heroic knights in tales of chivalry. She longed for romantic love. Yet e'en that was risky.

A cold knot of longing settled in Catrin's core. She shut her eyes, picturing Queen Eleanor, so in love with her royal husband and animated because of a coming child. Too many of the queen's children had died. Her daughters. Even the little prince was sickly. Catrin didn't want the sorrow. Better to keep her heart closed. Better not to love. Better never to marry.

Gwendolyn's arms pressed her waist and her maid's breath was warm on her neck. Catrin opened her eyes. Shifting in the saddle, she glared at the cloud-shrouded sky. Gray like Gilbert's burial cloths. Gray like her mood.

Aloft, a band of ravens soared, their black bodies contrasting sharply with the pall of the sky. Catrin grew anxious.

'Twas easier to give into hate than to love. Like the boiling of a cauldron, her fury flared. *The black knight. The King's Raven.* He was the cause of her latest anguish, no matter his claim of innocence.

Or suggestion that duty might turn to love.

Or her unwelcome response to his kiss.

"He will regret what he has done," Catrin spoke aloud.

"Milady?"

"We will bury my brother, Gwendolyn, and then I will discover who killed Gilbert."

"Aye, milady, God willing."

"God has nothing to do with it."

Catrin urged the patient palfrey into a comfortable amble. Vengeance was up to her and her alone.

THEY RODE in silence for many miles, attempting to make Clun before nightfall. Catrin let her mind drift while she rode, the comfortable pace of the palfrey lulling her into the netherworld between wakefulness and sleep. Gwendolyn's arms were warm around her waist. The steady rhythm of her maid's breathing imparted solace against the October wind.

Suddenly, a shout severed the early evening air. Catrin jerked the reins.

A rabble of men on foot burst from the trees.

"Outlaws!" Gwendolyn cried.

Cold fear surged through Catrin's veins. She watched in horror while her small band of men defended her. They were outnumbered two to one and taking the worst of it.

"Flee, milady! These are no common outlaws. They carry Norman broadswords!"

Gwendolyn's words were like shattering ice.

"My men!" Catrin froze, held by her sense of duty as well as fear.

"We do them no good."

Catrin hesitated.

"Go, milady!"

The note of entreaty in Gwendolyn's voice ripped into Catrin's consciousness. Quickly, she wrenched the horse's neck around, digging her heels into the flanks. The mare shot forward, back over the muddy road they had just traversed.

A hue and cry arose from the outlaws. Dread clogging her throat, Catrin bent low over the horse's neck, pushing the mare forward. The extra burden of a second rider slowed the gallant palfrey. Realizing this, Catrin pulled the animal off the road and into the deep forest.

"Our only chance is to hide," she said, her words coming in ragged gasps.

Gwendolyn clutched tightly to Catrin's waist. When she rested her head against her back, Catrin sensed the other woman's terror as if it were a living thing.

The tall trunks of the old wood proved a complicated maze. Slowing their pace, Catrin guided her winded horse through the coarse undergrowth. Even through the cold of her fear, she felt sweat trickle down her neck. Removing one hand from the reins, she laid a palm on the lathered shoulder of the laboring palfrey.

The din of battle had ebbed by the time Catrin pulled the mare down to a walk. In the distance, she heard the sound of horses plunging through the underbrush.

"They have our men's horses." Panic rose in Gwendolyn's voice.

Had the men from Clun and Gilbert's boy squire been overpowered? The thought of dying pricked Catrin's mind like a knife. Eleanor had promised her marriage would come upon her swift enough, and now, it seemed, so would death. Catrin accepted this reality as she accepted the severity of life.

Yet she would not bow to the inevitable. The thought of surrender soured her blood. Catrin reached into her purse to finger Gilbert's knife.

"Milady." Gwendolyn's hushed tone was spiked with urgency. "These men may mean to hold you for ransom. Give me your cloak and let me ride ahead while you hide in the woods. Perchance they will think both of us ride away and follow me. You'll be safe."

Catrin halted the horse and turned in the saddle. "No, we go on together."

Gwendolyn's fingers unclasped the heavy cloak from around her mistress's neck.

Through the murky half-light of the dying day, she saw tears in her maid's eyes. Catrin grabbed at her hands. "Gwendolyn! Have a care about what you do!"

"I do have a care, milady." Gwendolyn brushed her mistress's hands away. "Before your father left to fight the Welsh, he told me to care for you. You have no choice in the matter, for I do *my* duty."

In the blink of an eye, the maid stripped the cloak from Catrin's back and then shoved her. Caught off guard, Catrin fell from the saddle like a tinker's bundle, her breath knocked out of her lungs.

"Save yourself," Gwendolyn begged. "For my sake."

Unable to speak and struggling for air, Catrin pleaded with her eyes. Their gazes connected in a final farewell.

Gwendolyn moved into the saddle and tossed the cloak over her shoulders. "God be with you, milady."

With a nod, she was gone, goading the horse into a canter through the tangled wood. She made noise to draw the pursuit.

Numb and humbled by Gwendolyn's sacrifice, Catrin did as she was bid. Crawling deep into the underbrush, she hid beneath the rotting log of an oak tree. She shut her eyes and prayed.

~

WHAT FELT like hours could only have been minutes before several horses trampled past, the shouts of their riders adding to the sounds of the chase. Catrin shivered in her dank hole.

Digging her fingers into the woodland soil, she clutched the dirt, unmindful of the soil caking under her nails or the damp, earthy aroma of her hideaway. Guilt cut into her soul. Why had she let Gwendolyn play decoy? She should have prevented her maid's foolhardy heroics.

A distant hurrah sounded and then the pounding of the pursuit drifted over the crisp currents of air. Had the outlaws spotted Gwendolyn?

Soon a blood-curdling scream echoed through the forest. The shriek pierced straight into Catrin's heart like a well-aimed arrow.

Two horses and their riders approached from the road, halting in a clearing a scant fifty feet from her. Soon the original band of outlaws joined them. Catrin sucked in air and closed her eyes.

"Did you catch them?" demanded a deep voice as brittle as winter's death.

She knew that voice. But from where?

"Nay," another man answered. "The wench purposely rode her horse over a cliff."

Catrin shuddered. Gwendolyn was dead. She couldn't quite believe it. Not her surrogate mother and trusted maid, the woman who had care for her through childhood illnesses and knew her better than any other living creature.

Dear God, guide her soul. For Gwendolyn's sake, she hoped her silent supplication was heard.

"Are both women dead?"

"I know not, sir."

"Zounds! Find out!" The first man sounded forbidding. "I must have proof or your life will be forfeit as well!"

The troop of cutthroats clattered away, leaving a strange lingering silence.

Catrin's pulse pounded. She squeezed her eyes tighter as if to quiet the fear that threatened to rout whatever courage she still possessed.

A hair's breath away, horses' hooves trounced the underbrush. She heard the metal clank of chain mail, caught the scent of unwashed bodies, and sensed the intensity of the leader's purpose.

Was this man Gilbert's murderer? Was he the King's Raven? Were they the same person?

"They must be dead." The slap of a leather gauntlet striking a saddle emphasized the leader's point. "Harry, follow them and make sure those louts have done what they claim."

Another horse departed. Catrin opened her eyes and stared at the tangled brush like someone blind. She didn't know how long it was before the horses returned.

"Milady's cloak covered in her blood," a rough voice boasted.

Sickened, Catrin stifled a gasp.

"I climbed down the cliff face to retrieve it," one of them said. "I took me life in me hands."

"And her maid?" the leader asked.

"Dead as well."

"Harry?"

"Aye, my lord, I saw both bodies with mine eyes," his companion replied in halting Norman French. "Unless you knew they were at the bottom of the cliff, you would never see them."

The outlaws had lied and so had Harry. By his lie, the nefarious man had saved his worthless skin, for if the leader knew the truth, all these men would pay dearly.

The leader grunted. "I shall take the cloak as proof of our success."

"What about Rothmore's body?" Harry asked.

"Leave it. Let us ride!"

In a heartbeat, they were gone, the sounds of the horses fading fast.

All grew quiet. Catrin was alone.

Unable to quell the horror gripping her, Catrin crawled from her hiding place and slowly climbed to her feet. Was Gwendolyn truly dead? She had to see for herself.

Somehow, Catrin picked her way over fallen wood and through thick brush. She followed the path eked out of the forest by men and horses until she reached the edge of the cliff. Far below lay her dead horse. Nearby, Gwendolyn's lifeless and broken body was sprawled among the rocks.

Catrin began to shake. Her legs buckled and she crumbled to the ground. All those she loved died. She shut her eyes and sobbed, succumbing to the overbearing anguish.

'Twas better not to love or care.

Time passed slowly. Catrin hugged her knees, rocking back and forth, her head bowed to her chest. She crooned soft sounds of mourning.

Soon a chilly rain fell over her sorrow-shattered body.

Enough! She could weep no more. Catrin stood, and in a defiant motion, flipped her heavy braid over her shoulder. She raised her eyes to the heavens. Cold raindrops touched her upturned face, mingling with the salt of her tears.

She took a deep breath. Somehow she had changed. The world around her looked the same, but she was no longer the girl who had tied a favor around her brother's arm only a day ago.

What now? She dared not go to Clun Castle or return to court and face Isadora. Alive, her life might be in jeopardy still. Dead, she was safe and free.

The storm gathered strength, savage and unforgiving. The force of the wind pushed against her surcoat, wrapping the garment around her legs. Catrin welcomed the cold and bitter rain, for with its sting came her answer.

She could only rely on herself. Alone, she must find and punish the man who had murdered her loved ones.

Catrin fumbled for her purse and rubbed her thumb and forefinger over the smooth silk pieces inside. She had proof. The King's Raven had motive. She would start with him.

Yet she must first go to Northbridge Castle and tell Olwen not to worry. She was not dead at the hands of villains as someone evil had wished.

CHAPTER EIGHT

The second day after the attack, Catrin reached the wooded sandstone hills near Northbridge Castle. The rising sun was but a pink promise on the horizon when below her vantage point overlooking the valley she spied the broad water meadows stretching to the banks of the Severn. Beyond them, high on the western edge of an escarpment over-looking the river, a formidable Norman keep stood guard over the autumn countryside.

Catrin's hands fell to her sides. What remaining willpower she had used to navigate the distance at night and reach Olwen's castle drained from her with a whoosh. Now she only longed for a bath and a meal. The pang of hunger in her stomach was a familiar, but unwelcome, guest. Instead of seeking refreshment, she had to await nightfall and find her way into the castle without being seen.

Crawling into a thicket by the side of the road, she shut her eyes, overcome by weariness. Yet sleep did not come swiftly. Her mind replayed the events of the past few days. Father. Gilbert. Gwendolyn and her men. Dead. Gone. She loathed her enemies. Her hatred was as unforgiving as the Clee Hills she'd so recently traversed. Eleanor had given fair warning. *Still yourself against the fires of hatred, my lady.* N'er mind. Catrin preferred hatred to heartache.

She curled her fingers, her nails biting into her palms. Was the King's Raven to blame for her misfortunes? Did he employ a Saxon lackey named "Harry?" Many a boy was named after old King Henry. A small clue. The pieces of silk scarf were other clues—pieces of a puzzle. Surely, a greater purpose lay behind her brother's death, for whomever murdered Gilbert had tried to kill her too.

CATRIN AWOKE WITH A START. It was dark. A lone horse thundered past her hiding place. Only the brave or the desperate traveled the king's road at night.

Moments passed and the pounding hoof beats faded into the distance. When she thought it safe, Catrin uncoiled her cramped limbs from her hiding spot. She steadied herself mentally and climbed to her feet. Her neck and shoulders ached. Hunger pangs made her head woozy.

The normal sounds of nocturnal creatures and the sigh of the wind filled the air. Time to go. Lifting her chin for courage, Catrin stepped boldly onto the roadway and strode down the hillock into the valley of the Severn.

The darkness was a welcoming shroud. As she approached a cluster of humble huts gathered by the wooden bridge, a dog howled long and mournful. She heard a muffled curse and then a yelp. The dog quieted inside one of the huts.

Smoke from banked fires played in the air, tracing gray

finger patterns into the sky. Only one dwelling displayed a pinpoint of light, and someone snuffed it just as the clouds broke, allowing moonlight to illuminate her path.

Catrin quickly crossed the bridge. Her pulse pounded in her ears. A cartway wound its way up the escarpment to Northbridge, but she avoided it, choosing instead to climb the steep steps cut out of stone on the face of the cliff. Peasants made their homes in caves dotting the rocks. Catrin slipped quietly by these openings, maintaining a cautious pace.

Near the summit, she spotted a familiar rock masked by brush. She glanced over her shoulder, then slipped into the tiny opening of a secret cave, losing what light the moon had provided. With heavy gulps, she sucked dank air into her lungs and gathered her courage once more.

Trusting her childhood memory of summer games played with Olwen among the cliffs, Catrin placed a palm on the cold, clammy side of the cave wall. Cautiously, she moved forward step by step into the black hole.

Fear closed her throat. No. The forbidding tunnel would not overcome her. Creeping forward, she pressed a hand against the rock. 'Twas her only guide. Had she chosen the wrong cave? Surely this led to the secret escape passage Olwen's father had shown them long ago when she and her cousin were children.

Suddenly, her hand struck air, and she stumbled forward as the cave wall ended.

Catrin fought a stab of alarm. Her breath came in short, sharp gasps. She inched her right foot forward until the toe of her riding boot touched stone. Spiral stairs veered to the right. She placed her palms on both sides of the narrow wall and cautiously started up the steep ascent. How many steps?

Fifty, she remembered. Catrin counted them silently until she felt a solid, wooden door.

Dieu merci!

Without pausing to catch her breath, she tripped the hidden latch that threw the bolt. The door moved inward on well-oiled hinges hardly making a sound. Catrin shouldered aside a heavy damask wall hanging and entered the private solar of the lady of the castle.

One lone candle lit the murky darkness.

"Olwen?"

"Who goes there?"

"'Tis I. Catrin."

Her cousin emerged from the shadows, her pale face streaked with tears. Prayer beads dangled from a hand.

"Mercy!" Olwen crossed herself. "Catrin? Can it be you? We had word of your death!"

"You see that I'm very much alive," Catrin said with a laugh of relief. She opened her arms, and Olwen, sobs shaking her slim body, stumbled into them. "Do not cry so, cuz."

They clung to each other for many minutes. When the hinges of the solar door squeaked, Catrin stepped back, releasing Olwen.

"'Tis only Meg, my maid," Olwen said, wiping her eyes with the back of her hand.

The maid entered carrying a laver of water. She gaped, fingers flying to cover her mouth, and dropped the crockery. "A ghost! Lord, preserve us!"

"Meg, Catrin is alive!"

"We had word of your murder at the hands of outlaws." The maid dropped to her knees to pick up pieces of the broken bowl. "I have only now shown the messenger from your stepmother to the kitchen."

"Someone did try to kill me." Catrin knelt beside the maid. "Odd that word reached Isadora so fast."

"The messenger said Lady Rothmore learned of your death at Acton Burnell from my lady's betrothed, the one they call the King's Raven."

Anger wrenched Catrin's heart. "Why am I not surprised?"

"The knight said he came upon the scene of a battle," Meg explained. "He recognized the arms on the dead men's liveries, found your brother's shrouded corpse, and brought the body back to court."

They stood at the same time, and Catrin handed the maid the broken crockery she'd collected. "How did he explain my death?"

"The messenger said your bloodied cloak was with the dead men, outlaws he presumed, that he discovered on the highway."

"You say the outlaws were murdered too?" Catrin tried to understand. "Who killed them?"

"The messenger did not know," Olwen said. "He said the King's Raven did not know either."

Catrin glanced at her cousin. "I see."

"What are you thinking, Catrin?"

"From the sound of a voice I heard while hiding, I believe a nobleman wanted me dead. He must have killed the outlaws in his employ to prevent them from revealing their part in the plot."

Olwen wrung her hands. "Was that nobleman my betrothed?"

"I know not." Catrin wiped her hands on her soiled garment, feeling grimy. Her legs suddenly grew unsteady.

"Catrin, what's wrong?"

She met Olwen's gaze. Waves of hot and cold washed over her. Her head spun like dancing maidens on May Day. "I feel lightheaded."

"You are exhausted. Sit, cuz." Olwen ordered. She guided Catrin back toward the small chair near the fireplace. "Meg, be quick! Bring water, food, and mead. Do not speak of our guest. Catrin's presence shall remain our secret."

"Aye, my lady." Meg rushed from the room.

Later, after cleaning her face and hands and eating her fill of bread and cheese, Catrin rested by the fire. Heat radiated through her, warming her body, yet nothing penetrated her icy mood.

"We need to discuss what's to be done," Catrin said. Olwen sat opposite while Meg lingered nearby.

"Do you wish me to leave, my lady?"

"No, Meg. We may need your help."

Olwen leaned toward Catrin. "What do you plan to do, cuz?"

"The world believes me dead." Catrin drew a deep breath. Saying the words aloud sent a strange tingle through her body. "But I cannot hide away in this solar forever."

"Especially with my lady's coming nuptials," Meg reminded them. "Her betrothed arrives on the morrow."

Olwen's eyes grew cold. "I want nothing to do with marriage to one so wicked. I must go to the convent."

"Verily, 'tis the place for you, sweet, as we agreed," Catrin said, "but we have little time."

"I know." Olwen flushed and looked down. "I am sorry I had not heeded your advice sooner."

Trying to gather her uncontrolled thoughts, Catrin rose and began to pace the solar.

"Bran ap Madog's arrival poses a problem greater than you know." She dared not look at Olwen. "You see I have already angered him."

"How could you anger him? I thought you had never met him." Olwen shook her head, not understanding. "You said he did not come to the garden."

"I did not want you to worry." Catrin stopped and faced her cousin. "But he did come. He thought me to be you, and I let him believe it. And I angered him."

Olwen gasped and lifted trembling fingertips to her lips. "Oh, Catrin. What happened?"

"I called him a bastard to his face."

"You did not?"

"I did, Olwen." Catrin looked away. "Right after he kissed me."

"Catrin!"

"My ill-timed remarks have made it impossible for you to marry him." Catrin fought a chill of certainty. "He was furious because I spoke to him in such manner. He will still be angry. He will take it out on you."

"You must come with me to the convent, Catrin." Olwen's face grew determined. "We will both go."

How could she let this beast harm Olwen? Further, there was no assurance her cousin would be safe even in a convent. Church walls held no sanctity for one such as he.

She set her jaw with resolve. "I will not go to the convent."

"Where will you go?" Meg asked. "If people believe you dead, where can you live? Your life may be in danger still."

Catrin gazed at the two women. "I will go nowhere," she

said. "Catrin Fitzalan *is* dead. For the first time in my life, I am free of the constraints of society and, therefore, free to make my own choices."

"If the King's Raven arrives tomorrow, he will find his bride awaiting him." She lifted her chin. "I will be that bride, sweet cuz."

Olwen gasped. "How can that be?"

"Easy enough." The plot formed quickly in her mind. "Remember when I fostered with you as children, we oft traded places to confuse the servants? The other day, e'en Queen Eleanor commented how much we favor each other."

"You both have an uncanny resemblance," Meg agreed.

Olwen shook her head. "You talk foolishly. I cannot let you do it."

"There is no other way," Catrin said as her purpose firmed. "Someone must be here to hoodwink the king's man so he will not come looking for you."

"'Tis too dangerous."

"Maybe so, but I will make it work. He already believes me to be Olwen."

Olwen looked worried. "How will he not recognize you?"

"I do not think so," Catrin said. "I did see him at the tourney. At the time, I was dressed in a green gown. When he saw me later, thinking me you, I was dressed in your old gown. Both times he only saw my face, and I have already told him Olwen resembles her cousin Catrin."

"Who is now *dead*," Meg said, as if understanding the deception. "It may work, my lady."

"It must work!"

Olwen had gone pale. "'Tis a sin. You cannot do this. God will punish us both."

"God has already punished us." Catrin's voice was hushed by the weight of her words.

She had a plan, however dubious. It gave her a measure of control, however small. With it, she would not be forced to suffer her ill fate silently. She might meet it head on and fight like the warrior she had always wanted to be.

CHAPTER NINE

The callused hand of Father Ellis settled on Catrin's shoulder. "Walk with me." Olwen had insisted they take the castle chaplain into their confidence.

Together the priest and Catrin strolled toward the kitchen garden where Olwen grew her medicinal herbs— betony for the cough and diseases of the lungs, chamomile for headaches, and lavender for apoplexy and falling-sickness. Olwen cultivated her plants with care, picking them at full maturity and greatest vigor, and drying them for use when she tended the sick.

Catrin glanced up at the Father Ellis' plump and kindly face as they entered the open gate. Thomas de Belleme, Olwen's father, had installed the monk at Northbridge to shepherd the castle flock. That the clergyman was capable with his sums and could read and write had made him very useful in ways temporal, as well as spiritual.

The autumn had been warm, and the foliage of columbine was an island of green in the otherwise gray and barren garden. Catrin paused to take in the beauty of the small enclosure.

"If it is as you say, you have no certain proof the black knight killed your brother," Father Ellis pointed out.

Catrin's heart ached with an unrelenting sadness. "What about the second piece of silk scarf I found near my brother's body?"

"Mayhap you jump to conclusions," the clergyman suggested. "You know not who dropped it."

Catrin glared at him. She wanted to believe she knew the name of Gilbert's murderer—The King's Raven—for she had no other suspect.

"Your words of caution do not interest me, Father," she said with firm determination. "I shall avenge my brother's untimely death—an eye for an eye."

"Harsh words." The priest glanced down at her. "They do not become you."

"I am tired of having all of mine taken from me."

"Take care you do not let your anger and grief turn into hatred."

Catrin held his gaze. "Your words of counsel come too late."

"I do not like this," he said with a frown. "The Bible says, 'Everyone who hates his brother is a murderer; and you know that no murderer has eternal life abiding in him.' Catrin, I beg you to reconsider. I fear for your soul."

She let out a breath. Life had presented her without much control. All she ruled were her emotions. Hatred and anger hurt less than the sadness of loss.

She lowered her eyes, feigning submission. "I will consider your words, Father."

"Your scheme is risky and ill-advised."

"Is it not ill-advised to let my sweet cousin marry a man who is suspected of cold-bloodied murder?" Catrin glanced up. "Olwen clearly belongs in a convent."

Father Ellis regarded her, still frowning, but not denying her words.

"Our plan will work," Catrin declared. "The King's Raven already thinks me Olwen. We met at Acton Burnell. Few castle folk will suspect and those who do will be sworn to secrecy."

The clergyman grunted. "You are naïve. What of this knight? He is no fool."

"He will be the last to discover, and if he does find out the truth, I will follow Olwen to her place of sanctuary." Catrin shrugged, knowing full well the walls of the convent might provide an insufficient hiding place from a betrayed husband.

Father Ellis quietly considered her. "You are determined to do this."

She nodded.

"I cannot agree to officiate," he said. "To marry you 'twould be placing us both in mortal sin."

"I will not be thwarted in this! Think of my cousin's happiness and safety. Think of your duty to her." Father Ellis stiffened, and Catrin pressed him. "You baptized Olwen as a babe and educated her. You've seen her grow into a woman. You comforted her when her parents died. Do your duty, Father, and protect the only child of Lord Northbridge."

"Do not speak to me of duty," he rejoined. "Olwen is like my own child. For that reason alone, I have made arrangements at the nunnery of the White Ladies. I will take her there today where she will be safe." Father Ellis drew himself up and looked down his nose at Catrin. "In so doing I jeopardize my soul."

"Thank you." Tears welled behind her eyelids with relief. She didn't want to pressure him, but felt she must. Switching places was necessary as well if she was to learn the truth. Helping Olwen in the process was an added boon.

"I wish I could guarantee your safety, my child. I fear this false marriage will bode ill for you."

She offered a fatalistic smile. "We have no guarantees in this life. For the sake of my cousin and my family, I have chosen this path."

"You are foolish, but brave," he conceded.

Catrin sighed. "Nay, not brave. Simply stubborn, I think."

The old man's eyes glimmered with cautious humor. "Then I will pray for this king's man, for he knows not his fate."

THE SUDDEN EERIE STILLNESS, like calm winds before a coming storm, alerted Catrin to the arrival of the King's Raven and his entourage. 'Twas like the dying of the winds before a coming storm. Then chaos broke out in the bailey below. Dogs barked, grooms shouted, the trample of horses' hooves and the jingle of their trappings cut the quiet of the day.

Catrin abandoned her embroidery, slipping out to Olwen's herb garden, the blustery day more welcoming than the cold, damp confines of the castle. She had completed her transformation to Olwen only scant hours earlier. With the help of Meg and a reluctant Father Ellis, her cousin now resided at White Ladies, where she found refuge and, hopefully, a measure of peace.

So he had come. The carrion-eater. At Acton Burnell, he'd asked her to call him by his given name—Bran, the raven.

Her nerves jangled. Catrin raised her head and stared at the gray sky. The bridegroom had come to claim his bride, and Catrin, pretending to be Olwen, was that bride. As Olwen, she would take marriage vows, and then he would expect to bed her, as was custom with the traditional ceremony.

Unable to quell her sudden trepidation, Catrin picked up a garden hoe. Fear was best met by physical action.

What would she do? Delay? Play the virgin until she learned the truth of her brother's death? If circumstances were, as she believed, she would eventually exact revenge on her "bridegroom." If not, the Church could annul the marriage. A simple strategy.

Catrin smiled at her cleverness. In her year at court, she had studied the rule of present consent to better discuss holy matrimony with Queen Eleanor. The Church said both parties must freely give consent for the marriage to be valid. Vows given under duress or deception were invalid. Obviously, Bran ap Madog would exchange vows with an imposter.

In the eyes of the Church, they would not truly be married.

Catrin released a breath of sharp October air slowly. She mustn't question herself, her actions, or her motives. She must be brave, as Father Ellis believed her to be.

As she wanted to be.

AN HOUR LATER, Bran found her in the garden hoeing the dead stalks of summer's encroaching weeds.

"You did not come to welcome me, my lady."

She didn't glance up, hoping to put him off. "I am busy."

"Too busy to meet your bridegroom? 'Tis not well met, Olwen. I expected more courage from you."

Her head snapped up. "My whole life has been one of courage, my lord."

"Bran," he corrected and came toward her.

She stared at him in disbelief, for riding on his outstretched, gloved wrist—much like a nobleman carried a hawk—was a sleek raven. Her knuckles whitened on the hoe.

He stroked the glistening ebony feathers. "What think you of Mair?"

Catrin gaped at the black-clad figure and his hideous bird. To her, the knight's affable manner rang false. He held the bird of death. All she had seen and experienced in the last days settled like lead in her chest.

What have I done?

The import of her decision to switch places with Olwen suddenly struck her.

Could Father Ellis be right?

She was about to marry a man who approached so stealthily she had not heard him come. A man who carried a bird of doom. What if she proved unable to carry out the ruse and seek the revenge she sought?

Trreeck!

Startled by the raven's cry, Catrin dropped the hoe and lifted her arm to cover her face.

"Fie, bird!" The black knight flicked his wrist and in a whoosh of feathery wings, the raven flew upward to alight on a bare branch. "I must beg pardon, my lady. Mair won't hurt you, though she's oft protective of me."

How very odd. Catrin's gaze never left the face of her tormentor. He spoke of the bird as a friend.

She gathered her nerve and lifted her chin. "You talk with affection about such a terrible creature."

"Mair is not so terrible." He smiled. "We have much in common."

"Yea, you both live off rotten spoils of your victims."

His eyes narrowed, then he shrugged. "We are both oft misunderstood."

"So you remind me," Catrin continued in a terse tone. "I find it hard to believe you're not the fierce creature reputed by others."

"An image I have carefully crafted at the behest of our king," he said. "When you know me longer, you will learn the truth."

"'Tis not *that* truth I seek from you, sir."

"Bran," he prompted. "You forget again, *cariad*."

"Do not call me that!"

"What?" He arched a playful brow. "You want me to have no endearment for my wife and helpmate?"

The only help Catrin wanted to give him was a swift kick to send him on his way like the cur he was.

"Wife I may become, thanks to the king's command," she said with a defiant glare, "but I will never welcome an endearment from one such as you." She dared not call him bastard again, but he caught her meaning nonetheless.

He lifted an eyebrow. "Ah, so that's the lay of the land. I remember another day in another garden, *cariad*, when you welcomed my endearments. Do you not remember you promised to do your duty? How soon you forget."

"I forget nothing."

He looked down at her, his eyes merry. Did he think she flirted with him?

"Too bad, for I had hoped to remind you."

Catrin took a step backward. "I need no reminding."

"What a shame." He removed his leather gloves, a symbol of his power. She was vaguely aware of them dropping to the ground. "Will you not temper your intractable manner?"

"You may find my temper instead, my lord."

"Call me, Bran, *cariad*, as I asked."

His kiss, when it came, was as swift as the strike of a gyrfalcon after its prey. Caught off guard, Catrin was unable to flee. He seized her in his mighty grasp, pulling her toward him, upward, crushing her to his chest. As his mouth captured hers, she struggled to free herself.

Afraid of his overt masculinity, his strength, she fought against him. He devoured her lips, causing hot panic to rise in her throat. He was so powerful. The ultimate warrior. She was his quarry. Weak. Helpless.

"Do not resist. I'll not hurt you," he murmured against her mouth.

How could she believe him when he used his power against her? How could she fight him? The impossibility of her situation struck her like a deathblow. Catrin went limp in his arms.

"Ah, *cariad*."

His kiss gentled then, as did his grip. His questing lips softened on hers, but were insistent still. Releasing a shoulder, he reached up under her crespine, under her heavy, knee-length braid, and placed a strong hand on the bare flesh of her neck. Her skin twitched at his touch. As he pressed her toward him once more, his tongue sought her own.

Her stomach tight, Catrin felt sudden desire surge throughout her body. She recognized the sensations she feared, and her intellect rebelled. Yet her treasonous, arousing flesh paid no attention. A deep and needy pain throbbed inside. His lips continued to compel her response, and her lungs ached for air. A faint sound escaped from her throat.

Pulling back from the kiss, his dark eyes examined her face. She couldn't break the spell of his gaze. His breath was hot upon her eyes...her lips. He slowly lifted his other hand from her shoulder. His fingertips assaulted her, tracing liquid fire over her brows and down the curve of her cheek, and she forgot everything but a new heightened sensitivity that spread through her.

"The king has blessed me well," he murmured. "Do you know how I want to see more than the fair outline of your charming face?"

His lips took hers again. The silken heat of his tongue sent a quiver through her body. Catrin succumbed to his torture, returning his kiss with a growing excitement of her own. His hand strayed from her face into the folds of her surcoat. When his fingers brushed the wool fabric that covered her breast, shock waves reverberated up and down her spine. Her legs weakened. He caught her to him tightly. She felt the hard shape of him through the folds of their clothing. She felt her own melting capitulation.

She was his for the taking.

"Nay," he said under his breath, "we will be husband and wife first."

Bran stepped back a pace and dropped his hands. He appeared visibly shaken, his mouth open, his eyes glazed. In shock, she stared at him. Slowly, her fingertips strayed to her swollen lips.

What have I done?

"The king commands we wed immediately, my lady. He wants these lands secured. I find I agree, for I want more than *lands* secured. You will find I am eager to be your husband and will love you as is fitting for a husband to love a wife."

Catrin gathered what pride that remained within and looked upon him with disdain. "The king may bind us together, but he cannot order my heart. We may wed on the morrow, sir, but you will never secure that part of me," she taunted. "My devotion belongs to my cousin Gilbert Fitzalan, the late Earl Rothmore, whom many say you have murdered."

His countenance darkened. "I'm sorry for your grief, but I care not for your affection. I have my orders from the king, and I will do my duty."

She looked away and refused to answer. He retrieved his leather gloves and with angry deliberation pulled them on, his gaze never leaving hers, and then he whistled shrilly through his teeth. With a flap of wings, Mair swooped from the tree and settled on his outstretched, gloved wrist.

"Go. Make your preparations for the morrow when we will wed."

He left Catrin standing silently in the garden, alone with her anger and even more determined to prove him guilty of slaying her brother.

"This time I will not fail," Catrin vowed.

CHAPTER TEN

Anger hammered Bran hard. He curled his cold fingers around a goblet of good Bordeaux wine and drank deeply, hoping to ease his ire. The fire in the stone fireplace spit and popped, casting a small pool of light around the hearth. He stretched his legs out toward the scant warmth and leaned back in the lord of the castle's chair.

Long years of training had taught him to temper his emotion. His mind needed to be sharp, his hands steady, to do what he had been trained to do—kill the enemy. Whether symbolically on the tourney field or during the struggle of live combat, Bran always won. He bested his opponents, triumphant, but magnanimous in victory.

Until today.

Today, when the piercing blue eyes and the fair oval face of his betrothed overcame him, confusing him as if he were a green lad with his first love.

The mere memory of their kiss sent scorching desire coursing through his veins. He swallowed more wine, enjoying the sting of the dark liquor as it slid down his throat.

On the other side of the screen placed around him for privacy, the snores of castle folks, who had already taken to their pallets in the great hall, sounded strangely comforting. These were now his people. His responsibility.

A sharp thrill rippled through him. Tomorrow he would be wed. Tomorrow Northbridge and the surrounding demesne lands along the Severn River would be his. Property was the lifeblood of any man, and for years he had been bereft of true life. Now he would be wealthy beyond his wildest dreams. Property and heirs—offspring to carry on the only thing he had ever possessed until now—his name.

He would have all of it, if Olwen de Belleme proved as good a breeder as she was beautiful. Yet who was this maiden Edward had given him? The Queen called her quiet, childlike, a woman best suited for religious vows.

His experience had been wildly different. To him, she was an enigma, seeming rebellious, even coy. She was capable of arousing him with a hot, incautious compulsion that threatened to drive away whatever civility he possessed.

He had promised Queen Eleanor to be gentle. To go slow with his bride. But Olwen's mutinous behavior and her claim of love for another did not sit well. Not tonight. Not when everything he wanted was so close within his grasp.

Bran finished off the wine. He wanted more, but thought better of it. He needed a clear head for the morrow. Neither drunkenness nor anger at his bride would serve his purposes. If Olwen was to be won, he must follow Eleanor's admonition—control himself and go slow.

Frowning, Bran placed the goblet on the side table and stared into the sputtering flames until they blurred before his eyes. The death of Rothmore plagued him sorely. He had been implicated in the young lord's death. Now his bride-to-be taunted him with the lad's name.

Bran sat forward, clutching his cold fingers between his knees. Rothmore was dead now and so was the earl's sister, her life snuffed out by brigands on the king's highway. They were Olwen's cousins. 'Twas no wonder she was upset.

He let out a slow breath. Would his wife accept him? He did not like uncertainty, but he respected the brittle edge it gave him. He felt that brittleness now, gazing into the flickering firelight, thinking about the morrow. The most important battle of his life was to come, and he had no idea how to arm himself.

"I have brought a bath," Rhys said, rousing Bran from his reflection.

Brawny serving boys carried a large wooden tub around the screen, placing it near the hearth. Two more men carried buckets of steaming water. They emptied the contents of three buckets into the tub and sat the other one next to the fire, withdrawing when their task was complete.

"'Tis best that you wash before the morrow," the sergeant commented, laying out clean cloths and a new set of braes.

Then Rhys sprinkled flakes of sweet woodruff into the tub and the pleasant vanilla-like aroma filled Bran's nostrils. With a grin, he pushed to his feet. The firelight provided scant heat and only illumination, but 'twas enough for his purposes.

"You imply that my lady will refuse to wed me unless I bathe."

"The thought crossed my mind...my lord."

Bran's head jerked at the formal address. His stomach tightened. "True. Tomorrow I will, in fact, become *my lord*."

"Well-deserved," Rhys said. A smile lit his face. "And long enough in coming."

Bran agreed with his sergeant. He knew his place, just as he knew his worth in the scheme of things in Edward's kingdom.

Stripping off his clothing, he toyed with no false modesty. Bran stepped over the edge of the tub and sank wearily into the burning water that almost immediately pulled the tension from his back and shoulders. He took up a linen rag and soap and began to wash himself.

"Perchance you'll have a wife's hand to help you next time," Rhys said with a wicked chuckle.

"Be gone, knave!" Bran waved his soapy hand, dismissing the little man, who went away laughing.

Having enough problems with control, Bran did not need a reminder of what was to take place on the morrow. His deprived flesh had memory of its own.

Anticipation gripped him. At the same time, he mulled a sense of regret—Northbridge Castle, not Castle Dinas Bran. English property, not Welsh. Was he also to have a maiden whose heart belonged to another?

Anger flared again. Bran knew how to fight for what he wanted. Yet how did he fight with the specter of a dead man? A man whose death was attributed, by some, to him?

He must look for the murderer to prove his innocence. After the wedding, he would send Rhys out to spy for news.

Now steeled with new determination, Bran stood, water sloshing down his long limbs and over the edge of the tub. The trouble with sending Rhys away was that he had to attend to himself. He reached over and lifted the bucket of water. Slowly he splashed the now tepid liquid over his body, letting it rinse the soap from the hairs on his chest and the muscles of his thighs.

His manhood stood proudly, only tempered slightly by the cooling water.

God's teeth! He raised his gaze toward the old lord's war shield hung in decoration high on the wall by the hearth. How could he go slowly with his supposedly quiet and gentle bride when every part of him ached to consummate his marriage as soon as yon priest spoke the wedding vows?

CATRIN SHOVED her palm against her mouth, stifling a gasp, and jumped back from the squint, a peephole concealed by the war shield hanging near the fireplace. Had he seen her spying on him? It seemed as if he must, for those black eyes had looked her way almost as if he knew she was watching him bathe.

Her face flamed. She turned from the secret squint, feeling the heat shiver up and down her body. Fanning her cheeks with her hand, she slowly crossed Olwen's solar, the flagstones, covered with Castilian carpet, yet cold beneath her stocking-less feet.

After compline, Meg had taken her rest and now snored softly on a pallet at the foot of the tall, canopied bed. Catrin skirted Olwen's maid—her maid now—stopping at the side of the down-filled mattress piled high with colorful quilts and warm furs. Tomorrow night he would share this bed with her.

Bran ap Madog. The King's Raven. The warrior she suspected of killing her brother and father. Bran, the man who called her *cariad* and kissed her as she'd never dreamed of being kissed.

She stared at the lord's bed, aptly aware of its import. Heirs of Northbridge were conceived on yon bed. For years, children carrying the lord's name came into being there. Guilt pricked her ever so briefly. When he bedded her tomorrow night, he'd consummate his marriage with an imposter. 'Twas sinful what she was about, but Catrin hastily swept that thought from her mind the same way she brushed a piece of lint from her gown.

She had honorable intentions, saving Olwen from a fate worse than death. Mayhap she would soon discover the truth about Gilbert and her father as well.

Renewed with resolve, Catrin stripped off her shift, snuffed out the lone, tallow candle, and pushing back the soft fur coverlets, crawled into the high bed. Quietly, she let down the linen hangings, muting Meg's snores. Now she felt closed off from the world.

Sitting in darkness so heavy she couldn't see her hand in front of her face, Catrin drew her knees up to her chest and hugged them. Love was an ephemeral emotion, too dangerous, by far. She had never been in love, nor even formerly courted, because her father had been overly protective. Now, any girlish dreams she'd harbored were of no matter.

Catrin bit her lip. Why had she baited him? Why give him the impression that Gilbert had been her lover? The words had just slipped out.

Yet her inopportune words had prepared him for her hatred. 'Twould be much easier this way. He would have no false expectations of her loving him. Would that ease his anger when he learned the truth?

She doubted it. Nothing would stay the man's anger.

Wrapped in the closeness of her private cozy cocoon, Catrin smiled grimly.

She had to make him direct his rage only at her. Not at Olwen, nor Meg. Not at the good father, who would marry them against his will.

Hugging her knees even tighter, she rested her chin on them. In the silence, in the darkness, she felt the steady rhythm of her heart and heard the slow intake of her breath. The gentle scent of lavender on the bed clothing reminded her of Olwen.

Sweet heavens, could she manage this deception? Could she become Olwen—the shy, sensible, and holy maid?

She doubted that too. Not after seeing what she had seen tonight in the firelight of the great hall.

In that personal place between her thighs, a softening began—slowly—as if it was becoming a warm pool, opening and welcoming.

Fear sharpened Catrin's breath. She had seen men before. Heavens, she'd been raised with a younger brother. She'd watched curs coupling in the bailey. She knew what was expected of her on the morrow.

Catrin shut her eyes, suddenly dizzy. What she had not seen was the magnificence she secretly witnessed tonight, looking down on that proud stallion that was to be her husband.

Had he cast a spell on her? Standing—all of him—naked like a Celtic god? Why else did she ache in the place only he had stirred? Why else had memories of that kiss in the garden tormented her, scorching her cheeks and weakening her limbs?

Lord, help her. She pursued this deception willingly

enough, but now she wondered if she weren't the one to be deceived.

The King's Raven had worked his magic on her—as he had on all those other women—his spoils of war, the ones he so wantonly ravished.

CHAPTER ELEVEN

Father Ellis' dark robes mirrored his even darker mien. Catrin chose to ignore the nagging pangs of guilt, but the good father seemed unable to do the same. Thus, he'd ordered the ceremony to take place in the castle chapel, far from the customary church doorway and the trappings of the Church's high altar.

Bran ap Madog had agreed. After all, the king's decree ordered the nuptials to take place quickly. With no time for lengthy preparation, no family present, and the recent deaths of Olwen's cousins to consider, the union of the lady of Northbridge and the king's champion would likely be a somber affair. Ne'ertheless, Sir Bran had ordered all the castle folks to witness the event and bear testimony to its legitimacy.

Catrin waited for Olwen's betrothed near the massive stone hearth, keeping her head lowered and hiding her face behind strands of her unbound hair.

Meg had adorned her in Olwen's wedding finery—a blue gown made of silk from Sicily, cut full and long, hanging in folds, and a surcoat in a deeper shade of blue, made of baldekin and decorated with images of hounds and harts embroidered into the fabric with gold thread. The skirt of this outer garment was so long and generous that it covered Catrin's kid leather shoes and formed a small train when she walked.

Catrin's stomach complained loudly. Could others hear it? She glanced at those standing near and placed a hand against the folds of her surcoat, as if that gesture would ease her hunger pains. She had not broken her fast in preparation for the marriage communion. Now, with heat suffusing her face, she felt lightheaded.

Servants had hastily prepared the broad open space of the upper-story hall for the wedding feast. Rough timber floors had been swept clean and then strewn with fresh rushes and sprinkled with dried herbs—spicy basil, sweet-smelling balm and lavender, and refreshing hyssop. Tallow candles impaled on iron candlesticks flickered, casting splotches of stark light that failed to brighten the cavernous hall or alleviate the sudden chill in the October air.

Catrin sidled nearer to the roaring fire.

"He comes, my lady," Meg whispered.

Catrin's breathing faltered. Her bridegroom halted at the far end of the hall, hard-pressed by a crush of castle folk. Although Father Ellis had attended to Olwen's flock since the death of Lord Northbridge, they hailed the arrival of a true overlord, one provided by King Edward. Strength was always respected in troubled times.

Would she be discovered? Catrin kept away from the servants, letting Meg insist on privacy for the lady of the castle. Olwen's gowns fit well enough, and Catrin's hair and physical appearance gave credence to the charade. Yet

Catrin felt exposed and vulnerable. Was it because her hair was unconstrained, the symbol of a virgin, flowing in soft, shining waves around her face and down her back to her knees?

She watched him from under her lashes. The black knight was at ease with the servants and the lesser tenants, who had been summoned to the castle for the event. His laughter sounded effortless and genuine. How dare he win over Olwen's people so readily?

Welsh ruffian. Wizard. Caster of magic spells.

As if he had heard her thoughts, his gaze found hers, focusing on her like a raptor fixed on its doomed prey. She sucked in a breath. His hard eyes cut into her like talons. That dark stare penetrated her inner soul, almost as if he saw her failings, her lies, and her hate.

Bran ap Madog broke away from the crowd and, with the sweep of his black cloak, closed the distance between them in long strides. Everyone in the hall paused to watch. His footsteps echoed in the expectant silence.

Dressed from head to foot in black with no ornamentation except for the sapphire brooch clasping his cloak together across his broad shoulders, he stopped just inches from her. Meg stood a respectful distance away, and so did a small sergeant-at-arms who had followed his master.

'Twas as if they were alone amidst all the wedding guests and servants.

Her heart racing, Catrin had no trouble pretending to be the shy Olwen. She could but glance at him, hastily, and then lower her gaze, as any demur maid would.

"Ah, *cariad*, you are lovely," he said so softly only she heard.

Her head jerked up. "I told you never to call me that!"

He assessed her, silently, his face unmoving. What was he thinking? Pinpricks of tension held her erect. She lifted her chin and stared back at him.

"I warned you, as well." His words, when they came, were a quiet hiss between his teeth and meant for just her. "You will act the part of my wife, if only for the sake of your good people here." He swept an impatient hand, indicating the assembled crowd.

She drew a sharp breath. His threat wasn't idle. She saw it in his resolute stance and in his eyes, those raven's eyes. Bran ap Madog was a hired killer, the king's mercenary as well as champion. He would think nothing of wrecking havoc on Olwen's people if she failed in her scheme. She must succeed, conceal her fear, and go forward as planned.

"I will do my duty, sir, for I know my obligation," she said, letting him see by her own icy gaze that having his way with her would not be easy.

"Your duty is to call me by my given name. I am Bran to you, Olwen."

Olwen. Sheets of chilly fear paralyzed her. She played a deadly game. Yet he had stopped calling her *cariad* and that was victory enough for the moment.

She bowed her head. "As you wish...Bran."

He accepted her simple gift and nodded. "Father Ellis awaits." He took her right hand gently in his. "Come, let us both do our duties."

Before the sixth hour, the ceremony began inside the tiny chapel with Mass. Bran, as she now tried to think of him, presented the formal decree from King Edward to Father Ellis. After that, the clergyman announced the terms of her dower and the dowry. Catrin paid scant attention, not caring what was said nor promised. She concentrated solely on the way her bridegroom's massive grip swallowed her hand.

His fingers were long and tapered, strong and tanned from days in the sun. Still, she felt no safety with her small hand in his. Conversely, she felt dizzy, her face hot and flushed. 'Twas as if smoldering embers somehow extended from his fingertips, shooting up her arm and down her body, and bursting into flame somewhere near the core of her being. That place where last night she had yearned for him—nay, lusted for him—so much so, she had gone without sleep, dreading the day to come.

Now, they stood side-by-side facing the priest who appeared flustered and ill at ease. He had every right to be so, knowing what he was about to do was a sin before God and holy church. Catrin thought only of the man beside her who was casting his dark spell upon them all.

Father Ellis crossed himself and glanced pointedly at her. Catrin stared up at him. Would he go through with the ceremony? Would his courage falter?

The priest looked at Bran and then began slowly, "Since it is your intention to enter into the covenant of Holy Matrimony, join your right hands, and declare your consent before God and his Church."

Jolted by the gravity of the words, Catrin fought hard to attend to the priest's pronouncements. Was she actually doing this? Marrying Olwen's husband? She could no longer ignore the import of what she was about to do. The weight of her wrongdoing nearly buckled her knees.

His soft brown eyes turning bleak, Father Ellis looked at them. Pointedly. At one and then the other. "I require and charge you both," he said, "as ye will answer at the dreadful day of judgment, when the secrets of all hearts shall be disclosed, that if either of you know any impediment why ye may not be lawfully joined together in Matrimony, that ye confess it now."

Lawfully joined together.

She wasn't Olwen, the heiress of Northbridge. She had no entitlement to do what she was doing. Only her own gut-wrenching conviction told her this was right. She must wed to pursue justice. To protect her cousin.

Catrin held her tongue and held to her purpose. She glanced once more at the unyielding countenance of the black knight who stood straight and motionless beside her. He already held himself like a lord. His loose hair, longer than fashion dictated, bespoke his Welsh heritage, a heritage she shared, but denied.

Once again, she tempered fear with determination, and drawing a breath, turned back to Father Ellis, carefully repeating the vows when asked.

Yet she could not shake the deeper dread that settled in her stomach when she thought of the coming night.

CHAPTER TWELVE

"You eat little, my lady," Bran said, leaning toward Catrin, not quite touching her. Still, his warm breath brushed the side of her face. He smelled of wine and a faint scent of woodruff.

"I am no longer hungry, my lord," Catrin replied with a stiff nod of her head.

He failed to heed her dismissal and sliced a piece of venison from the joint on the trencher they shared. She had long ago satisfied her hunger during the first course of their wedding meal. Now, some hours later, they lingered over a third course, amid the noisy, joyous castle folk and freemen who feasted with them in the great hall, eating and drinking their fill.

He offered her a wicked, indolent smile. "You will need your strength for what's to come this night."

She eyed her new husband who sat relaxed beside her at the cloth-covered trestle table. Her jaw muscles tightened. Heavens! She wished she were so relaxed. His attentionnay, his very presencecramped her belly and twisted her nerves.

Now he expected her to eat more. She was wise enough to understand *his* subtleties. The mere thought of climbing into bed with him made her want to flee.

"I am not as needing of strength, my lord, as forbearance," she said with a sniff, maintaining her stiff posture. His gaze rested on her face. Feeling it heat, Catrin glanced away. "I have proven I will do my duty."

"Then do your duty as etiquette demands and let me tend you." He scrupulously wiped his hands on a linen napkin and picked up the freshly cut morsel between two fingertips. "You'll find this venison quite tasty."

Catrin looked back at him feeling trapped like a rabbit in a snare and let him feed her the tidbit she did not want. His fingertips grazed her lips, lingering there almost intimately while she accepted the meat and began to chew it slowly. She stared up into his penetrating eyes, feeling as if she would melt from their intensity. Reading his mind was not hard. She knew he thought of stolen kisses. He thought of tonight when his kisses would not be stolen, but legally his. Tonight, when she must do her duty as his wife.

"You see, 'tis a lovely cut of venison, without that gamy taste," he said. "Your cook should be congratulated, my lady."

Catrin swallowed and patted her lips with her own napkin. "As you should be congratulated, my lord, on your persistence." She reached for the cup of wine.

He laughed and seized the cup from her very hands. Then he lifted the goblet to her lips, offering it so that she could take a sip. Catrin drank, seeking to wash down more than Cook's tasty meal—but rather her fear, her repugnance, her hate.

She was anxious to be gone from the hall and longed to be done with the approaching night, instead of waiting like a condemned murderer for the executioner. She had made her bed, so to speak. Now she wanted to lie in it, simply to ease the pounding in her head. Surely, the consummation would not be as terrible as its anticipation.

Catrin shut her eyes. She was fooling herself. Everything about her groom bespoke a certain mastery of the subject that threatened her very sanity. Bran ap Madog, the King's Raven, was a master of blade and lance. And master of women as well.

"You are bored," he stated. "By merest chance, may I tempt you with something sweet?"

Her eyes flew open, knowing full well he had been watching her, wondering about her, wanting her. In truth, his sultry gaze confirmed what her senses perceived.

"Nay, I fear I cannot eat another bite," she said, tilting her head away from him.

He motioned with his hand to his sergeant-at-arms who stood near his left shoulder. Like magic, the wiry man produced plates filled with various treats—pastries topped with pine nuts and white sugar, marzipan cakes with almonds, plus a variety of costly figs, pomegranates, and dates.

Queasiness washed through her already tense body. Catrin shook her head declining the sugarcoated date he'd plucked from the plate and held to her lips.

"Nay?" Bran brought the foreign delicacy up to his mouth and lazily took a bite, his gaze never leaving her face. "You know not what you miss." He chewed with deliberate slowness as if he were tantalizing her, promising her of more delights to come.

So keenly aware was she of his every movement—the slight lift of a dark eyebrow, the way his throat moved when he swallowed, the exciting timbre of his deep voice—Catrin caught his double meaning.

Bran finished the morsel and wiped his hands once again on his napkin. "Then, let us have entertainment. Rhys, what say you?" He turned to his sergeant who hurried off to do his bidding, returning with a motley troop of travelers who included a juggler, several nimble acrobats, and a young troubadour with a lute.

To the approval of those in the hall, the acrobats tumbled between the tables and in front of the lord and lady of the castle, springing high into the air and flipping frontward and back. Applause rose as each one of the brightly clad men finished a maneuver. The juggler balanced wooden balls on a stick and then tossed four of them in the air at one time. Moving them in a circle between his hands, he never let them fall to the rush-strewn floor.

For a moment, as her attention turned toward the enter-tainers, Catrin's nervousness eased. Even Bran applauded the diversion. She found the performers provincial and simple. As a member of Queen Eleanor's entourage, she had once seen a magician with slanting eyes who had come from a faraway place. He had made fire appear from the very air, something both frightening and wonderful.

Surely, her new husband, a former Crusader, had more sophistication than to let these local players captivate him. She slid her glance to the left, catching the untroubled look on his face. The fine lines by his eyes crinkled now with laughter and the brooding look was gone from his gaze. Why should he not be diverted? Bran had gained what he wanted. As Olwen, she and the lands of Northbridge were his bounty.

And tonight? That unbidden thought sparked fire

between her legs. To ease it, she reached once more for the cup and drank deeply of the tart Boudreaux wine, soon draining it.

She motioned to the sergeant. "What is your name?"

"Rhys, if it pleases, my lady." He bowed very smartly for a Welshman.

Catrin handed him the silver goblet. "More, if you will, Rhys."

His eyes lowered respectfully, he took the cup from her. "Wine from my lord's private stock?"

"Yea, I find it flavorful." With that remark, she recaptured Bran's attention, but she did not care. Defiantly, she raised her chin. The drink had emboldened her, taking the edge off the unholy fires ignited within and bringing a feeling of relaxation, the feeling her new husband came by so easily. She needed something to tolerate the sharpened gaze of the man beside her.

With her unbound hair drifting over her shoulders and without the protecting headdress, as was fashionable, Catrin felt naked at his perusal. He bent his head near and took her hand, sliding his thumb across her soft skin.

"Your fingers are long," he murmured. "You have pretty hands. Do you play an instrument?"

"Sometimes a harp." Her breath stuck in her throat and she offered a quick prayer that he wouldn't ask more of her or notice the tiny knife cut on her thumb or the blisters on her palm.

"So you like music?" With his free hand, he signaled for the young troubadour who came eagerly forward. "Play for us, lad. Something suitable for a wedding feast."

"Aye, my lord. Perchance something from my travels?"

Catrin couldn't miss the lad's impertinent wink, two

lustful men making sport. She was the prey. Incensed, she tried to pull her hand from Bran's grasp, but he held it tightly.

The troubadour played opening notes on his lute. Then the lad turned soulful eyes toward the heavens and began to sing in high-pitched Norman French, "Bacchus can soften / Feminine obstinacy / And bend it to / Willing consent...

Feminine obstinacy? Catching the meaning, Catrin set her jaw. Where were the sweet endearments? The courtship? She was angry for Olwen's sake. Her sweet cousin would have had to face such a shameless display as she endured now. Would this have been her fate, too, had she been forced into marriage? No thought of love or tenderness, just a rutting, randy buck for a husband.

Rhys returned with a replenished cup, placing it on the table before her. Catrin jerked her hand free and reached for it. When Bran moved to stop her, she cast him an angry look. "What, my lord? You disapprove of a *willing* bride?"

He had the grace to flush and sit back in his chair. Picking up the goblet with both hands, Catrin brought the cold silver rim to her lips. As she drank, she defied him over its rim with her rebellious gaze. He watched her silently, and this time she could not read his thoughts.

Sated for the moment, she placed the cup back on the table with a thump, sloshing wine over the sides onto the tablecloth. Then casting a glance at her husband, she raised her hands high and clapped for the lad with the fine tenor voice. Others at the banquet turned to stare and then joined in with their own applause.

"Sing us another song," Catrin called, ignoring the pointed look Meg shot her from across the hall.

Sweet, pious Olwen would never behave such. But sweet,

pious Olwen was safe in the arms of nuns, not facing a wedding night in the arms of the King's Raven. The man's slight smile and dissolute gaze encouraged her misbehavior.

"Yea, let us have more such songs," he said, nodding to the lad and stretching his arm possessively across Catrin's shoulder.

His very touch fueled the fire she was trying to bank. Through the roughness of his sleeve, she felt his warmth. It seemed to scorch the back of her neck, burning all the way to the tips of her toes. As the boy's voice rose again in song, she grasped the goblet and drank more.

CHAPTER THIRTEEN

"'Tis a pity you have no fine ladies to attend you on such a night," Meg said, fussing with Catrin's hair.

The maid had brushed the long, heavy strands for what seemed like hours. Catrin thought each one must sparkle and pop like the roaring fire that bathed the solar in an eerie glow and caused her head to ache from the stuffiness the heat created.

"No family. No friends," Meg prattled on.

Catrin shut her eyes and held her tongue. Did Meg chatter to quiet her own nerves? She couldn't begrudge her maid that comfort. Why remind the well-meaning woman of the strangeness of her circumstance? Catrin was not Olwen. She had neither mother nor sister to ease her into womanhood with the bedding ritual. Perchance Meg was doing her best as a substitute.

The maid had helped her bathe in the morning, and now along with the hair brushing, Meg had liberally doused her with a traditional love potion made from one part lavender flowers, orris root, and musk seed and one-half part cinnamon and rose petals.

Catrin seriously doubted whether her groom needed such enticement. From what she had seen and felt, his arousal was certainly assured.

She lifted the goblet she'd been holding to her lips and once more let the tart liquid slide down her throat.

Meg frowned with disapproval. "You drink too much."

"Ah, yes. Sweet Bacchus will take the place of mother and sister," Catrin said, her words slurring.

"'Tis not the god of wine you need," Meg snapped, "but our Holy Father's blessing."

Catrin cocked her head. "I could use that too."

Heaven knew she needed all the help she could get to see her through this night.

Almost as if her wishes had been heard, a sharp rap sounded on the solar door and Father Ellis pushed his way into the room without so much as a "by your leave."

"Your husband sent me to bless the wedding bed." He was unsteady on his feet.

So, Bacchus had made his rounds. Catrin handed her cup to Meg and turned on her stool, the long strands of her hair shadowing her eyes. Pulling her robe around her shoulders, she watched the monk stagger across the room to stand, however wobbly, beside the great bed.

"Bless, O Lord, this sleeping chamber," Father Ellis began, making the sign of the cross. "Watch over thy servants who rest in this bed, guarding them from all fantasies and illusions of devils; guard them waking that they may meditate upon thy commandments; guard them sleeping that in their slumber they may think of thee."

He droned on for a few moments longer, sprinkling the bed clothing with holy water before turning from his task.

Now oddly sober, he leveled a stare at Catrin. "You will not deny him his due," he said in a hushed voice. "He must not suspect the switch. All of our lives depend upon you playing your part."

"'Tis no need to warn me, good Father. I am well aware of my duty." She lifted her head haughtily, brushing back her hair with a finger, and glared back at him.

"'Twas your idea and now this scheme must work," he whispered in warning.

Catrin swallowed the lump in her throat. What could she say to ease his anxiety? Or her own? The priest's hands shook and his face paled. No wonder he had hidden behind the pagan god of drink…as she had.

Catrin rose and went to him. Father Ellis was a big man, softened by years of living at Northbridge. "Never fear. I will do my part," she told him.

"I do fear," he whispered. "For my soul."

Catrin swayed, but straightened her spine with effort and confronted the man's fear with a hard look.

He met her daring glare by pulling himself up and puffing out his chest. "Make ready," Father Ellis snapped. "He will soon come."

Rotating on his heel, he left the solar and shut the massive oaken door behind him.

Gazing after him, Catrin's eyes lost their focus. The room blurred. Her head began to spin. Meg approached, slowly stripped the robe from her shoulders, and led her, naked, toward the marriage bed.

A THUMP on the stone steps prompted Bran to look up from where he stood studying the crackling fire. Father Ellis, his flowing black robes billowing behind him, descended the stairs. With his head ducked, he did not meet Bran's eye.

"'Tis done," the priest mumbled in passing.

Bran watched him scurry away, surely back to his cup from whence Rhys had extracted him. The wedding banquet had ended what seemed like hours ago, trestle tables put away, and revelers taken to their beds to sleep off the effects of too much food and drink. Bran stood alone near the hearth and stared with longing at the stone steps that coiled up the tower wall to the lord's solar.

Lady Olwen had no woman-folk of her station to properly witness the bedding and he had no hale companions with whom to drink and carouse before heading up those steps to prove his manhood. And claim her virginity. The Lord had blessed him in that he had no such witnesses. Verily, the thought of spectators on such a valued night had almost sent him seeking his own drink.

Yet he had forborne the temptation, knowing full well he would unlikely rise to the occasion if too deep in his cups. Not so concerned were most of the servants nor his fair bride, it seemed. He had to smile. His wife was fast becoming inebriated when he saw her last.

Bran held out his hands to the fire, his palms warming to the heat. A muscle flexed in his jaw. He was by no means unsympathetic to Olwen. Had not the queen warned him of her timidity? Had not she advised him to go slow? In faith, he had not objected to refilling her cup after understanding her reason for drinking. As the lad's song said, Bacchus would ease her way, just as surely as it would hinder his.

He curled his fingers into fists, letting the heat redden his knuckles. The fire played before his eyes and cast a bright aura around him. All he had worked for was finally within his grasp. He had only to climb yon stairs and take the lass who awaited him. He had only to consummate the vows they had spoken. Then this castle and these lands would truly be his.

Excitement surged through him. He hardly could contain himself, nor contain the sudden rise of his cock. Bran wanted to throw back his head and chuckle. Why had he worried and sworn off good wine? Tonight he would have no problem with the task required of him. Making his long-sought wishes come true would be easy.

Suddenly, he could wait no longer. Why had not the maid come down? What were the two women doing? Impatience prodded him, and he paced in front of the hearth, his boots muffled in the rushes.

"My lord?"

Bran turned quickly to glare at the maid. He lifted an eyebrow, questioning.

"My lady is ready." She bobbed a curtsy and darted away.

Not all the castle was so skittish. Just the priest and this maid. Most of the inhabitants had welcomed his arrival, vowing their loyalty and their service.

So much for idle conjecture. He would win those two over before long, for they were important servants to his wife. Now, he had other matters to attend.

Anticipation filled him, sending an empty feeling throughout his stomach. Grasping a candlestick, he started up the steps, slowly, without haste. He dared not frighten Olwen, or his task would be made more difficult.

Bran entered the solar, shut and bolted the door. Nothing but silence greeted him. Turning, he gauged his surroundings, shadowy in the dim light of candles on two wall sconces and the one he carried. As befit the lord's station, there was an enormous four-posted canopy bed in the middle of the room, already curtained by linen hangings. Other than that, the contents of the room were a few stools and chests, Castilian carpets on the stone floor, and a tapestry suspended on the far wall.

As he gazed across the room, eagerness almost overcame him. He controlled the fires that threatened to explode within and walked forward, placing the candlestick on a chest for safety.

Where was Olwen? A heady floral scent filled his nostrils. Preparations had been made for him that was certain. He surmised she was awaiting him in bed.

In a hurry now, he sat on one of the stools, wishing for Rhys attendance, and pulled off his boots. Rising, he stripped off his outer surcoat and the tunic beneath. Standing in only his braies, his feet upon the cold stones, he stifled the need to cry out with joy. Undignified as it was, he could hardly suppress the strange emotions that ranged through him.

Elation, eagerness, anticipation merged within his chest. He was a lucky man. His work and loyalty would pay off better than he could ever imagine.

Bran fumbled as he untied the strings that held his undergarments around his waist, and then dropped the clothes to the floor. Cool air bathed him, soothing his over-heated skin. He approached the high bed, his heart thrumming mercilessly in his chest.

"Olwen?"

No answer. He grasped the linen hanging and jerked it back.

Somewhere in the midst of the sable coverlets, his wife slept, her gentle breathing music to his ears.

"*Cariad?*"

Unwilling to disturb her, but impatient to see her, Bran lifted the candlestick and brought it nearer to the bed. The soft light spread a dim illumination, enough for him to see Olwen's gentle brow, peaceful now in slumber. Her fair lashes touched her high cheekbones, her full lips relaxed. Her hair, feathering around her, was smoothed so that it created a natural drape for her ample breasts. Her arms outside of the covers were pale and her fingers long and tapered.

Bran reached across the bed and touched her velvety hand, fascinated by its beauty. This woman belonged to him. Legally. Physically. He was in awe of her for that reason. Gently, he slid his fingers under hers, holding her hand, rubbing her short, sturdy nails with his thumb. The pad of her right thumb was roughened, almost as if something had nicked it. The thought of any injury coming to his precious possession angered him.

Filled with an instant, overwhelming need to protect her, Bran snuffed out the candle and placed it aside. Carefully, so not to awaken her, he climbed into bed, leaving the hanging drawn back. The mattress sagged beneath his weight. He slipped under the heavy coverlets, feeling the cool sheets on his warm skin, and stretched out, pulling the fur over both their shoulders.

His wife sighed in her sleep and turned on her side to face him. He studied her in the dim light that was left from the dying fire, inhaling her intoxicating floral scent, feeling her breath against his face. How he ached to draw her to him—to feel the swell of her breasts against his chest. To feel his swelling inside her.

Bran forced down his aching arousal. Snuggling deeper under the coverlets, he shut his eyes. In a moment, he would awaken her. In a moment, he would do what needed to be done and consummate his marriage.

"DON'T MOVE!"

Awake in a heartbeat, Bran's eyes opened with alarm, his senses suddenly alert. Something sharp pressed against his throat.

She loomed above him, straddling his hips, her naked body outlined in the shadows.

"You have me at your advantage, my lady," he said as courteously as if he'd been at court.

"So tell me, My Lord Raven," his wife hissed. "Why did you kill Gilbert Fitzalan and his father Earl Rothmore?"

CHAPTER FOURTEEN

She straddled him, as she would ride astride her palfrey. Her knees and her inner thighs pressed against the sable mantle that covered his hips, gently chafing her skin. 'Twas an odd sensation—the softness of the fur coupled with the hardness of his hipbones—and it produced a dangerous excitement and an aching awareness within her womanly place.

Catrin forced aside those alarming feelings, concentrating instead on her brother's small, but sharp dagger she gripped firmly in her hand. She pointed the blade at the base of his throat, nicking his flesh and drawing a spot of blood.

"Your lack of trust, my lady, becomes you not." He spoke with anger, the muscles in his jaw firming, his lashes masking his eyes. "I did not kill the young earl."

"How can I trust the word of a mercenary?"

"And how can I trust my wedded helpmate when she points a dagger against my neck?"

In the blink of an eye, the knight sent the knife soaring across the bed. One quick movement more, and Catrin found herself rolled in the sable, wrapped up to her chin and trapped beneath the hot, suffocating weight of her former captive. Her chest heaving, she struggled for breath. She squirmed, only making her predicament worse. Fear clouded her vision.

"Let me go!"

His hands pressed the bed on either side of her head as his breath seared her face. "Lie still."

"Let me go!" She fought tears of fury and frustration.

Earlier in her alcohol-induced stupor, she had awakened to find him in bed with her, his breath brushing her cheek as he slept. To make matters worse, she had burrowed near his shoulder, cuddling close to his warm body in her sleep. Very unnerved, she'd first feared he had already taken her, but her body felt unchanged. Her psyche did not. Why had she turned to him in her sleep? Why did she feel an odd solace when she snuggled next to him?

Catrin had stiffened, outraged by her traitorous mental and physical response, and then devised a plan, hoping to take him unaware. If he admitted killing her brother, 'twould be fitting to take her revenge. To kill him fast as she might a bug.

"How quickly you forget your holy vows." His eyes flashed and his face now seemed cruel in the gloom. "I had a mind to be charitable, considering your maidenhood and obvious concern I had for you, but now I'll not wait. I will take what is mine."

His mouth seized hers, descending as swiftly as a viper and consuming her. What a fool she had been to imagine she was physically a match for the King's Raven. He was too big. Too overpowering.

On instinct, she fought, moving her head left and right until his hands captured the sides of her face, stilling her movement. His whole weight rested on her. She couldn't breathe. Panic engulfed her.

He must have sensed her terror, for he released her face. Placing his hands again by her head, he lifted his bulk from her chest, leaning on his arms but still pinioning her body with his. The fury with which his lips ravished hers continued unabated, devouring her with a kiss so long, so filled with anger, she had no time to feel anything but the weight of him.

She had never been kissed as this man now kissed her. In her youth, there had been only chaste pecks on her cheek, stolen along drafty corridors while she ran errands for the queen. Game-like kisses, flirtatious, never meant to be serious. Nothing like this. Nothing like this kiss that filled her whole being.

Soon, the tenor of his assault changed, lessening, relenting. His breathing became labored, and she felt his arousal— hard against the soft fur that even now covered her. He lifted his mouth, and she gasped for air. He seemed unconcerned, just staring down at her with dark eyes full of passion.

Bran lowered his lashes, seeming to know he had revealed too much. "I would know all of you." As if to imprint her on his mind, he grabbed a fistful of her hair, entwining his fingers in the blond strands, lifting it to inhale its fragrance. "Your scent. Your taste. Your maidenhood."

Trapped as she was in the fur cocoon, she could do nothing but glare up at his lowered face, and feel the rise and fall of his chest and the press of his man part.

"How will you punish me?" She hated the pleading note in her voice.

"What is my right as your husband?"

Her fate was sealed, yet she rebelled against it, not wanting to be his bounty. "You will force me."

"Nay. I will court you."

As he slipped off her body, Catrin looked away. Strands of his black hair tickled her cheeks. A sudden desire goaded her. Perversely, she longed to slide her fingers through his hair as he was doing to hers. She longed to pull his mouth toward her once more and feel his savage passion.

Bran flipped the heavy fur back from her body. Cool air washed her heated skin, scant relief, as he continued to woo her. Relaxing on his side, his thigh trapped her against the soft sable. She refused to look his way. Yet, she felt his hard manhood against her naked thigh and heard his harsh breath. She knew he was watching her.

Gently, he caressed her eyebrows and face, drawing her chin toward him so that she was compelled to look at him. The black depth of his gaze immobilized her as surely as his muscular limb. A tight ache clogged her throat, even as, tenderly, he let the fingers of one hand trail down her neck, resting briefly at her pulse point.

Then he moved his fingers lightly across her chest until he cupped her right breast completely in his strong grip. He circled the tip with a thumb. She sucked in her breath as he recited the words of the boy troubadour. "When I glimpsed her breasts / I want to cup them in my hands / Play with each nipple in turn."

He dropped his mouth to the other nipple, circling it with his tongue, wet and warm. Chills rippled through her, seeming to burst into fluid heat in the part of her where she kept her virginity. Her body writhed uncontrollably.

They both were breathing heavily now. She was long past denying him, and she knew it. Part of her mind resisted, but her body betrayed her. Flush with excitement, she concentrated only on his tongue, his fingertips, the rocklike promise pushed against her thigh.

"Desire urged me to kiss her mouth," Bran said, continuing the troubadour's song, but with no tune, no music. Yet somehow they made their own. "To kiss her, to kiss her, to kiss her mouth," he repeated, each time tempting her now swollen lips with his.

Someone whimpered. Catrin recognized her own sound. Her body was spinning, free-falling, wanting. She tried to quiet her trembling, outraged by her out-of-control body. She tried to remember the final words of the ballad. The boy had sung them, almost defiantly, as any man would. "Delighting to mark her as my own," the troubadour had trilled.

Bran planned to mark her. She tried to remember he had that right as Olwen's husband. And she was simply playing a dangerous sport full of heavy consequence.

He straddled her now, his form covering hers, his hard flesh pressing against her. Unceasing, he kissed her again and again, not long angry kisses, but tiny ones, filled with a pent-up yearning, the prelude to the ultimate finality. Somehow it seemed right. Her hot, swollen, aching body complied.

She felt his hands touching, coaxing, and opening her. Strangely, they did not seem to violate. She was his, wasn't she? As Olwen, she belonged to him.

Suddenly, he pushed into her with his arousal. Surprising pain engulfed her. She cried out. He thrust again and again, entering her deeper with each stroke until she was surrounding him. Resting a moment, as if to let her catch a lungful of air or perchance to recoup his own wind, he stared down at her with such raw emotion in his eyes she thought she would weep.

She returned his gaze, wide-eyed. He throbbed within her. She was joined with him. Linked together in the primal dance of life. She was his. Not Olwen, but Catrin. She had been foiled by her own plans.

Tears seeped from the corners of her eyes. What had she done? She couldn't think. Swept up in the moment of his lovemaking, her woman place ached for something she could hardly fathom. She needed relief.

"Myn Duw!" he cried. "I cannot wait."

As he drove into her repeatedly, she circled his neck with her arms, hoping to hang on. An unbidden impulse caused Catrin to lift her legs locking them around his hips. She drew him nearer and nearer and arched to meet him. All thought fled. She was awash in the rhythm of the moment—hot and frenzied—until finally his body jerked.

Bran threw back his head and roared the primeval cry of conquest. He shuddered, relaxed, and collapsed upon her. His pulse thudded against her breast. His manhood still inside, he stroked the curve of her cheek, murmuring sweet endearments.

Having accompanied Bran on his wild ride, Catrin held on to him for dear life. Strange sensations enveloped her. What was that dull ache? That feeling of disappointment? She longed for something more, a final release.

Had she been the one to give him that something she longed to find? That something she lacked, but he had gotten from her.

Had the King's Raven been so easily tamed?

❧

BRAN HAD MARKED HER. Her blood had spotted the sable. Now Catrin cringed when he called Father Ellis at first light and presented the fur mantle to him.

"Take this, good father, as proof that Bran ap Madog, the king's faithful servant, has fulfilled his marriage vow with Olwen de Belleme, who as all can witness, was a virgin."

The new Lord of Northbridge preened himself as if he were his treasured raven.

The Augustine monk blushed scarlet, but received the fur, holding it away from himself so as not to taint his holy robes. "I accept this as proof, my lord, and will vouchsafe its authenticity to anyone who inquires."

Father Ellis sent a cautious gaze toward Catrin, who remained in bed, her hair in tangles over her shoulders and the sheets pulled up around her neck to protect her modesty —or what was left of it. At his glance, she flushed warm with shame, crossing her arms over her scantly covered breasts. Had she diminished the good Father's fears? She had done her duty. Yet, there was a beleaguered quality about him, as if he regretted the part he had played.

Remorse trickled through her. She jutted out her jaw and returned Father's look. He would not sway her from her mission. She had done what she must do to protect Olwen and search for the truth.

"Will you be at Mass?" Father Ellis asked.

"Nay, let us forego chapel today," Bran said, pressing a coin into the priest's palm. "For the poor in honor of our wedding."

Father Ellis fisted the offering. "Thank you, my lord." And then bowing his head, he backed out of the room.

"That man acts as if I'm about to take off his head," Bran complained and crossed the room to stand before her.

He wore only his braies, something Catrin was used to seeing, for she had brothers, but not brothers with such a broad, muscled chest. His look of smugness filled her with ire. She ached where her maidenhood had been and her temples pounded. Moreover, Catrin's grumbling stomach told her she needed to break her fast.

"Your reputation precedes you, my lord," Catrin rejoined, lifting her chin, not in the mood for his possessive stance.

He lifted a black eyebrow, considering her. "And yours, my lady, does you no justice."

What did he mean? He confused her, just as much as he angered her. She had watched him with furtive glances as, earlier, he had padded naked around the room, acting as if they had been married for years. He was a magnificent male. She would grant him that.

In a pout, she turned away from Bran's troublesome gaze. How she hated the feeling of hot and cold that coursed through her body. She reviled her weakness. Why hadn't she been born a man? Her whole life she had chafed at her ill fortune. If all had been different, she would have been in control, not controlled. She would have found release, instead of throbbing from frustration, longing for something she did not understand, because she'd ne'er experienced it.

Catrin whipped her head around to glare at him. How could Olwen have survived such brutish behavior? She'd barely endured it herself.

"'Tis a shame that in your service to the king, you never learned courtly love," she said, and lifted a fingertip to still the pulse beating in her temple.

"What?" He did not seem dismayed by her impudence.

"Did I not offer you sweets and provide diversion for you? Tumblers and a troubadour from France?"

The boy's naughty song echoed in her ears. "You know what I mean."

Did she have to spell it out for him? He should have been courting his wife as Tristan had courted Isolde.

Bran took a step nearer, his physical presence overpowering her in a way she had never thought to experience. His muscular forearms, the strength and the gentleness of his hands, the feel of his lips consuming hers—all of this she remembered from last night. When she saw the flicker of lust in his eyes, she lifted her chin a notch.

"*Cariad*, I know what you mean," he acknowledged softly. "In my anger and my rush, I failed to satisfy you."

Looking down to hide a frantic flush, Catrin fought bewilderment and annoyance. She did not want to admit he had not satisfied her in the way he spoke. She knew only that she was not pleased. Not only had he forced her, but also in the offing, she had failed to learn the truth about Gilbert.

"Nay, I am not satisfied by the king's command," she said, purposely ignoring the true intent of his remark. She lifted a shoulder to shrug. "Yet I will obey with my body as any loyal servant."

She left the implication lingering between them. She may give her body to the king's mercenary, but no one could make her give her heart.

"The battle is joined." His lips twisted into a slight smile. "So be it, *cariad*."

"I told you to not call me that!"

He stood his ground. "Olwen, then."

"Nay!" Her stomach swayed. "*My lady* will do for you, *sir*."

The pettiness did not become her. Yet she could not stop herself from sniping at him. She had but one-way now to fight her enemy. Words, sharp barbs to prick his manhood, letting him know she would ne'er succumb to his charm. For e'en now, he lured her with the look he gave her—the challenge in his eyes, the cocky tilt of his head, and the bulge in his braies seeming to grow as she watched in horror.

She had done her duty. Their marriage could no longer be called into question unless she chose to reveal her true identity. Until then, she had one more task to complete now that Olwen was safely in hiding. She must discover the murderer.

A wave of inspiration struck her. Mayhap if she denied yon randy knight who stood in front of her poised like a ready stallion, she could persuade him to reveal the truth she sought. Forcing him had certainly not worked. A little feminine blackmail, perchance? She was not above such action.

"*My lady* it is." He executed a deep, mocking bow that looked comical, naked as he was above his waist.

Catrin hugged herself fiercely, angry at the insult, as he intended. Her breasts tingled in response to his heated gaze. Nay! She was stronger than her wayward body. She would never again let him do to her what he had done last night.

He must have read her defiance for he stepped nearer, suddenly solemn.

"My lady, we have a long life ahead." He reached across the bed and caressed her cheek, sending sparks of awareness whizzing through her. His voice lowered. "I care not if you fight me, but I will have my rights as your husband."

She shook her head to rid herself of his hand. "I cannot stop what you take by force, my lord."

He would not be gainsaid, but caught her chin in his firm grip. "'Tis your choice," he said with a nonchalance. "'Twould be easier on you if you accepted what fate has bestowed."

"I will ne'er accept my fate."

The tips of his fingers bit into her flesh. "Then you tempt fate, if that is your will."

"You know not how I tempt it," she murmured, staring up at him.

They stayed that way a moment, locked in silent combat until the sound of strident anger drifted up the stairs from below. Catrin recognized the shrill voice of Meg and the lower, lyrical lilt of Rhys. The two servants burst into the room together. They had evidently butted heads though the day was only hours old. Bran dropped his hand from her face, then turned away from her.

As he walked toward the intruding pair, Catrin could not stop her gaze from skimming the muscles of his shoulders and traveling down his back to his trim buttocks and strong thighs. She swallowed and ripped her gaze away, trying to attend to the linen bed hangings, the hunger pangs in her stomach, the brightening day—anything but the dull throb between her thighs.

Meg came immediately to the bed carrying a tray that she sat aside. "That foreigner Rhys is an ignorant buffoon," she growled. "He dares question my authority here."

"'Tis best to accommodate our new master." Catrin tried to be diplomatic. "As you know, things have changed."

"Faith, I know it," Meg said with a lift of an eyebrow. She busied herself by filling a laver with water so Catrin could wash her hands.

Across the room, Bran's back was turned as Rhys dressed

him, attending to his morning needs just as Meg tended hers. Glad for the respite, Catrin dipped her hands into the tepid water. How she longed for another bath, her second in as many days.

"Father Ellis said you were not coming to Mass, so I thought you would want to break your fast." Meg gave her a towel and then offered a chunk of bread slathered with butter.

"Bless you, Meg, for I am starved." Catrin dried her hands and accepted the warm bread. She tore off a portion, chewing it slowly so she savored each bite.

"Father also brought down the fur mantle."

Catrin caught her maid's understanding gaze and felt herself flush again. The entire castle knew the deed was done. "Mistress Olwen" was a virgin no longer, and control of Northbridge had officially changed by king's decree. Wiping her fingers on the towel, Catrin lifted her hand to her temple where the affects of too much drink still pounded sharply behind her eyes.

"I knew you would have a headache." Meg pursed her lips. "If I were your mother, I'd say you are rightly served."

Catrin smiled. "If I had a mother, I wager I would not be in this position."

She glanced at her husband, now fully clad in his customary black. Troubling warmth surged through her at the thought of the real "position" she had found herself in, smothered beneath that fur coverlet with him riding atop her.

"Even so, my lady," Meg continued. "I brought you willow bark tea for pain relief."

"Thank you, Meg." Catrin accepted the cup of tea. "Olwen is lucky for such a faithful maid."

She sipped the hot tea, remembering her own maid Gwendolyn. No greater sacrifice was there to give than one's life. Along with the tea, Catrin swallowed her sorrow, knowing she could not allow herself to give into such sadness. 'Twould not honor Gwendolyn. Only catching the maid's murderer would do that. Silently, she renewed her hatred and her resolve.

Meg glanced over her shoulder to see if they were being watched and then turned quickly back. She whispered, "How was it?"

Vexed, Catrin did not know how to answer Meg truthfully. She parried the question. "I'm afraid I don't remember much of it."

Meg accepted her answer and went away clucking about the evils of too much drink.

Catrin shifted under the sheets, suddenly tired of remaining in bed. Alas, she remembered last night all too well. How was it indeed? Frightening. Amazing. Frustrating.

She had been a fool to think herself a match for the King's Raven. Perchance she may have gentled him for a moment, but she had not tamed him. How quickly she had forgotten her purpose under his demanding touch.

She would have to be more wary now, on guard at all times lest she lose more than her virginity to this warrior, the man the kingdom now thought of as her husband.

CHAPTER FIFTEEN

Bran's index finger tapped impatiently on the arm of the lord's great oaken chair. In front of him stood the castle cook, who literally held a scruffy kitchen boy by the ear. Hopping on one foot, the boy cocked his head to one side in order to ease his obvious pain. His mouth was tugged into a tight line of even more obvious distaste.

"My lord, this urchin is lazy and shiftless," the cook wailed. She then recited a list of the lad's offenses.

Bran tuned out her strident voice but nodded his head from time to time so he appeared to be attending. Already this morning, he had heard the grievances of two freemen whose cattle had strayed into each other's fields, condemned a murderer to death, and settled another land dispute. All before the noonday meal.

He had no idea how tedious the process of securing his lands would be. For someone who had ne'er owned more than good battle armor and a string of fine horses, he found it ironic that in the space of one day, he was now called upon to resolve petty complaints as well as life and death matters.

He much preferred the not so tedious task of securing his heiress.

Satisfaction filtered through him, causing him to smile. For a glorious moment, he relived the feel of the fine texture of Olwen's hair and her unconscious responsiveness to his touch. How he had loved the sensation of her lying in his arms.

He had not had a woman in so long, and now this woman was his.

A twinge of regret pricked him, tempering his male pride in ownership. He knew full well his lady wife hated him. Because of his reputation. Because of what she thought he had done to her uncle and cousin, and whatever love she bore for the reckless young earl.

Bran gripped the arms of the chair. He did not need Olwen's affection, but he did need her obedience. *That* he would secure.

The castle steward stood at his right shoulder. "Cook oft finds fault with this lad," he whispered in Bran's ear.

"Then why has nothing been done about the boy?" he demanded, frowning in displeasure.

Father Ellis looked up from where he sat behind a rough-hewn table, transcribing the day's events. "Christian charity, my lord," he said. "The boy is an orphan."

Bran had been an orphan once. After his mother had died, his grandmother had raised him. When she died, by chance, his father's aunt arranged for him to be fostered in East Anglia, far away from his native Wales and any embarrassment he could bring to his princely father.

Bran shifted in the lord's chair and leaned forward to assess the young scullion. "Stand straight," he ordered.

Cook released the culprit's ear and the towhead boy stiffened his spine and squared his shoulders. Although dressed in rags, the lad returned a look of rebelliousness.

"What is your name?"

"Will." The boy spit out his name as if a curse.

Bran glared at him. Minutes passed and those around them stilled, watching the drama unfold.

Finally the boy understood the unspoken message. He dropped his gaze and stuttered, "Will Tabor, my lord."

"Why, Will Tabor," Bran wondered aloud, "do you defy yon cook and the charity of the good Christians of Northbridge?"

The boy sulked, shifting from one foot to the other. Then he mumbled, "Because I dislike washing dishes."

Bran hid a smile with a scowl. "'Tis not because you are naturally lazy and disobedient?"

"No, my lord. I just don't like it."

"Have you another preference?"

The boy glanced up, his eyes widening. "I would much prefer working with horses."

"Harrumph!" The cook reacted but dared not speak, cautious in front of the new lord.

Bran sat back in the chair and surveyed the scene before him. The eager lad, the surly cook, and the curious castle folk all awaited a decision that would brand his tenure as lord and master. For sure, he had no use for a shirker or for someone who defied orders at Northbridge.

In spite of that, the destitute scullion evoked an empathy Bran thought to ne'er feel again. Verily, he had tried to put his homelessness behind him.

Bran brought his fingers up to his chin in the fashion of a steeple, his thoughtful silence deepening. Afore he had not been master over others. He did not count Rhys, for the sergeant-at-arms was more friend than servant. Granted, he led other knights in battle, but this new power o'er the lives of those who served him and owed him homage was new to him.

So why did he delay? This lad needed discipline. Yet something stirred within as he admitted a deep truth to himself. By rights, he had not put his early, orphaned days behind him. It drove everything he did. E'en now, it colored his view of the defiant boy.

"Rhys, take this lad to the stable. Put him to work. Tell the groom to flog him if he disobeys even once."

A murmur of astonishment spread through the hall. Rhys collared the lad and dragged him away before the startled boy could mutter thanks.

The cook, however, was another matter.

"I am now one less worker in the kitchen, my lord," the woman protested. "Where am I to find more help?"

Bran deftly evaded the issue. "Yesterday, I paid tribute to your fine venison," he said heaping on the praise. "I told my new wife that in all my travels, I have not seen such a fine presentation or tasted such a flavorsome dish."

The cook bobbed a curtsy, pleased by the compliment. "Thank you, my lord."

"Father Ellis will reward your efforts on behalf of our wedding feast with a small token of our thanks." He glanced at the monk and then rose to his feet ending the audience. "I am near famished. Let us have our dinner."

The servants sprang into action, and the great hall buzzed with the business of preparing the room for the major meal of the day. Bran stepped out of the way, retreating to the hearth, where he stretched out his hands toward the fire.

Visions of the fire in Olwen's eyes intruded upon his thoughts. He stared at the flame, reliving his wedding night, her drunkenness, and her challenge to his rights. Would she have killed him? In truth, what was this Gilbert to her?

Had her cousin Gilbert courted her? Made promises and maybe done something more? Nay, Olwen was a virgin. He had proven that. Mayhap, the two held a fantasy between them, nothing more than chivalrous words and secret messages of children growing up together.

Was this why did his wife wanted courtly love? He knew not how to sing or write poetry. She was his now, and he need not bother himself with such whimsy. Further, he need not cultivate such prettiness of speech. Had not he experienced her body ready for his? Had not his simple touch ignited the passion she thought could be roused only by pretty words? Why her contradiction?

Olwen was not indifferent to him, no matter her hostility. This pleased him. Yet he knew he must go slower, bring her to the peak so she toppled over the edge before he reached his own climax.

Bran brushed a strand of hair from his eyes. Aye, he had rushed her, because of his long privation keeping himself pure for his wedding night. Tonight would be different. He would take care to satisfy his wife's needs. He knew a well-sated body went far toward tempering a churlish disposition.

"My lord?"

Bran started and turned to find Rhys beside him. "You have not forgotten your training," he said smiling at his friend and servant. "Furtiveness has long been one of your greatest skills."

"'Tis not hard to sneak up on someone whose thoughts lie between the sheets." Rhys chortled and clapped Bran on the back. "Look there. I see you will be kept busy while I am gone."

Bran's senses gave a bound. He followed the direction of his sergeant's gaze. Olwen had entered the great hall with her deportment stiff and correct, her head high, almost haughty. She wore again an elaborate headdress that banded her chin, and a golden net crespine confining her hair. He was sorry for that. He liked her hair draped around her breasts and crushed in his grasp.

"I unlocked her chaste treasure last night," Bran admitted, letting his pride unfasten his tongue.

Rhys laughed again. "We know."

Olwen was no longer a virgin, and everyone recognized the fact, thanks to the fur coverlet he had sent down with Father Ellis.

"I find myself desiring my wife's charms."

Rhys nodded. "As any bridegroom should."

His sergeant understood him well. Gratitude rose within Bran. And love. He tried to curb the intensity of his emotion, knowing 'twas best to remain detached, even from one as faithful as Rhys.

Silently, they watched Olwen circle the room, keeping her distance from them. She greeted each one of the servants politely, even regally, as if she were forcing herself to appear untouched by her change of status.

How did it feel to be exhibited as a man's trophy?

The question drew him up short. No matter, she was his. He had earned her.

Bran brushed aside the prick of disquiet. His concern for her feelings should have died the moment he awoke with the tip of a dagger biting into his throat.

Now he cared only for the rumble in his belly. "Come, good friend, let us eat, and then I'll send you on your way."

OUT OF THE corner of her eye, Catrin inspected her husband and his sergeant standing near the hearth. She kept her distance from them, focusing on the castle folk she met, making sure she didn't do anything to give away her identity. She had not been to Northbridge in two years, and although several of the inhabitants had changed, many remained the same. 'Twould not do to slip and reveal herself by mistake.

She would do better to remain closed up in the solar, but the cheerless atmosphere weighed heavily upon her mood.

Or was it the recollection of what had transpired there in the early hours before dawn that shamed her?

Even thinking about it drew heat to her face. Flustered, Catrin nodded her head in a perfunctory manner at a chambermaid, hoping beyond hope the old woman saw nothing amiss.

When the sound of the Welsh sergeant's laughter punctuated the hall, heads turned. Even Catrin stopped and looked. Bran leaned near in the manner of long-held camaraderie, telling his small companion something in confidence.

Jealousy stabbed her, and she turned away in dismay. Why should she care if that beast whispered secrets to his sergeant? In truth, he probably bragged about the wedding night, making ribald boasts, as men were wont to do.

Fury now assailed her. And panic. Fighting to regain her composure, Catrin pulled herself up even straighter and pasted a smile upon her lips.

"Lady Olwen?"

Dread surging through her, Catrin whipped around to face the man she'd falsely wed. His black eyes flashed before he bowed as if he really was a courtier, and then he offered his arm in invitation.

"May I have the honor of escorting you to dinner?"

"You had my *honor* last night, my lord, if I recall," she said.

His head snapped up and smiled. "I find that I am *hungry* still."

She grasped his double meaning. Two could play the game. "Then you shall have to eat heartily at dinner." She lifted her chin as she placed her hand lightly on his sleeve. "For *I* shall not satisfy you, my lord."

Catrin looked away from him and smiled stiffly for the benefit of those assembled. The castle folk watched them and possibly overheard. She tried not to think. She tried not to react when he covered her hand possessively with his. Why did his very touch ignite smoldering embers of desire?

Bran led her in a stately procession around the room to the high table on the dais. 'Twas his statement of ownership. Of his new authority. He seated her then took the lord's chair. Trestle tables had been hastily assembled and covered with cloth. Below them, as servants and tenants clambered over the benches finding seats for themselves at lower tables, the noise level rose. Better to drown out her thoughts.

And bank the flames she fought hard to control.

It did not help that Bran was so imposing, sitting beside her, smelling of woodruff and a musky, manly scent. Neither did it help that she was forced to dine with him, to spend several hours in his presence, when all she wanted to do was escape.

She should learn to accept this forced intimacy as penance for her deception. If only she could discover the truth, the sacrifice of her virginity would be vindicated.

Rhys brought a towel and a basin filled with water. Bran offered the basin first to her, and she dipped her fingers into it to clean them.

"I know not how I will manage without you," Bran said after he washed his hands and returned the bowl and towel to his sergeant.

"You have always been self-sufficient," Rhys said with a grin. "Now your new wife will attend to you while I'm gone."

Where was Rhys going? Catrin had too much pride to ask. Instead, she feigned indifference, ignoring Bran's chuckle and lifting her chin while surveying the great hall with all the haughtiness she could muster. Fortunately, Father Ellis rose for the blessing.

After he finished, a procession of servants began, each one bearing food. First the pantler marched to the head table bringing white bread and butter. After serving the lord and lady, he turned to distribute barley bread to the rest of those assembled. Next came the butler and his assistants, who carried wine for the head table and beer for the rest. Catrin eyed the brimming cup of Boudreaux placed before her on the table, her stomach heaving.

Perchance she would go without wine at this meal.

Unlike the wedding feast, today's meal was simple and blessedly not as lengthy. The first course consisted of chunks of Stilton cheese and a clear chicken broth that they ate with wooden spoons from wooden bowls. Catrin sipped the broth and nibbled at the cheese but dared not touch the brimming goblet.

"You do not drink, my lady," Bran observed, his shoulder dipping much too close to hers, his wine-scented words whisking across her face.

"I am not thirsty." How much straighter could she sit? Surely, her posture transmitted her message of disdain.

He murmured a low sound of amusement and drew the goblet away from her. "Rhys! See that my lady has a good claret, flavored with honey and cinnamon." He turned once again to speak like a parent. "The claret will aide your digestion and relieve your soreness."

Heat suffused her cheeks. "You had my maidenhead," she whispered sternly, "but if you please, do not reference it for all to hear."

He tilted his head and sat back away from her, seeming to relent. Only the grin upon his lips told a different story.

Rhys brought a new goblet. Then he cut the trencher, a thick slice of day-old bread, separating it into two pieces to provide place servings for the lord and the lady. Next, two young men carried a whole deer impaled on a spit. Having been spit-roasted all day, its steaming juices dripped onto the rushes. Rhys served his master a hunk of venison.

"Ah, Cook! Thank you!" Bran called out. "The aroma is enough to whet even the most finicky appetites."

Catrin saw his sidelong glance. Her eyebrows drew into a frown at the off-handed tease. All morning she had watched him from the squint that overlooked the great hall.

He had dispatched the cases brought before him as lord of Northbridge with wisdom and justice.

Bran sliced a juicy morsel of meat and, like yesterday, offered it to her with his fingertips.

"I wondered why you allowed that kitchen boy to go to the stable," Catrin said before accepting the bite with her lips.

"Did I please you as I did last night?"

The dual meaning of his words overwhelmed her. Chewing slowly, as she was once again forced to succumb to his offerings, just as he had forced her last night, Catrin fought for a pointed comeback. "I take my pleasure in many ways," she replied. "One is by helping the poor and down-trodden."

"And I by remedying a prickly situation," he said smoothly, as if it held no import. "'Twould not do well to flog one so young. This way I gain a stable hand and rid yon cook of a scallywag."

So much for her thinking he was somehow moved by the boy's plight. "Are you always so calculating?"

"When it suits my purpose."

Catrin turned away and grasped the goblet. The spicy claret went down easily. She sat the goblet aside and patted her lips with a napkin. "Does it not suit your purpose to show Christian charity?"

He sat forward. "If it will please you, then I shall be more forthcoming with my benevolence."

She grunted. "Nothing you can do will please me."

"*That* you have made perfectly clear." His voice became lower, menacing. "'Tis why I send Rhys to search for the murderer of your cousin."

"To what point?"

"To find the truth. To clear my name." He smiled slightly. "To make my life with you tolerable, Olwen."

She lashed out, "Never call me that!"

He bowed his head, mocking. "You have my apologies, *my lady.*"

Why was she so upset? Didn't she want to learn the truth? Wasn't that why she switched places with Olwen? She hadn't expected Bran to also seek the truth by sending his trusted servant away. It reeked of artifice. She didn't trust him. How could he honestly seek Gilbert's murderer, being the killer himself?

Catrin turned to him, her eyes narrowing. "I had two cousins, my lord. Outlaws surprised Lady Fitzalan on her way to Clun. They killed her and her serving maid. Will your sergeant search out their murderers as well?"

"I had heard of Lady Fitzalan's tragic death, but not of her maid." He steepled his fingertips together under his chin and surveyed her. "Do you believe 'twas something more than highwaymen?"

Catrin swallowed, fearful that she'd betrayed too much. "Call it woman's intuition," she said. "I have oft been known for my innate skills of divining the truth." There, another little lie would do little harm. She didn't want him to learn she had intimate details of the ambush.

Bran raised an eyebrow. "Are you a witch?"

"Witch enough to provoke you, it seems," she scoffed.

Why remind him of last night? Because he goaded her, making her impatient. He brought out her foul mouth, causing her to recall words her brother's randy friends had bantered and making her want to use them on him.

"Is that why I want to have you?" he mused. "Because you are a witch?"

She lowered her eyes to hide an impulsive flush. So be it. She had gone this far. She would go farther.

Catrin glanced up. "Suggest to Rhys he search for a noble lord attended by a Saxon named Harry."

"Harry?" Now it was Bran's turn to snort. "How many Saxons are named 'Harry' after our king's father?"

'Twas the only clue Catrin had. E'en so, she dared not acknowledge any more of the truth.

"Laugh if you will, my lord," she said. "The name came to me in a dream. As if my dead cousin spoke it to me."

Sacrilegious. Dangerous. What she suggested was serious, especially if Father Ellis heard. But 'twas far better to let him think her a soothsayer than for him to learn he had married the wrong woman. Woe unto her when he learned the lands he so desired were not, and never could be, his because of her deception.

CHAPTER SIXTEEN

Sitting on the stool before the hearth, Catrin watched the firelight play across the stone floor of the solar. She wore only a chemise. A cold rain had started to fall after the meal at midday and now the October evening felt dank.

"He sent the little Welshman away," Meg said with a grunt. The maid had helped Catrin undress and now stood behind her, brushing her hair with long, easy strokes. She moved the brush from Catrin's scalp down the length of her fair curls that fell to her waist.

"Aye," Catrin murmured, drugged by the motion of the brushing. 'Twas a hypnotic thing, filling her with lethargy and a peacefulness she knew to be unfounded. "Rhys goes to find Gilbert's murderer."

"What? I thought you suspected Lord Northbridge of slaying your brother."

Catrin sighed. "That is the mystery. I only have Court gossip to rely on and the scrap of cloth found by Gilbert's body."

Memories of that hideous day flickered in Catrin's mind

like the firelight dancing before her eyes. The red blood of her brother and the black of the fierce raven on Bran ap Madog's red war shield all meshed, leaving only the impression of horror and sadness.

"But you say he claims not to have done the deed," Meg said.

"I suppose he may be telling the truth," Catrin admitted. She was tired of the worry and heartache. Tired of the verbal battle between her and the man she had falsely married.

The day had been a long one. After dinner, Bran disappeared outside with Rhys, but the dreary weather kept her indoors by the fireplace. She picked up Olwen's needlework to pass the time. How she hated the wearisome sewing. Anyone with half an eye could discern her crooked stitches from the careful, even ones of the real lady of Northbridge Castle.

With light waning, she and Meg retreated upstairs to eat their evening meal in privacy and prepare for bed. Thoughts of the night to come troubled her, for Catrin vowed no cooperation, planning to coerce a confession from him by withholding her favor. Bride she may pretend to be, but she was neither willing, nor eager.

A sudden commotion erupted on the stairs. She glanced up at Meg, whose face mirrored her perplexity.

Without comment, the maid strode to the door and swung it open. "Who goes there?" she called.

"Water for the lord's bath."

Catrin jumped to her feet, toppling the small stool. She hugged her body with her arms, a niggling fear prickling the back of her neck. "Your new wife will attend to you while I'm gone," Rhys had said.

Strapping serving boys burst into the solar, carrying a large wooden tub and several buckets of steaming water. Catrin sprung out of their way. They sat their burdens down near the hearth and waited for instruction.

She did not have to look to know when Bran entered the room. His presence filled the solar with a spark that electrified her senses. She glanced up to see him surveying her with shuttered eyes, assessing her from afar as a falcon scouted its prey.

"Pour the water into the tub," he commanded. "Leave one bucket by the fire." The boys scrambled to do as they were bid. "Now get out!" He turned to Meg. "Even you."

Meg seemed about to speak, mayhap to challenge his orders, but she thought better of it. Darting past him, she fled with the others, leaving Catrin very much alone.

"I have not finished with my maid," she said, glaring at him in defiance. "My hair needs tending."

"I will tend it." Bran shut and bolted the door. Then he came toward her. "And you will tend me."

Dread filled her. She might as well have been naked for all the cover her thin chemise gave her. Whereas moments earlier, she'd been sleepy and at rest, now all of her nerve endings crackled with tension.

"Nay!" she defied him. "Tend to your own needs."

Catrin turned away. Hearing him cross the room, she was unprepared for the way he grabbed the fleshy part of her upper arm and jerked her around. Anger burned in his eyes and something more.

His gaze left her face to scorch her body, traveling down to her bare toes. "I am tired of your willfulness."

She glanced down. Her flesh paled white where his fingers bit into her arm. "And I am tired of fighting you."

Bran threw back his head in laughter. "Well met! We are only one day wed, and we are both in agreement."

He dropped his hand, leaving her arm suddenly bereft of warmth, and turned from her to start undressing. "I am glad you will cooperate."

Cooperate? 'Twas the last thing Catrin wanted. She stared at his back, watching him strip off his tunic and braes. Soon he stood stark naked before her, the taut shape of his buttocks testifying to years in the saddle.

She swallowed. Fascinated by the curve of his back and his well-muscled shoulders and thighs, she fought the low, insidious lust inching its way to where she had lost her maidenhead only hours earlier.

He faced her, and Catrin could not help but gape at him. Grinning like a cocky page, Bran stepped forward and brushed a hand over the top of her head and down the side of her face to hold her cheek.

"I will not force you," he murmured, his black eyes growing even darker. "In faith, I have another bauble to give you once I give you this one."

Catrin flushed to the tips of her toes. She knew what bauble he referred to—the one thrusting so proudly before him.

Her breath grew labored. The flesh where his fingers touched her cheek sizzled. She must resist him, but it made better sense to go along with his game. For the moment.

And for the moment, his gaze entranced her, pulling her in, mesmerizing her. Swaying, a deep stupor engulfed her. When he bent his head to kiss her, she let him, drowning in the soft pressure of his lips.

He broke off with an audible sound of regret. "The water cools."

Bran left her. She teetered, licking her dry lips. He climbed over the edge of the tub and sank down into the steaming water. Too tall to fit comfortably, he bent his knees so they peeped out of the water.

Glancing back, he raised an eyebrow. "I am waiting."

Snapped out of her trance, Catrin lashed out, "I am no serving wench."

Leisurely, she bundled her hair by tying it once into a loose knot thereby getting it out of the way.

Expensive lavender soap from London and a linen rag lay beside the tub. Bran reached over the side, picked them up off the floor, and extended his hand, offering them to her. "Rhys usually adds woodruff to the water," he said matter-of-factly as if they had lived this way for many years.

Well, then let the sainted Rhys tend you! But she dared not speak this bit of boldness. 'Twould serve him right to smell like lavender flowers.

Had he heard her thoughts? She tipped up her chin and firmed her jaw, hesitating. Her knees felt weak, but as before, something about him enthralled her, melting her reluctance and moving her step-by-step toward him.

Taking the soap and rag from his hand, Catrin settled on her knees at the side of the tub. She dipped the rag into the water and then soaped it, working up a rich lather. Slowly, afraid to touch him, she caught his long hair with her left hand and lifted it from his shoulders.

"I thought crusaders wore short hair because of the clime," she said, faulting him for going against fashion.

"'Twas short at the time," he replied.

Catrin patted his back with the rag. Trembling slightly, she rubbed his muscled shoulders, made strong from the wielding of his longsword, leaving the sweet-smelling lather covering his skin. Then she followed his spine until she reached the water.

She suppressed the need to gulp. "Why not now?"

"It suits my purpose."

More calculation. Marriage to Olwen was part of his purpose. There was something satisfying about knowing he would get his comeuppance some day, no matter the cost to her safety.

"Extend your arm, if it suits your purpose," she directed, releasing his black locks so they fell against his wet neck.

Bran complied, and she ran the soapy cloth from his shoulder down the length of his left arm until a ragged red scar near his elbow stopped her. "Where did you get that?" she asked.

He glanced down. "I think that's where a Saracen almost severed my arm."

His words chilled her.

"Why?" He smiled slightly and lifted an eyebrow. "Do you care about me?"

Catrin jerked back. "As much as I care for anyone in my household."

Bran caught her wrist, his fingers seeming to burn to the bone. "You don't disappoint, do you, *cariad*?" Catrin pulled back but couldn't break his grip. He growled, "I thought you were tired of fighting."

She shot him a look. He didn't seem to mind her reluctance but simply drew her hand toward the curly, black hairs on his chest.

"You are not finished," he said.

Helplessly, Catrin touched the rag to his chest. He dropped her wrist and rested his arms on the side of the tub, settling back. She scrubbed the place between his breastbones and then up to his throat. Going down again, she passed over his nipples that hardened at her slight touch. Seeing them tighten, Catrin felt warm shock waves wash through her womanly place.

She no longer stopped the gulp that escaped her lips. Her throat ached. She felt out of her skin—cold and hot, flushed with a fiery lust she could not hope to control. Washing the hard planes of his stomach, she was all too aware of the heat in her face and in his even hotter gaze that landed possessively on the thin fabric covering her breasts.

When she came to the water once more, she stopped.

"Tend to it all." His voice was rough with what she took to be desire.

Was his man part fully erect in the water, hiding just beneath the surface, taunting her?

Catrin sprang to her feet and slammed the rag into the tub, splashing water into his face. "Do it yourself!"

She ran from him, as far as the confines of the solar allowed. A flickering thought crossed her mind. The secret steps. Escape! But where? She was barefoot and practically naked.

Her mouth dry, Catrin turned and saw him rise from the tub. He stepped over the rim onto the stone floor and came toward her, slowly and menacingly. He seemed in control of himself. Did he take pleasure in the game? After all, what man did not enjoy conquest, especially of a woman?

"Queen Eleanor pegged you wrong." He crossed the floor to where she cowered at the window seat, her hair now loosened and falling around her face. "She told me to go slow, for you were inexperienced and innocent. Faith, you have fooled her highness."

Catrin's fingers curled into fists, her nails biting the pads of her palms. What had she done? By her simple acts of defiance, she was giving him cause to doubt her. Soon he would figure out he had taken the wrong cousin as wife. Her head or those of the servants who helped her would not be safe.

"You bring out the worst in me," she snapped.

"And you bring out the best in me."

Without more ado, he caught her by her shoulders and dragged her to him. He crushed her to his wet body, suffocating her with a kiss that devoured her lips and invaded her mouth. She resisted only briefly before the same hard-breathing desire exploded within her. She kissed him back, seeking satisfaction, exploring his mouth and hating herself for her own insatiable hunger.

He broke away, panting, and as she breathed quickly, he lowered his head once more, raking his lips down the tender flesh of her throat. Angered by the thrill that trailed through her when he found sensitive targets, Catrin had half a mind to resist again. Instead, she brought her trembling hands up to his chest to brace herself, and gasped aloud when his mouth found her nipples beneath the ineffective chemise.

"*Myn Duw!*" he groaned.

She felt like groaning too, her hands clawing at his solid chest. She ached and throbbed. On instinct, she sought release, pressing her hips toward his man part. Only it could give her what she suddenly could not do without.

Bran dropped his hands to her buttocks, pulling her toward him. Breathing fast, he forced her back against the chilled window seat.

"You make me a mad man," he admitted with a growl.

Catrin was mad too. Mad with a desire she'd never thought to feel and for a man she had no reason to love.

He took her then. Up against the drafty window,

thrusting hard. But she did not care. 'Twas her penance. Her punishment. Bran pulsed inside her, full and hot. She rode him, her chemise pushed up around her stomach, her legs wrapped around his waist.

"*Cariad!*" he shouted, grabbing a frantic breath before he jerked once, twice, and then shuddered like a sobbing child as once more he came within her.

Catrin clung to him for dear life, feeling limp and incomplete again. She longed for her world to be different. For this black knight to have been dressed in white. For this man who brought her to the height of desire to be her lover. The man who could give her what she could not even begin to know she needed.

CHAPTER SEVENTEEN

Will Tabor, the new stable boy, held the sleek, black raven on his outstretched gloved wrist. "She's not a bad bird, my lady," he said.

Catrin eyed the horrible, screeching creature with a doleful look. "Perchance I would rather keep a large hawk," she murmured. "I see no purpose for such a creature."

"In the fields they eat rotten carrion. They're quite clever," the boy explained. "I once saw a raven steal food right from beneath the nose of a dog."

Pulling her cloak more tightly around her, Catrin marveled at his enthusiasm. The lad, who had been lazy and shiftless under the care of the cook, was now responsible for Bran's treasured bird.

"Do you want to touch her?"

She took a step nearer and stretched out her fingers, keeping them away from the scary beak. Carefully, she smoothed the slick feathers on the raven's head. As if she knew she was facing a stern test, the raven behaved herself, regarding Catrin with beady black eyes.

"She's called Mair, my lady."

"So I have heard." Catrin had also heard ravens possessed a great gift of perception. They were soothsayers, as she claimed to be. Did Mair know the truth about her brother's death? Did she know who ambushed her on the way to Clun?

"Thank you for showing the bird to me, Will," she said with a smile.

The boy bobbed his head and returned to the mews, empty now except for the raven.

At a loss for something to do, Catrin wandered toward the stable. For days she had been confined inside by the constant drizzle. Therefore, when today broke fair and clear, she donned an old pair of men's braes under a woolen gown, surcoat, and cape. After morning Mass, she escaped into the bailey, where much of the real work of the castle took place.

Restless now, hoping to find peace in the quiet of the stable, she walked the dirt aisle between two rows of stalls. As she passed Bran's string of prize horses, black as midnight, they lifted their heads from fragrant hay bags, and stared at her with wide eyes. Her husband was rich in horse-flesh, if nothing else, she thought with a sigh.

After taking her hard and fast on the cold window seat and then coupling with her much more gently in midst of the lord's great bed, Bran had called a silent truce. He'd not touched her since. Always up before dawn, Bran left the bed while she slept. Not bothering to eat the midday meal in the great hall, he returned to the castle long after she crawled into bed for the night.

When she queried Meg, Catrin learned her husband traveled the length of the lands, surveying the tenants, settling disputes, and providing the strong hand Northbridge had lacked since the death of Olwen's father. Bran rode out in the rain by day and by night sat in front of the hearth in the great hall. Catrin watched him from the secret squint, wondering why he suddenly avoided her. Had she grown three heads and added bat wings?

A dark bay mare, almost black but for the brown around her muzzle, stuck her head over the restraining rope that kept her within her stall. Catrin stopped and offered the palm of her hand, letting the well-bred mare snuffle at her straight, outstretched fingers. Gentle brown eyes surveyed her. Catrin looked into them, sighing, and then moved her hand to the well-muscled neck.

"I have no carrots to offer," she murmured, rubbing her palm over the shiny coat "I'm sorry, girl."

The horse pawed a complaint and bobbed her head up and down. 'Twas quiet here, but for the movement of horses in the dim light. An uneasy calm came over Catrin amidst the smell of hay and horses. Marriage to Bran had accomplished only one of her goals. She'd saved Olwen from a difficult fate, for her cousin couldn't have abided the rough coupling she had withstood. Olwen's gentle spirit would have broken from it.

As if hers would not!

A fretful knot twisted in her stomach. Catrin soothed herself by soothing the mare, crooning soft words with no meaning and stroking the dark neck. She must admit her new fear, if only to herself. Why did Bran leave her alone in bed, only to join her for short periods when she was already fast asleep? Why was he avoiding her? Did he suspect the truth? Had she done something to cause his suspicion?

That she even cared what he thought was troubling.

Anger stiffened her spine, and she turned away from the

mare lest the animal sense her disquiet. Aye, why did she care? And why had the woman part of her ache and pulsate as she stealthily watched him through that secret squint?

Catrin crossed the aisle to survey a striking black stallion with the distinctive feathering of a horse from Freesland. She did not dare approach such a vicious creature, wary of him as she was of his master.

"Ride with me, my lady," Bran's deep voice vibrated through the cavernous stable. "The destrier I call Taran, which means Thunder in Welch, needs exercise."

Catrin whirled around. "Is that a command?" she asked, her face feeling hot.

He shook his head. "Nay, a simple request."

She studied him, watching the muscles flex along his jaw line. She heard her pulse beating in her ears and wondered once more about her reaction to this man. They battled silently, their gazes colliding.

Finally, she lowered her eyes. "I would like that."

'Twas almost as if he too held his breath. He remained motionless staring at her. All of a sudden, Bran sprang into action calling out instructions. Grooms appeared from nowhere, bustling about, readying the horses.

"Saddle Merch for my lady," Bran ordered. He turned to her. "'Merch' means 'girl.' I think the palfrey will suit you fine."

Catrin stood in the middle of the aisle while a stable boy saddled the dark bay mare she had just stroked. She turned in circles, watching the commotion, wondering about the efficiency the servants of Northbridge exhibited so soon after the arrival of their new lord. Had Bran instituted such change?

"I will ride Taran," he told the head groom. Turning to

Catrin, he asked, "Do you think you can handle a frisky mare? She's been cooped up because of the rain."

She lifted her shoulder with disdain. "I think you know I can ride anything, my lord."

Bran laughed aloud. "You're right! I have found your horsemanship to be excellent." He stepped nearer so only she heard his words. "In fact, I fear you may geld me with your competence."

He left abruptly to check the girth on the mare's saddle. Her face flamed at his remark. Still her heart danced nervously, and she marveled at him. Today Bran seemed in a fine mood, even joking about their lovemaking.

Nay, she refused to think of it as such, for love she did not feel. Copulation. The mating of two animals. 'Twas all it was. And if he found her so experienced, why did he leave her alone for so many days? As if he had disappeared into a cave of his own making, sour on the world?

Bran led the mare from the stall and handed the horse over to the groom, who held the reins at the head.

He came toward Catrin. "My lady, I will help you mount."

Catrin spotted the twisting of his lips. Still joking and using sexual references, was he? *Fine.* She could rise above his rough coarseness. She had survived Gilbert's common male language, after all, those many years.

Lifting her chin as if she were the queen herself, Catrin placed her hand in his, allowing him to usher her toward the mare. Her gown and surcoat were split on the sides, allowing her to ride astride, the way she liked it. Fortunately, a stone mounting block was nearby, and she didn't need her husband's help or his hands upon her body. Catrin climbed aboard Merch, gathered her reins expertly, and adjusted her skirts and cape. Then she jabbed her heels into the sides of the mare, bolting forward out of the stable.

Catrin carefully maneuvered through the bailey and out the open gate picking her way past huts clustered on the plateau near the castle keep that made up the high town. Her bold action must have surprised Bran, who still had to saddle his stallion, mount, and follow her. She didn't care. For once, she felt carefree with the little mare between her thighs and not a rutting knight.

The sandstone cliff fell steeply to the river below. Catrin took the winding cartway she had avoided on the night of her arrival. By the time she reached the bridge, Bran had caught up with her.

"You should not go out alone."

His brows furrowed, and his lips drew into a thin line. He was angry now. She didn't care.

They crossed the wooden bridge, the clomping of the hooves sounding hollow above the roar of the rushing water below. Although the river had risen because of the rain, the Severn still retained its boundaries. On its banks, mallards and geese gathered, searching for food.

They turned left, passed through low town, and followed the riverbank. Soon, leaving Castle Mount behind, they entered woodland, the trees already winter-bare. The air was crisp and smelled of smoke and fallen leaves. A wild excitement stirred Catrin's blood. Her horse wanted a good gallop, but she carefully controlled the mare, letting her settle into a comfortable amble for a few strides. Bran relaxed his stallion into a prancing walk. His horse's head tossed up and down as the animal fought the bit.

Catrin knew the stretch of ground ahead was flat. "Let's run them!"

Before he could utter a reply, she kicked her horse into a gallop, leaned forward in the saddle, and urged the mare into a faster pace. The wind whipped her cloak behind her like a battle flag and stung her eyes and her face. The illusion of freedom spurred her on. She wanted to shout with joy.

In only a few strides, Bran caught up with her and rode precariously side-by-side with her on the narrow dirt track. She glanced over her shoulder at his wind-reddened cheeks, his eyes alight with pleasure. Like a boy released from his studies, he grinned mischievously, seeming to goad her forward.

Soon, the road grew muddy and Catrin slowed, fearing for the safety of the gallant mare. She caught her breath, feeling winded like the horse, her mind eased of its worries.

"You ride well, my lady."

"Ha! High praise from the King's Raven! I am honored."

He frowned at her sarcasm. "You give no quarter, do you?"

"I have none to give. This marriage is not of my choosing. The king selected for me."

They rode a little way in silence until they reached a shallow ford of a millrace. In the distance, a mill emerged through the trees, the sound of its wheel groaning as it turned, providing the power to grind grain into flour. They paused to let the horses drink.

Bran shifted in his saddle. "I want to give you something."

"I want nothing from you, but the truth." Her answer sounded curt.

"And I have given you the truth."

"Then spare me more gifts." Catrin raised the mare's head and turned toward Northbridge.

"Be that as it may, I want to give you a morning gift."

His words stopped her. A morning gift, or a thanks offering, was meant to pay the bride for the loss of her virginity.

"If love passed between us, there would be no need for such a gift," she said.

"Love is not part of the bargain I seek."

"Only my *cooperation*."

Scowling, he reached into the folds of his black cloak and pulled forth a jewel. He let out an exasperated breath as he handed it to her across the gap between the now restive horses. "'Tis a brooch to pin together your cloak."

Catrin accepted the beautiful bauble in the palm of her right hand. She smiled at the irony of it for he had given her another one in their marriage bed.

The silver-encrusted brooch was made from red jasper, a stone symbolizing love. Did Bran realize that? Surely not. He wanted love from her no more than she wanted it from him.

"Thank you, my lord," she said with a proper bow. "I will treasure it as long as we are married."

His lips pressed tightly together, Bran spurred his black horse into a gallop, leaving her to pick up her gait and sprint after him. She clutched the red jasper brooch in her hand along with the reins.

As they retraced their ride, she speculated about their change in mood. Gone was the cheerful exuberance of the earlier gallop. How quickly did their differences manifest between them. What could she expect, given the circumstances of their marriage and her deception?

Catrin knew something was amiss when they trotted silently side-by-side into the bailey now crowded with retainers all bearing the Rothmore crest. A groom took her horse's reins, and Meg ran across the courtyard toward her.

Fear stabbed Catrin in the gut.

"My lady." Meg reached the mare and looking up, whispered, "Your brother, Earl Rothmore, has come to Northbridge Castle!"

CHAPTER EIGHTEEN

Her half brother Richard, Isadora's son, was now Earl Rothmore. Catrin wanted to flee, for his presence at Northbridge boded ill.

Did Meg read the panic in her stare? She must, because Catrin saw her own fear mirrored in the eyes of the faithful servant.

The maid clutched the hem of Catrin's cloak. "My lady, the boy is not well."

Alarm seized her as she slid from the mare. "Where is he?"

"In the hall."

Sparing a quick glance at Bran, who watched her with curiosity, Catrin picked up her skirts and with Meg sprinted across the bailey. Servants scattered to let them pass. Together they climbed the sandstone steps to the door of the keep and entered the dimly-lit hall. Inside, several Rothmore retainers clustered in a group cast dubious glances at the sparse furnishings of Northbridge's great hall. The lands and property Bran had claimed by marriage to "Olwen" paled in comparison to the lavish holdings Catrin's ten-year-old brother had inherited.

Seeing so many people she knew, Catrin halted at the entrance. Meg seemed to understand her reluctance and uttered a soft, "Courage."

Catrin squared her shoulders and gave the maid a slight smile. "Keep this for me." She handed Meg the jeweled brooch.

Then she strode down the length of the hall, passing the new arrivals with her head high, her cloak whipping behind her because of her haste. She hoped her air of confidence would dissuade even the most suspicious.

Richard sat in the lord's massive chair near the fire. He was a thin lad clad in the flowing robes of an adult. His face appeared paler than usual for all that he was always sickly. Eyes wide with trepidation and shadowed by dark circles, he cast sharp glances around the hall.

Catrin's soul filled with a cold ache. Richard had the look of her father and Gilbert. He was a Fitzalan. He was her brother, no matter his mother.

She went to him, dropping a curtsy, her eyes downcast. "My lord."

Richard acknowledged her gravely with the nod of his head. Yet, when he spoke, it was with the voice of a child. "You may rise, cousin."

As she stood and looked him full in the face, she heard him gasp. With his thin hands grasping the arms of the chair, he propelled himself upward to stand before her. "Catrin?" he whispered.

Compassion ripped her heart anew. In a foolhardy move, she went down on her knees and gathered her little brother in her arms, hugging him tightly and feeling the very bones of him beneath his garments. "Aye, I am alive," she whispered. "But do not react for our enemies are all around. I will explain when we are alone."

Richard nodded. "I have been afraid." He caught himself before saying her name. He was wise beyond his years.

"As have I." She looked at him. "You must be brave, for you are to take Gilbert's place."

Richard's lip trembled. "I would rather not."

"As with much in this life, you shall have no choice." Catrin pulled him even closer.

"I know," he whimpered. "I try to be brave."

Slowly, she became aware of the heat radiating from her brother. Catrin rocked back on her heels and, holding him at arm's length, placed a palm on his scorching forehead. "My lord, you are ill."

He nodded his head. "I know, but since I am sick so often, I didn't want to trouble anyone."

Catrin rose abruptly, searching for Meg. Instead her gaze slammed against the speculative one of the Guy de Hastings, Lord Leighton.

She lifted a haughty chin. "My lord?"

He bowed with mock formality. "Lady de Belleme."

"'Tis Lady Northbridge," Catrin replied sharply, for her natural dislike of him rose within her like a striking viper. "I am now married."

He smiled with condescension. "Yea, the king's man. Where is your new husband, my lady? I have business with him."

"What do you want, Leighton?" Bran's voice boomed above the chattering household. All those in the great hall fell silent as the new master of Northbridge advanced through the crowd. He came to a halt in front of them, looking very much like the wild Welsh warrior of his reputation. "You have reason for your visit?"

Tension popped between the two men. Why this animosity? Bran's lips pinched together with evident hostility, his stance rigid and unyielding.

Lord Leighton seemed no better disposed to be pleasant. He looked down his aquiline Norman nose at the darker, heavier knight. "Lady Rothmore, Richard's mother, sent me to make sure her son arrives safely, what with Welsh raiders crossing the border murdering innocent English women."

"What is the purpose of the earl's visit?" Bran gave no quarter nor acknowledged the slur.

Lord Leighton's eyes burned. "At the king's command, I have brought you this dispatch." He offered a sealed parchment to his host.

Bran took the missive, glanced at the royal seal, and then lifted his gaze to search the onlookers. "Where is Father Ellis?"

"What's the matter, my lord?" Leighton scoffed. "You cannot decipher our liege's message?"

Catrin's stomach gave a sickening lurch. What if Bran could not read? Learning to read did not figure into the training of a common soldier. And wasn't Bran a simple soldier before his elevation in rank by the king? That she knew so little about him pierced her conscience for an instant.

Bran remained stonily silent in the face of Leighton's obvious satisfaction. Catrin's aversion to the pompous neighbor of the Fitzalan family was magnified a hundredfold because of his humiliation of her husband. Her pulse quickened and so did her protective instincts.

"May I, my lord?" She extended her hand, wanting to end

the standoff, but knowing as she did, she might humiliate her husband more.

His jaw clenching, Bran handed over the parchment, much as he had earlier offered her the brooch. She took it from him, their fingertips touching, and she quickly turned away, breaking the red wax seal bearing the king's crest. Nearby, Richard coughed a dry hacking sound that testified to his poor health.

Once more, while Catrin scanned the Latin text, appreciation welled within her. Her mother's dying instructions to her father were for him to promise that both her babies be taught to read and write—the girl as well as the boy. Illiterate herself, her mother had known her daughter's half-Welsh heritage could be tempered by education. Thus, she and Olwen had spent many days under the tutelage of one tutor after another, often learning more aptly than Gilbert, who had oft been schooled with them.

Catrin looked up from the message, a mixture of dread and excitement seeping to her very core. Now, even more, the implication of her deception weighed upon her. As Olwen's husband, Edward was honoring Bran.

If he was not the one who killed Gilbert, she wronged him sorely by pretending to be Olwen. The earlier glee she felt knowing Bran's world would crumble some day when he found out the truth now ended abruptly, for she had involved her only remaining brother in the deception.

"King Edward has given you the guardianship of Richard Fitzalan, Earl Rothmore," Catrin said, her voice growing husky with emotion. "He is to foster with you, learning the tasks and duties of a high lord of the realm."

Bran stood a little straighter, letting the news sink in. Catrin saw the depth of feeling in his eyes. He would know the responsibility and the great honor of the king's decree. He also would know of the wealth that came to him because of it.

Leighton knew it too. His nostrils flared and his eyes flashed. He hid his anger by narrowing his eyes.

He could not hide his fisted glove.

Tense silence followed, both men measuring each other like two barn cats protecting turf.

"We must return to Oswestry," Leighton spoke, finally ending the standoff. "Yet, it grows dark early these days."

Was he seeking an invitation? Good manners, as the lady of the castle, bid her to ask the king's courier to stay. Fear held her tongue. With so much at stake, she didn't need the prying glances of Guy de Hastings.

Bran's look reproached her. She should speak. Swallowing her unease, Catrin murmured, "We will have our midday meal soon. Please dine with us, Lord Leighton. You and your retinue can start out early on the morrow."

"I can never resist a beautiful lady," he said bowing slightly and favoring her with another rude and speculative glace.

She thought Bran would take off his head.

"'Tis settled," her husband said. "Let us eat!"

Hungry servants sprang into action at their lord's command, dragging out trestle tables and benches for the largest meal of the day. Catrin sent Meg to check with the cook and called for the butler to offer ale and wine to her guests.

Then, her visitors attended to, she turned back to Richard. The boy slumped in the chair, looking more wan and pathetic than she'd ever seen him.

Before she could go to her brother, Bran stepped to her

side and caught her arm. "You were quick to shame me in front of Leighton," he growled close to her ear so no one else heard.

Catrin bristled. "What would you have me do? I tried to save you from embarrassment when I realized you cannot read."

"You miss my meaning," Bran countered. "You were slow to do your duty as wife and mistress of Northbridge. Word travels fast, and Lord Leighton has designs at court. Should we send him away without the hospitality of a full belly and a good night's rest?"

Catrin flinched at his angry tone. She didn't need this, not with Richard's illness to deal with. She met Bran's gaze, refusing to back away. Not even with the touch of his hand branding her flesh, his breath hot upon her face, his manly outdoor scent embracing her. Not even when she trembled with unwanted desire and then hated the way her body betrayed her.

"Mayhap, if you acted less like your hot-blooded ancestors, we could discuss this civilly," she said with a pointed glance at his grip on her arm.

Something flickered in his eyes. He removed his hand. "I have treated you with respect."

"You, my lord, have treated me as your raven namesake."

Had they been alone in the hall, she knew he'd take her then and there. The anger in his gaze was a palpable thing. "I can play your pretty games," he said, "but you will also play mine."

"Fine. Then play the magnanimous host. Tend to our guests while I see to Richard."

Pointedly, she turned her back on him. She felt him leave, for the air around her seemed to lighten as the charged energy of his presence vanished. Catrin knelt once more beside Richard and placed her hand against his forehead. Her mind whirled with concern and confusion.

She took a shaky breath. Could Bran be jealous?

Quickly, she checked that disturbing thought. And the notion that Lord Leighton's voice sounded so strangely familiar to her.

Bran sent Meg to fetch Olwen from the solar where she'd taken the boy Richard. Now his tardy wife chatted with Leighton, her head demurely down, her laughter tempered, almost as if she responded politely when expected, nothing more. Still Bran was not amused.

He slouched in the lord's chair, one arm draped over its back and the other rising every few moments when he brought a silver goblet to his lips. His irritated stare swept the two of them.

Damn Leighton! First the whoreson challenged him in Paris at the French king's tournament, forcing him to best one of King Edward's subjects in order to maintain his disguise. Now, Leighton challenged him with his pretty new wife, blatantly flirting with Olwen and making her laugh. Did she not know the man was a schemer? Prone to taking what he wanted?

Frustration rippled through him and he bit back a curse with another swig of ale. Leighton had a silver tongue. Bran had not the gift, nor the inclination. Olwen wanted courting and what had he done? He'd fair raped her the last time they'd been together. Damn his uncontrollable lust!

Damn her for making him feel so out of control!

Bran knew what she meant when she said he had treated her as his raven namesake. In the slang of the day, to raven a woman was to copulate with her roughly or even brutally. His gut twisted with shame. He had never meant to treat her so harshly. He wanted to go slow and bring her to climax.

Instead, she had bested him with her beauty and her innocent passion. They fed off one another, with anger, surely, but also with a sweet, insatiable desire. She had made him hunger so that he couldn't stop wanting to feast on her charms.

This was his reward. To watch his young bride trifled with by the damn self-seeking lord.

He had stayed well away from Olwen for days; unable to be near her for fear he'd lose his control once more. Even now, a simple glance at her sent his pulse racing and his cock rising. She had that kind of effect on him.

Was it because he had long been without a woman? Now that he had a wife legally, his lust mounted because of his pride of ownership. Verily, he need not fear fathering a bastard ever again. Olwen would not think kindly of his pride in her as his possession.

He did not want to believe there was more to his obsession.

"Madog! Your bride has quite a wit!" Leighton waved a shank of venison in the air and then bit into it, ripping the juicy meat from the bone.

Bran's hackles rose. His noisy guest was unashamed in his insult, for Bran was now Lord Northbridge and deserved to be addressed by that rank.

"Lord Leighton," Olwen said with a sweet smile that Bran mistrusted, "please have more of my husband's wine brought from Boudreaux. You'll find it tasty as well as potent."

Olwen darted a glance his way, revealing an amused tilt to her lips. With a clunk, Bran slammed his goblet down on the table and scrubbed his hand down his face. What was she plotting? He sat forward, suddenly intent on watching his bride.

He watched her pinch a piece of dark, crusty bread and bring the bite up to her lips. Her movements were restrained and feminine much like her features, the simple oval of her face and bright blue of her eyes. Her pale hands were refined and elegant with long, tapering fingers meant, perchance, to use on a musical instrument. He could imagine them plucking the strings of a harp, a small Celtic one like his grandmother used to play.

Memory of those hands upon his back and the soft fullness of those lips on his mouth excited his passions. He could not stop wanting her again...and again...with a hunger not even close to slacking.

CATRIN KNEW BRAN WATCHED HER, just as surely as Guy de Hastings did. Their guest had known her, for however briefly, as Catrin. She doubted he had known Olwen, but discovery 'twas a chance she dared not take, and she was uneasy. Leighton's suspicions must be thwarted.

Carefully, she toyed with Leighton as if she were a pawn in chess, manipulating him with a filled cup and murmuring sweet, nonsensical words that pumped his ego. All the while, anger simmered beneath the surface, and she was cautious not to show her contempt. Rumor said Leighton and Isadora were lovers. Both had denied it, but why else had her stepmother entrusted him to deliver her son to Northbridge?

Richard. Worry plagued her. She had come to expect her brother's frequent illnesses, but this was different. He burned with a fever she knew not how to ease. Thankfully, Meg was with him. She longed for this interminable meal to end.

"Welshman," Leighton called, leaning on the table and pointing his eating knife at Bran, "the king honors you well with the care of Earl Rothmore."

Bran's eyes narrowed. "I am well aware of the king's grace."

"Lady Isadora means to make certain of her son's welfare."

"I would expect a mother to care thus for her son," Bran answered evenly.

The sudden rush of pride she felt surprised Catrin. No wonder Edward had used Bran for his purposes. Her husband possessed the judgment of a diplomat and kept his thoughts well controlled.

Not so their guest. Wine loosened Leighton's tongue. He turned to Catrin as if confiding in her. "Lady Isadora worries Richard will not be strong enough to learn the fighting skills of a knight. Further, she wonders how a barbaric Welshman can pass on the finer skills her son needs as a lord of the realm."

Catrin drew a sharp breath at the blatant insult. Bran closed his fists upon the arms of the chair and looked as if he were about to rise. The fierce black knight of the tourney field had returned.

Men! They thought nothing about the welfare of poor Richard. They thought only of their silly pride and selfish greed.

"My lords, this meal has ended!" Catrin stood, placing

her hands on the edge of the table. "I must go now to Richard, who you, Lord Leighton, brought to us with a raging fever."

Leighton was not pleased by her indictment. "Harrumph! The foolish boy is always ill." He swallowed more wine and glared up at her.

Anger rankled Catrin. "Please give Lady Isadora a message from my husband and myself when you see her on the morrow." She glanced quickly at Bran. "Tell her she can rest assured that her son, my cousin, will be safe in the household of Lord Northbridge."

Catrin pushed back her chair and gathered her skirts, pausing a moment to stare down at Bran. "And you, my lord," she said softly, bending down as if to kiss him but letting no one else hear, "may take your rest elsewhere tonight, for I have given Earl Rothmore the lord's great bed."

With that, she whisked past him, head held high.

All the while, she attempted, unsuccessfully, to banish the thought of the hurt flitting, however briefly, through Bran's raven eyes.

CHAPTER NINETEEN

Catrin sighed, thankful at least that the loathsome Lord Leighton had left early in the morning, and she had one less worry. She stared at her brother's haggard face. Richard's hand clung to hers. His skin felt hot and dry, his slender fingers mere bones beneath pale flesh. His eyes were shut, and his lashes lightly touched his cheek. He was almost feminine in appearance.

How would he ever stand the rigors required of a lord of the realm? Now that he had been fostered with Bran, his knightly training would begin. Unlike Gilbert, so sturdy and spirited, Richard possessed none of the qualities of a warrior. He should be called to the clergy, by rights, becoming a scholarly monk, shut away from life's hardships and pursuing his love of learning.

She must explain this to Bran. Surely, he would listen. Surely, he would temper the boy's physical education at her behest.

Catrin could never imagine her brother raising the Rothmore sword in battle, nor staring down a black knight who glared through the sights of his great helm.

"This is but a common contagion," Meg said, coming to stand behind her. "One that children are wont to contract. His doesn't have griping in his bowels or flux."

Meg's words didn't ease her worry. "That may be," Catrin acknowledged, "but Richard was e'er a sickly child. I fear his convulsions will return."

Richard's eyes popped open. "I only have them when I'm overly tired," he said. "I have not had one in a long while."

Catrin squeezed his hand. "I am glad."

Richard's convulsions had indeed tapered off with age, but they were still frightening because no one knew when the demons within would strike him. In this, Isadora had proven to be like a mother bear, fiercely protecting her son from slander and gossip. Few knew of the debilitating condition that caused his eyes to roll back in his head and his body to shake as if possessed by the devil himself.

As much as it pained her to admit, Catrin recognized the sincerity of his mother's love.

"Never worry, sister." There was a sly twinkle in Richard's eyes. "I want to get well so you will tell me the story of your escape from the outlaws."

"'Tis a promise," she said with a grin. "I will tell you all as soon as you are out of this bed. But you must call me 'Olwen' and remember only Meg and Father Ellis know the truth."

"I am glad Olwen is safe," Richard whispered. "Everyone knows she wants to be a nun."

"Aye, she is safe." Catrin nodded.

"Is Bran such a bad man?"

Startled, Catrin glanced over her shoulder at Meg, who

turned her gaze away, unwilling it seemed, to help her answer Richard.

Catrin didn't know how to respond. Who was she to judge? Certainly, Bran had been "bad" to her, taking her as forcefully as any wild stallion, but hadn't she provoked him? Like a mare in season? Didn't they feed off each other as if an unholy destiny existed between them?

Her cheeks flamed at the thought of their coupling. She had wanted him as much as he wanted her. Her flesh burned with desire and sinful lust, fueled by the wickedness of her lies and false oaths to God with the marriage vows she had uttered.

"I do not know if he is bad," she said softly. "I only know what people have said about him."

"But what was his motive? His purpose for killing Gilbert?"

Catrin stared down at her half-brother, wise in so many ways. She had secretly asked herself the questions that came so quickly to his keen mind. In faith, what would be Bran's purpose when he looked to have received everything his heart desired in marriage to Olwen—land, a castle, and power?

That his "wife" had not come willingly, clearly, was another matter Bran had not foreseen. Further, she hadn't considered her response to him. Trying to suppress the stirrings of her sinful nature kept her constantly on pins and needles.

Still, why *would* Bran want to kill Gilbert? She would name a better purpose from the feckless Leighton, whose lands bordered Rothmore holdings, or even from Isadora. Her stepson's untimely death meant *her* son inherited the earldom.

Yet why would either one of them want her murdered? Isadora was soon to be rid of her through an arranged marriage. The king would have seen to that if she had "lived." Then Catrin would no longer pose a problem to her stepmother. There would be no more conflicts in the household, and she would no longer remind Isadora of the Welsh woman who had first won Earl Rothmore, John Fitzalan's devotion, and borne him two children.

Guy de Hastings had even less cause to kill her, a mere woman, heir to nothing of value.

"I know not Bran's reason, dear one. I only know people said he sought revenge for Gilbert's dishonorable behavior on the tourney field." Catrin offered Richard a smile she did not feel. She didn't want to disclose the presence of the second piece of scarf, her only true evidence against Bran.

"'Tis a true puzzle," the boy said, his mind already seeming to plot the answer. Then a fit of coughing took him. Concerned, Catrin looked up at Meg.

"Force him to drink," the maid instructed.

Richard shook his head, for the curative concoction Meg had fixed for him had a foul taste.

"You must, Richard," Catrin said. "You are in my care, and I want you to get well."

Richard sighed and did as he was told. Then Catrin soaked a rag with tepid water and bathed his face. She continued until her brother fell into a fitful sleep. She put the rag into the laver and sat back in the chair, worn out with worry and little sleep.

Meg touched her shoulder. "I will watch him for you."

"Nay, I will stay."

"You need your rest," Meg insisted.

"I will rest later. You go."

She would not leave Richard. That was all there was to it. He was all she had in this world. All those others she loved had died. Father. Gilbert. Gwendolyn. Even Olwen was lost to her now.

She'd failed to protect those she loved, except for Olwen, and that success might be short-lived if Bran discovered the truth and went after his true wife. A sudden fear knotted in Catrin's throat at the thought.

"I will bring your supper," Meg whispered.

"My thanks," Catrin said, watching the maid slip from the room.

All was quiet, but for the sound of her half-brother's raspy breathing. He looked so small amid the majesty of the master's great bed—small and out of place. A lone candle burned at the bedside, its faint light sputtering in the draft.

She, too, was out of place in that room and in that bed, where for several nights she lusted after the King's Raven, giving him all the pleasure he wanted, but failing to find any satisfaction for herself. Why? Not from his wont of trying that she was unable to topple over that hill of passion he pushed her up.

'Twas her punishment. Just as Richard's illness was her penalty for the sin of lying in front of God and then wanting another woman's husband.

The wayward thought provoked her spirit. Nay! Olwen would not have been this man's wife, no matter the king's decree. So, why, of a sudden, did she think of him that way? She licked her dry lips, in her mind's eye seeing the form of *her* husband as he chatted with Father Ellis, dispensed swift judgment to a wrongdoer, and lightly stroked the arched neck of his black stallion.

A great yearning overwhelmed her. Catrin sat up

straighter, denying the warmth she felt, repudiating the raw need snaking through her body.

She wanted him.

'Twas just lust, was it not? Nothing more. Bran ap Madog was nothing more to her than a suspect in the murder of her brother and father. He was nothing more than a means to an end.

The throbbing in her temple would not cease. Neither would the part deep down in her soul that questioned her conscious thoughts. Why did she protest so much?

A strange lethargy enveloped her. God help her. What had she gotten herself into?

She had come to think of Bran as *her* husband.

Catrin put her head down on the side of the bed and shut her eyes. The rough breathing of the small boy in the bed lulled her until she fell into a fitful sleep.

BRAN PAUSED at the open door, letting his eyes grow accustomed to the murkiness of the solar. Evil vapors filled the room with the scent of sickness. A medicinal aroma clung to the very fabric of the wall hangings and coverlets. He gagged and almost failed to enter. What this room needed was light and fresh air enough to chase the contagion away.

Crossing into the room, he spotted Olwen sitting by the bed, her head resting on the side, her face turned toward the door as she slept. He walked toward her, carrying her supper. Meg, the loyal servant, was loath to let go of her duties, but he was master here after all, and the maid could do naught but curtsy and accept his decree.

Now he stood beside the bed holding a tray containing this day's savory stew and freshly baked bread. Looking down at his wife, a strange awe enveloped him. She had removed her headdress, wearing only a silver net crespine confining her hair. Olwen had attended her young cousin for two days, not coming downstairs, not resting. No wonder she slept the sleep of one exhausted.

Bran placed the tray on a side table and returned to steal clandestine glimpses of his wife. A sharp pain of regret clobbered his gut. Ah, that he could inspire as much devotion as this boy!

What was it about these Rothmore men that they managed to inspire such loyalty and affection? First the sister with the handmade favor and now her cousin Olwen. Both were women who protected and fought for the men they loved.

Bran let out a breath that was much too close to a sigh. He never tired of looking at Olwen. Her comely face was a pale oval of perfection with its straight nose and pert mouth. Now her sapphire eyes were shut, unable to flash at him with anger or with passion.

His fingers curled at the thought of Olwen naked above him—the tiny knife in her hands, so easily overcome. How he longed to have her ride him like that, of her own free will, not taken so forcefully that, although his manhood exploded with pleasure, he came away each time edgy and angry with himself and with his lack of self-control.

The more he resolved to do better, the more his vices overcame his best intentions. 'Twas better to stay away from her. Doing so was his frustration and the penance he had meted out for himself.

Yet 'twas impossible to remain aloof from the one possession he had failed to conquer.

SWATHED in the remnants of an erotic dream, Catrin opened her eyes. She was immediately catapulted from a cocoon of dreamy pleasure into harsh reality. Blinking again, she stared up at the dark, foreboding visage of the man in her dreams. This same man scowled darkly at her, his male scent of woodruff almost a slap to her face.

"What do you want, my lord?" She kept her voice low, but it sounded harsh even to her own ears.

Standing up quickly, she swayed for an instant before gaining her balance. Her throat ached, and she swallowed. Then, before he could answer, she raised a finger to her lips. Bran's mouth tightened, so he surely caught her meaning. Catrin shooed him backwards toward the window seat, far enough away from the bed so as not to disturb Richard.

"I have brought your supper," he said, so stiff that no emotion crossed his face or marked his eyes. "And I have come to see how you do."

Catrin did not want his concern. "You can see I am doing well enough, my lord."

"Aye." He nodded, his regard sweeping from her head to her toe. "How is the boy?"

She drew in a breath, suppressing the need that touched each part of her body with that glance. "Richard is still ill," she answered, "but I have hope for a full recovery."

"What about yourself? Will you take your supper downstairs? With me?"

Annoyance crawled along her spine. "My duty is to Lord Rothmore."

"What about your duty to your husband?" Bran's jaw clenched with evident anger.

She lifted her nose in the air. "I have done that duty, my lord."

"As you are wont to tell me time and again."

His long hair, glinting in the fading light from the glazed window, tempted her. Catrin longed to run her fingers through its length. She stared up at him, at the grim set of his mouth, the mouth that had ravaged hers and seared her breasts. Unbidden, her body came alive with desire.

Her heart squeezed unbearably. "Would you rather we tell the king we did nothing to help his grievously ill vassal? Two in my family were lost to Edward this year."

He rested a hand on her sleeve, lightly, as if coaxing. "Coming downstairs will not hinder his lordship's recovery."

Catrin felt the heat in his touch. She trembled, outraged at the ache of longing that spiraled through her body. "Thank you, my lord, for your concern, but I choose to see to Richard's nursing myself," she said, trying to make her tone dismissive.

"Your devotion is noble." Harsh light burned in his eyes. "Have it your way—for now. But be aware, I have prepared the solar in the opposite tower for your cousin's use while he remains at Northbridge."

"Now?" Panic rose in her voice. "Richard must leave this room now?"

"He may stay here until he is well. But this is our room, Olwen. This is where we seek our privacy. Where we know each other as husband and wife. I want this room returned to what it was before he came."

She lowered her lashes, hoping to cover the surprise that might show in her gaze. "I'm sure Richard will appreciate that you have given up your bed for him."

"And what about you, Olwen? Do you appreciate what I've done for him?" His gentle pressure on her sleeve increased as his warm breath skimmed her temple. "And do you not long for what we can have in that bed?"

Bran's hand connected them. Yet his fingers were merely a tease. She hated herself for wanting more of what they promised to do to her—what they could do to her in that bed. "What we can have, my lord? I do not understand. Our coupling is as any wild creature might have, devoid of any spark of love."

"Love I cannot measure, but I give you my respect and devotion as my wife."

His eyes shifted back and forth, his gaze scorching her face, forcing her to tighten her jaw in an attempt to withstand the pull he exerted on her resolve. God help her! If he dropped his lips to hers at that moment, she would kiss him back.

Richard's coughing broke the spell between them. Catrin sucked in a breath. "Go, my lord, lest you catch the contagion as well. This is no time for discussion."

"I will go now," he said, his voice full of angry authority. "But I will return. I am master of my house, Olwen, and you would do well to remember that."

CHAPTER TWENTY

Two days later, after All Saints Day had come and gone without his wife leaving the solar, Bran marched upstairs.

He found Richard sitting up in bed with Olwen by his side. When he entered the room, she shut her mouth much too quickly and turned a book face down on her lap as if not wanting him to hear what they said.

"You do not knock, my lord?" Olwen asked, her voice sounding thin and wispy.

Bran read the panic and defiance in her eyes, and a pang of regret stabbed him. "This is my room too, my lady, remember? Yet you should have no fear." He smiled at the irony. "I can't decipher what you are reading. You have no need to hide it from me."

Turning from her shocked visage to the face of the wide-eyed boy, Bran bowed slightly. "I am glad to see you so much improved, my lord."

"Aye," the child acknowledged with a shy grin. "I have felt more like myself today."

"I'm glad," he replied. "Olwen has tended you faithfully."

"Aye, my lord." The boy glanced sharply at his wife. He hesitated. "My…er…cousin is loyal to a fault, I believe."

Bran gazed at the young earl, deciding the lad's clear eyes bespoke a keen intelligence. He nodded. "I find all of your family to be loyal, my lord."

"*Fidelitas usque ad mortem.* Loyalty 'til death. 'Tis the Rothmore motto," Richard said with a touch of pride.

"And a fine motto, to be sure." Bran smiled. "I am Lord Northbridge, your guardian."

"I know who you are, my lord." Richard brightened. "You are the King's Raven, his majesty's champion. You are to teach me what I need to know to become a knight and a lord of the realm."

"I will teach you the ways of a warrior, for I have first-hand knowledge of it," Bran said with a nod. He glanced at Olwen. "But first, I am taking your nurse away from you. For all of her devotion, my wife needs fresh air. She has been too long cooped up."

Amusement sparkled in the lad's eyes. "You have my permission, my lord."

"Richard!"

"You know I am better, *Olwen*," Richard said, emphasizing his cousin's name.

"The day is fair, my lady. Ride with me. We shall not have many such days this winter." Bran wanted to touch Olwen, to grab her hand and pull her out of the sick room and into the light. He hated that he had to plead with her, that he *was* pleading with her. She was his, by rights, was she not?

Slowly, she stood, looking wan, shadows smudging under her eyes. She lowered her lashes submissively. "I will go with you, as you request, my lord."

Bran swallowed, wanting her to go with him because she

wished to. "Fine. I will have Merch saddled and brought to the bailey. Dress warmly."

Before she could nod, Bran whipped around and departed the solar. Silently, he cursed the feelings gnawing at his insides. Why couldn't he name these strange feelings? All he knew was that he wanted his wife to be his wife in more than name. He was not a patient man. He didn't want to give her time to forget her sorrow. He didn't want to go slow, as the queen suggested.

Bran curled his fingers. "*Myn Duw!*" He swept through the great hall and down the steps to the bailey.

These feelings were swallowing him up, making him forget his good judgment. Making him behave as wild and dangerous as his Welsh ancestors his wife so despised.

THEY RODE AT A HARD GALLOP, Bran astride Taran, his black destrier, and Olwen on Merch. When they reached the place where he had given her the brooch, Bran pulled his horse down to a walk. She slowed the mare.

"So, what is it that you say to the earl?" he asked, turning in his saddle to gauge his wife's expression. "Why do you hide it from me?"

Color flushed her cheeks. The ride was doing her good. She no longer looked as pale as in the solar. He was right about forcing her out of the sick room. 'Twas doing him good to be with her as well.

She did not answer, looking suddenly unsure of herself. Or was it of his reaction?

He guided Taran in a sweeping circle around her as she

and the mare continued a flat walk. "You need not fear me, my lady."

Still no answer.

"You have my word."

She licked her lips, seeming to catch her breath. "I speak to him of the tales of Tristan and Isolde, Arthur and Genevieve, tales of courtly love."

He lifted a questioning eyebrow. "Your choice of entertainment matter *is* curious, for I doubt the king wants the lad's head filled with such nonsense."

"Nonsense? The queen and her ladies listen to the reciting of romances," she replied, tipping her adorable little nose into the air.

"'Ladies' being the operative word," he pointed out. For some reason, he enjoyed baiting her. "You cannot think the subject is fit for Earl Rothmore?"

"Tales of chivalry and courtly love are always good instruction."

Bran caught her meaning. She was being critical of him. Of their relationship. Yet, his heart was light, and at the moment the darker implications of her words did not trouble him. That she was talking with him at all pleased him, so much so that he wanted it to continue. He wanted to connect with her on a level other than the purely physical.

At the small stream, he reined in Taran. "Let us rest and give the horses a drink."

Olwen halted her palfrey. She nodded, lifting the back of her hand to her brow. "I could use a moment to catch my breath."

He dismounted, finding it easy without the normal weight of his mail and helm. He neared the mare and his wife. Those strange feelings clogged his throat once more.

"Let me help you down." He reached up for her and circled her tiny waist with his hands.

She swayed toward him. For one brief second, that seemed almost an eternity, she searched his face.

"My lady," he whispered, awestruck by her beauty.

Then she jerked and cried out, her horrifying scream of pain reverberating in his head. She collapsed like a child's rag doll into his arms. Going down on one knee to cushion her fall, he sank with her weight.

"Olwen?" Could she not hear him? "Olwen!"

Her eyes were shuttered, and her chest rose and fell slowly with each laboring breath. Bran cradled her and climbed to his feet holding her in his arms. His wife's blood soaked his surcoat.

"*Mon Dieu!*"

Frantic, Bran scanned the horizon, looking for the hunter who shot the wayward arrow penetrating his wife's shoulder.

CHAPTER TWENTY-ONE

"Her lungs are full of infection."

Bran looked at his wife's maid with stark disbelief. "What does *that* mean?" he whispered, knowing full well.

He had kept Olwen's wound from festering but he couldn't keep contagion from her lungs. The harsh reality washed over him like a cold North Sea wave. With the help of Meg, he had saved Olwen's life after the hunting accident. Keeping Father Ellis' leech away from her, he had staunched Olwen's blood flow and stitched and dressed her wound himself, applying a poultice as he'd learned in the Holy Lands. That she had not died in the first hours had been a miracle.

Through it all, Bran had been so preoccupied he had failed to search for the dimwitted hunter who'd shot his wife. Olwen's recovery had meant more to him than seeking out the person responsible.

Meg shook her head. "I know not what to do now."

The resulting silence lengthened between them. Bran stared at his wife, lying in the master's bed, her eyelids closed, unaware of her surroundings as she slept fitfully. Her full lips were slightly parted and her face was flushed from the new fever. Her hair hung loose and tangled. She twisted her head side to side and struggled to breathe.

She was so lovely. Even in her sickness, Olwen's exotic beauty drew him. He reached out and smoothed a strand of silky hair away from her eyes. He touched her brow, feeling the softness of her skin and the ever-present heat. Stroking his fingers over her cheek, he caressed her and trailed his fingertips lightly over the flesh of her jaw and chin. Could his touch extract the contagion? Heal her?

Nay, he had not the gift. His grandmother had possessed it. His mother's mother. 'Cepting Nain was not here. She had died of old age and deprivation years ago in a hovel near Castle Dinas Bran.

"I once knew of an herbal tea used for such ailments," Bran spoke softly, his voice hushed by emotion. "Mayhap you have the ingredients."

Meg looked up at him. "Tell me. I will find in the village what I do not have."

"Make a tea from meadowsweet flower, wild thyme, licorice root, plantain leaf, and another ingredient I do not remember." Bran paused in his recitation, wishing he had paid more attention to his grandmother's concoctions. But that was so long ago. He'd been but a child. A boy prone to playing at war with sticks and stones.

He shut his eyes a moment, summoning his grandmother's spirit. Nain's love. Her acceptance.

"Elder flower," he said at last. "Add a touch of honey to make it palatable and soothe the throat."

He met Meg's steady gaze. What did she know about the deepest secrets of her mistress? Did she know if Olwen truly despised him? Was his wife's desire to enter a convent too great for him to overcome? Could he ever bend Olwen from her belief that he had murdered her cousin and uncle so she would accept him as her husband?

His questions were moot. If Olwen did not shake this contagion and recover from the dreadful wound, nothing mattered.

"I will find the ingredients, my lord."

"Thank you. You are Olwen's faithful servant," Bran said, noting the strange look shifting through Meg's eyes. "I will stay with your mistress until you return."

She bobbed a quick curtsey and hurried from the room.

Bran took the chair by the bed, sitting where Olwen had sat nursing Richard.

When Bran had brought his unconscious wife up the stairs that day, the lad had quickly jumped out of his sickbed, gladly forsaking it and the stuffy chamber. He was too weak yet to do much more than rest, but now he accomplished his recovery in the second solar overlooking the bailey while Bran nursed his cousin.

Young Earl Rothmore had not complained about the move, his concern only for Olwen. There was a pluck to him Bran liked, never mind he'd been so sickly upon his arrival.

Yet Bran did not think long on his ward, because the laboring sound of Olwen's breathing blocked out all other consideration. She had to get well! If not, he would...

What would he do?

Bran swallowed the panic that rose in his throat. Granted, he'd known fear before. Fear as he rode into battle. Fear when his grandmother died and he was taken from Wales to live with strangers. But never had he been afraid for another. Now the concern for his wife obscured all else.

She *might* die. 'Twas a possibility. With contagion in her lungs and after so much loss of blood, Olwen had no guarantee of survival. That was the raw truth of it, and its implications roiled roughly in his gut.

Life had been tough for him. He could take that. Yet he wanted nothing to harm the woman King Edward gave to him. He wanted to protect his wife, keep her safe. Love her.

The word *love* plowed in the deep furrows of his mind. At first, he didn't comprehend it. Bran ap Madog did not love. He loyally served at Edward's pleasure. He was the King's Raven. His duty was to the king, and any love he bore to another human being must go to Edward. And Rhys. 'Twas permissible to feel affection for his sergeant-at-arms, he told himself.

But love a woman?

He had always kept romantic love out of his vocabulary. He bore no tolerance for courtly love and tales of star-crossed lovers. Practicality weighed too heavily upon him.

Devotion and respect he gave her full measure, surely. But love? Olwen wanted love. She'd told him so. 'Cept she wanted not his.

She hated him.

'Sides how could he love her when she made it perfectly clear she loved another—a young knight he'd fought on the tourney field and, if rumor were true, slaughtered in cold blood?

As if she felt his thoughts, his wife moaned in her sleep. Bran watched her with a distress that clogged his mind. He was worried about her. Nothing more, he told himself. She was his property. His entrance into the world of the landed nobility. 'Twas right for him to protect his property.

If that was true, then why was he hovering at her bedside

when he should be out personally hunting down the miscreant who had damaged what was his.

AFTER MEG RETURNED with the potion brewed into a hot, steaming tea, Bran shooed her away. Olwen was his, and he would tend her. He sat on the side of the bed and lifted her head, forcing her to drink the hot liquid. Letting the steam rise to her nostrils, he urged the fluid down her throat.

She was a poor patient. Querulous. Petulant. Her fever raged, and her cough deepened. Most of the time, she was unaware of him, simply fighting off the "nurse" who tended her, her eyes dull and unfocused.

Bran stripped her of her clothing. He piled on the blankets when she shivered uncontrollably. He removed them when she grew hot. When she burned with fever, he bathed her, carrying her naked to the tub, making sure the water was neither scorching hot nor freezing cold, but tepid, so it gently drew out the fever.

When she could not breathe, he held her in his arms, propping her up so the pressure on her lungs eased. He hoped his arms around her brought some comfort. Comfort she neither acknowledged nor possibly knew existed.

He did what he could for his wife as days passed into nights and nights into days.

Bran lost track of time. His only bond to the outside world was the faithful Meg. He asked not about his castle. He cared not about the people he had ruled so very briefly. Nothing mattered if Olwen died.

Yet, she did not die. One day, she opened her eyes and

stared him full in the face with a look of recognition so poignant that it made him flinch.

"My lord," she said in a weak voice.

"Olwen?"

She stretched a pale finger toward him. "Your face."

Bran scrubbed a hand over his jaws, feeling the heavy growth of beard on his normally clean-shaven skin. "How do you feel?"

She glanced away, letting her hand drop feebly to the coverlet. "Like a damp rag wrung dry of water."

"You were wounded in a hunting accident, and you have been ill," he said, scrambling to recover the formality that had characterized their lives together. If he dared show how his heart had softened toward her during her sickness, she would take his new devotion and shred it with indifference and hatred.

"Wounded?" She seemed flustered.

"Aye, by a stray arrow from a poacher's longbow."

"What day is it?"

He did not know. "I will ask Meg."

"Meg?"

"Your maid." He sighed with relief. Her confusion did not trouble him. She'd struggled so gallantly. Her mind would recover now that her body appeared to rally.

CATRIN DID NOT UNDERSTAND. What was Bran doing here, sitting beside her, looking as disheveled and careworn as a stray puppy? She turned her face away from his penetrating scrutiny. He embarrassed her, making her scalp tingle with the heat of his worried gaze.

Vainly, she ran her hand across the rumpled coverlet, feeling its softness. That she was once again naked in the lord's bed should trouble her if she had the strength to care. She did not. She had not lied to him when she said she felt limp and exhausted.

Catrin glanced back at Bran, who stared at her still, shifting his sharp scrutiny across her face until she felt her flesh begin to burn.

"How is Richard?" she asked weakly.

"Fine. Recovered." Bran straightened himself and stood.

"I want to see him."

"When *you* are recovered," he said in a low commanding growl.

She narrowed her gaze. Why did he deny her so forcefully? Richard was her brother, after all.

Then a pain of awareness sliced through her. No. Richard was her "cousin." Bran had called her "Olwen." The game continued.

"I want Meg."

His eyes dimmed. "I can tend to you, my lady. Tell me what you want."

She frowned. "I want Meg. She can attend me."

He bowed, stiffly, almost as if he had been sitting too long. "As you will."

And then he was gone, turning to leave so quickly he almost flew from the room. Catrin shut her eyes. It took too much effort to keep them open.

BRAN DIDN'T WANT to stay away from her.

His presence in the great hall signaled his wife's recovery, and the castle folk buzzed with excitement. He ignored them all, preferring the solitude of a good, hard ride on Taran. Returning to the hall long after snores of sleeping servants filled it, he sat in the lord's chair and stared for hours into the fire, finally dozing restlessly until a distant noise snapped him awake.

Standing, he knew he must defy Olwen's wishes. He could no more keep away from her than he could refuse to breathe.

Quietly, so as not to awaken anyone, Bran ascended the stone steps to the solar where the wooden door stood slightly ajar. He took a deep breath and slipped inside the room, immediately smelling the familiar scents of sickness and wood smoke. Meg's gentle snores drifted from the pallet in the corner. All was dark. Why had the candle burned out?

Suddenly, a muffled noise drew his gaze toward the bed. Olwen grunted. A shadow moved.

His warrior's instinct seized him. "Halt! Who goes there?"

Bran charged toward the bed where a shadowy intruder held a pillow over his wife's face. The man whipped around, seeming to measure his chances, and then sprang over the bed to the far side, trampling over Olwen's body in his effort to escape. She whimpered and Bran halted because of his indecision.

In that moment of hesitation, the prowler sprinted around the end of the bed. He shoved past a sleepy Meg, who now stood in the way, and fled through the door. Bran let him go, concern for Olwen filling every fiber of his body. He flung the pillow aside, and, now as he bent over her bed, Bran saw the horrible truth in her wide, frightened eyes.

Someone had tried to kill his wife.

CHAPTER TWENTY-TWO

Someone wanted to kill her. *Again.* Catrin needed only to shut her eyes to see once more the sharp, single-minded glare of her attacker and smell his unwashed body and foul breath. She shuddered, remembering his harsh hands restraining her and the pillow smothering her face. Her weakened lungs had burned, and she had grunted in fear.

Then she was set free. Suddenly. Thankfully. Bran's face bent over hers, and she stared into the look of fright in his eyes.

He saved her life. Now guards were posted outside her door and another serving wench helped Meg with her care. She was never alone. Even now, as morning sunshine bore through the glazing above the window seat, her room was crowded. The bright light diffused the vision of her black-clad husband who stood beside her bed looking down at her with an expression of odd disquiet.

"Because someone tried to smother you last night, I took another look at the arrow that was imbedded in your shoulder," Bran told her.

She squinted up at him to see his eyes shuttered, giving her no glimpse of the love she saw there the night before. Had she dreamed it? And what of the other dreams she faintly remembered? Of someone strong and caring, bathing her and holding her tight, sustaining her will to live with his very conviction.

Catrin rubbed her right hand across her eyes. Her left shoulder ached like a firebrand, restricting her movements. Still weak, she lay against the linen-covered pillows, sinking deeply into the cushions, weary from a profound, abiding exhaustion.

She dropped her hand to the coverlet. "What did you find?"

"'Twas not a hunting arrow as I had earlier assumed," he said.

She lifted her eyebrows, startled. Bran appeared ill at ease.

"The arrowhead had not a y-shaped forked hunting head, but a larger, bodkin head usually used for war. The fletching was made of pinion feathers, much larger than those used for hunting."

Catrin absorbed his information. The frightful implications of Bran's discovery settled in her stomach. "A yeoman skilled with a longbow and using an arrow made for war can be deadly accurate. Yet I was only hit in the shoulder."

"I believe your movement to dismount ruined the bowman's shot." Bran raised his gaze to hers, transmitting an uncharacteristic anguish. "Mercifully," he said softly, almost in an afterthought.

Catrin studied his face, her breathing shallow. Confusion spun in her head. She didn't know what to make of Bran's revelation. His concern.

"Verily, 'tis a miracle the arrow did not strike me in a more critical place," she said, "and that I did not die."

Bran nodded, frowning at her. "In the confusion, I failed to investigate your attacker."

"You thought it was an accident."

"I should have not assumed."

Bran gave himself no quarter. Angry now, he spun from her to pace the room, his black robes whipping around him with each stride.

"Because of my neglect, you were almost murdered last night." He pounded a fist against the wall. "I will not let that happen a third time." He turned to face her. "I protect what is mine!"

Her perplexity ended. Catrin lowered her head. "Aye, my lord. 'Tis proper you protect the things that are yours."

She felt him take a step toward her, but he hesitated and did not come nearer. Keeping her eyes cast downward, she gave no quarter either and would not look up. What made her think the King's Raven, the knight-errant who sought land and property above all else, would find concern in his heart for her? A mere woman.

Aye, what made her want for something more from him? He was her enemy, was he not?

She sensed his departure. The energy level in the room evaporated. She felt depleted once more. Finally, Catrin raised her head, sadly craving more than she had a right to expect from the man she had tricked so foully when she married him.

RICHARD CAME FOR VISITS. Many of them. Between his sessions with Bran, her half-brother sat beside Catrin in the solar, so full of life, chattering and laughing. He read haltingly from the Arthurian romance to ease the boredom of her slow recovery.

"I have never seen you so happy," Catrin said to him one day a fortnight later. She had regained more use of her arm and shoulder and had recovered enough to want to leave the confines of the solar.

The boy paused, thoughtful. He glanced at his sister as if judging what to say. "Lord Northbridge has made me his page," he said. "I know some of my duties, because Father allowed me to learn them, even though Mother was against it."

"I remember you were a very good page," Catrin said, thinking back at the serious way Richard had attended his father at dinner, bringing the wine and carving joints of meat.

"Lord Northbridge—Bran—says that I am behind in my fighting skills," Richard said as if he suddenly wanted to talk about it. "He started teaching me how to care for his armor and has given me my own to wear."

Catrin pushed herself up in the bed. Bran was right. Richard was long overdue to be fostered. Isadora had begged her husband not to send the boy away, using the excuse that he was ever sickly. Earl Rothmore, older and indulgent, had conceded hoping to please his young wife and keep peace. Much in the same way he had indulged Catrin, his only daughter, not demanding her marriage, John Fitzalan had failed to make a decision until she was almost beyond marriageable age.

That Richard was now learning the art of war, three

years behind other boys of his age, gnawed at Catrin's heart. His military schooling must be started, yet it troubled her. Like Isadora, she feared for his safety.

"I pray he will not push you beyond what you can do." Catrin stretched her hand out toward him.

Richard pulled back, the pride of his young manhood showing. "Bran says a boy must leave his mother's side, for 'tis her natural tendency to keep him with her. Else he will never become a man."

Catrin shrugged. "There is wisdom in what Bran says."

Richard's small jaw jutted forward. "Bran guides me with a wisdom and charity you fail to appreciate. He is not a bad man, Catrin, and he is right. I am sorely lacking in my skills. I must know the art of war if I am to tend to my land and people." The young earl's jaw remained firm.

Catrin dropped her hand. Like so much in her life, others controlled what she did. Or society dictated it. Bitterness rose in her throat. She couldn't prevent Richard's growing up any more than later on she could prevent him from riding in a tourney or into battle. Her lack of control was magnified by her desire to protect the one person she had left, her very determined young brother.

"You must not worry so," Richard urged after a moment when she failed to speak. "If you opened your eyes, you would see the worth in your husband."

Even Richard, who knew the truth, called Bran her husband. Not Olwen's husband. The irony bit into Catrin's conscience. She smiled. "Then tell me about your guardian, this veritable paragon of virtue."

Richard was no lackwit. He caught her sarcasm and bristled at it. "Do you not remember how Bran nursed you night and day, never letting any other tend you?"

Catrin sat back. Even the plush pillows could not cushion her shock. "I thought Meg tended me. When I awoke, Bran was in the room, but he sent Meg to me soon after."

Seeming eager to prove his point, Richard persisted, "You're wrong. Bran let no one else attend you. He was with you morning and night, nursing you through the shock of the wound and then the contagion."

She took a deep breath, settling against the pillows, allowing Richard's words to sink in. She hadn't known. Not really. Bran hadn't told her. Neither had Meg, for that matter.

Her memories of that time were hazy. Incomplete. She thought them dreams. When she closed her eyes and thought back, she had the sensation of strength around her. A tender caring. A determination. And love.

Love had brought her back. She knew that now with a certainty. Yet had it been Bran's love? Surely, not! He thought of her as he would his destrier Taran or the lowly scullery boy who worked in his kitchen. She was his possession. He owned her. In truth, if he had fought to save her life, he was only doing his duty, as any chivalrous knight.

Catrin battled hard to keep hatred burning brightly in her chest. She couldn't let herself believe anything positive about her husband. 'Twould be too costly.

Richard watched her, his eyes narrowing. "This makes the third time someone has tried to kill you," he said simply.

Wrenched out of her musing, Catrin reacted with a frown. "Nay, *Catrin* is dead, remember? These last two attacks came against our cousin *Olwen*."

"I see the right of that," he said with a nod. "Are you going to tell Bran that you are not Olwen?"

"Do you want me to?" she asked, biding time to regain her clarity of thought.

He nodded again, looking down. "'Tis not fair for him not to know."

Bran had an ally. Surprise rendered her speechless for a moment as fear gnawed inside. "I cannot tell him the truth," she said at last.

Richard's head jerked up and his gaze slammed hard against hers. "Why not? He saved your life. He cares for you."

Catrin recoiled. "He cares about Olwen, the wife the king gave him."

Her little brother made a dismissive snort. "You are wrong."

She sat forward. "Think this through, Richard. If I tell him the truth, he goes to find Olwen and takes her away from the safety of the convent of White Ladies."

"Think again. Mayhap he plays the game," he suggested. "Content with the truth, maybe he'll let the real Olwen live in peace."

"He is the king's man. We have exchanged marriage vows. I have sinned in doing so because I'm not Olwen. His ignorance will be no excuse to the church or to the court. Bran will be punished if authorities find out the truth."

Cold fear cramped Catrin's stomach. Richard failed to see reality. Could filling him full of tales of chivalry and King Arthur have been wrong?

"Where, then, does it end?" he asked with a wisdom that amazed her.

She stared at him, wondering herself. "It ends when we discover who killed Father and Gilbert," she whispered.

Richard rose abruptly. "You are a silly female to have placed yourself and Bran in this predicament. All I know is that Bran did not kill Father and Gilbert. There is too much honor in him. Someone else did it, probably the same person who tried to murder you." He stood beside her bed like the dangerous knight he was to become. "Bran didn't do it or else he wouldn't have saved your life!"

He turned his back on her, muttering something under his breath, and then marched from the room with the righteous air of a Crusader.

"Richard," she called out. "Do not be angry with me!"

As so many men were wont to do, he didn't stop to listen, to discuss.

Fighting the burning tears threatening her eyes, she turned her head away as the new maid entered and smiled uncertainly at Catrin. What a mess she had made of things. By discovering the murderer and protecting Olwen, she'd only wanted to do what was right and noble. How could she have known she would dig herself into a deep hole from where no logical escape existed?

Some part of her had begun to suspect Bran's innocence. For one thing, he had been with her when the arrow had struck her. That someone was now trying to kill Olwen, as well as the rest of her family, meant someone was trying to eliminate the whole Fitzalan family. Olwen was a Fitzalan through her mother. She had a stake, however small, in the Rothmore earldom. Which meant Richard was in danger too.

Catrin curled her hand into a fist, thoughts of crying gone. Richard was next—unless it was for Richard the killing was done.

Sudden pangs of fear and bewilderment bolted through her. Who stood to gain from Richard's inheriting the earldom? Besides Richard himself, of course? The boy was too innocent and naïve to scheme to put himself forward. He would never stoop to murder.

But his mother Isadora might.

Catrin's native animosity for her stepmother surfaced. Still, she tried to consider the situation once more with dispassion. Her assumption fit, however. Isadora now had new standing as a widow owning one-third of her deceased husband's property for life. Further, she had power as the mother of the young earl.

What if the obnoxious Guy de Hastings was aiding her?

The more Catrin considered her theory, the more she came to believe it. Yet what was she to do about it? For one, she couldn't tell Richard unless she had proof. Isadora was his mother, after all, and although Catrin despised her, Richard didn't hate his mother.

And then there was Bran. The thought of telling him sent ripples of fear through her veins. To explain her accusations, she must admit the truth of her deception.

"I am sorry, my lord, but you have married an imposter," she would tell him. *"I am not Olwen de Belleme, the woman King Edward gave you as reward for your service. You have married the wrong woman."*

He would stop her there and not let her finish. The implications of just those few words were many. Bran would no longer hold the lordship over Northbridge and its lands along the Severn River. All that he worked for would be lost. Catrin doubted whether he'd be able to see much past *that* ugly truth.

She had her own ugly truth. As Catrin rested in the master's bed, watching the new maid sewing by the fire and seeing the bright sunshine fade into the light of late afternoon, she honestly examined her actions. What had she done?

Shivering because of the ever-present winter cold, Catrin slid down in the bed and snuggled deeply under the covers. Clutching a pillow, she turned on her side and shut her eyes.

She couldn't reveal to Bran her identity simply because she didn't want to see hatred and anger cloud his dark eyes, the ones that so recently held concern.

Dare she hope he loved her?

She sighed. The simple fact was she didn't want to tell Bran the truth because she was beginning to care for him.

And that fact scared her more than the thought of taking another arrow in her shoulder.

CHAPTER TWENTY-THREE

The newfound knowledge she harbored a growing love caused Catrin a sleepless night. Next morning, she sat propped up in the master's bed watching the firelight dance among the shadows of the room and feeling the weight of an overwhelming weariness. So much time had passed while she had lain near death. The mere thought rendered her speechless.

Not so Meg who chatted gaily about the coming twelve days of Christmas. Bran ordered the festivities to proceed as usual, the maid said. While Cook prepared for the many feasts, servants were in the forest selecting the Yule log.

Was this another proof the new lord of Northbridge concealed a generous heart? Catrin struggled to deny the black knight possessed such an instrument of caring. If she saw him strike a horse out of anger or scold the stable boy, she'd find it easier to retain her loathing. Like her strength, her hate was fast seeping away.

Of course, her tiredness could result from the prolonged inactivity of illness. She was bored. Moreover, she had spent many idle hours in fantasy, imagining Bran's strong arms around her and reliving that look of love that flitted so briefly through his eyes when he looked at her.

She had also spent many hours despising her whims because she believed in such make-believe.

"I will go downstairs," she suddenly announced, tossing off her lethargy.

Meg halted near the fire, raising her head, a look of concern in her eyes. "Do you think it wise, my lady?"

"Wise or not, I am going." Catrin threw back the coverlet. A rush of cold air chilled her through her thin shift. "I will be surrounded by castle folk. No one will harm me."

"'Tis not that." Meg came toward her and placed a hand on her forehead. "I fear you aren't well enough."

Catrin brushed the maid's hand away. "Neither am I ill enough to stay in bed! I will dress and go downstairs." She softened at Meg's look of anxiety. "I know you mean well, dear Meg, but it will do me good."

Meg nodded and helped her climb out of bed. Shame flushed Catrin's face. She need not be rude to the woman who cared for her so diligently.

"Here are your slippers, my lady." Meg placed the soft kid shoes on the floor by the bed.

"Thank you." Catrin pushed away glum thoughts and slid her feet into the slippers. "Now, please help me dress."

At least, she maintained a small measure of control over her person. After days of being near the brink of death, this tiny victory felt like a triumph.

~

THE GREAT HALL bustled with activity. Servants dashed hither and yon, carrying out their assigned chores. Catrin halted at the foot of the spiral steps and, bracing herself, placed her hand against the cold stone wall. Dizziness played with her sense of balance. She struggled against it, wavering slightly, hesitant to step into the chaos within the hall.

Ah! But what a feast for her weary eyes. Festive garlands of holly, ivy, and laurel draped the walls, adding touches of green to remind all present of the infant Christ. Someone had dragged the Yule log near the hearth. 'Twould be added to the fire tonight and burn for the whole twelve-day celebration. And something smelled heavenly, wafting up from the open-air cook pits near the walls of the tower keep below.

She had felt so isolated from this endless hubbub that was everyday life. Once more, a sense of gratitude washed over her. She was on the mend. Alive. She was charged with excitement and vowed to say an extra prayer of thanks at Mass tomorrow.

Richard looked up from where he sat near the hearth with Bran's great helm in his lap. She saw him mouth her real name and then glance around in fright when he realized his mistake. But no one seemed to hear for there was too much noise.

Then her brother sprang to his feet and dashed toward her. He wore a mail hauberk and mail chausses on his legs. His sleeveless surcoat mirrored an adult's, reaching to mid-calf and slit on the sides for riding. "Olwen, you've come down!"

His eyes were bright, this time with pleasure, not sickness, and his cheeks and nose were splashed with red from the chill. Cold was ever-present in the winter, and Catrin suddenly felt it, more so now than when she was healthy and active. She drew her fur-lined cape around her.

"Aye, sweeting, I have come down," she replied with a smile. "I found boredom an unhappy companion."

Richard looked chagrinned. "I'm sorry I didn't come visit you today." He took her hand and, as if already a courtly knight, pulled her toward the warmth of the hearth.

"You've been busy." Catrin acknowledged his handiwork with a tip of her head. Bran's dented battle helm gleamed like a jewel.

Richard settled beside her and took up his task again. "Not only that, but Bran has let me wear this set of armor. It is just my size," he said proudly.

Catrin tucked her cape around her feet. "I noticed. 'Tis not too heavy?"

"Nay." He was matter-of-fact. "'Twas made for a boy about my size, Bran thinks. I do not find it heavy or cramping. I can move about freely."

"Are you made to wear it all day? Won't you grow weary?"

"Bran says I need to get used to its feel. He's going to instruct me this afternoon in the use of a sword."

Sparks, like the ones that popped and crackled in the fire, shot through Catrin. She tried to be indifferent to Richard's news. Bran had kept away from her once he stationed the guards outside her door. Now that she might see him again, she fought to control her eagerness.

"What else have you done today?" she asked for diversion.

Richard brightened once more. "Bran took me to the stables. He introduced me to a boy named Will who is about my age. Bran told Will to teach me about the workings of the stable and all about the horses. Bran even let me feed his raven. Then I helped Will saddle the black destrier."

"Taran?"

"Aye." Richard nodded. "I held Bran's stirrup while he mounted."

Certainly, her brother glowed from the honor bestowed on him. For that Catrin thanked God. She smiled fondly. "What else?"

"Bran and his men-at-arms hunted for wild boar."

That explained the heavenly smells from the bailey below.

"He said he'd take me some time," Richard finished with pride.

Alarm shot through her. Catrin sat straighter. Hunting wild boar was dangerous. "Richard, do you think it wise?"

Her brother pulled a frown and turned back to burnishing Bran's war sword. "He will take me when I'm ready."

Rebuffed, Catrin sat back. They had already discussed her over-protectiveness. She was a mere woman, after all, unschooled in these things. Frustration rippled inside. Let him go, she told herself one more time.

Bran this and Bran that, Catrin thought. The black knight truly made an impression on Richard. Would he also be a good influence?

After a moment, Catrin put these thoughts aside and grew content just watching her brother's careful attention to detail. He took seriously his job as page. She drew in a deep breath and nestled into her warm cape. Lulled by the heat of the fire and the silent companionship, she let a sigh escape her lips and shut her eyes for just a moment.

"Why are you here?" Bran barked.

Catrin awakened, her eyes flying open. She had not heard him approach. Tamping down a sudden panic, she straightened herself in the master's chair and looked up at the armed knight looming above her. Under his black surcoat, Bran was covered from head to foot from his mail coif to the mail chausses on his legs, and he presented a fearsome sight.

"You're not well enough to be here," he accused sharply.

"That is for me to decide, my lord." She tilted up her chin in defiance, struggling for control over her emotions.

"'Tis not safe."

"I am perfectly safe with Richard to guard me."

He grunted and turned from her but not before she caught a look of resignation in his eyes.

"Richard, time for your lessons."

"My lord, I am ready." Richard stood stiffly by the hearth and lowered his head in a brief acknowledgment of respect.

Bran carried a small sword by his side. "I found this sword in the armory. You will practice with this every day." He then held out the sword hilt first.

Richard almost jumped out of his mail with excitement. "For me?"

"Take the pommel in your hand and check the blade for balance."

Richard grasped the sword in his right hand, holding it up and away from him as if he knew by instinct what to do.

"'Tis not too heavy?"

Richard shook his head. "Nay, my lord."

"Not now, anyway." Bran glanced at Catrin and grinned as if to share an inside joke. She accepted his quick camaraderie and tension left the back of her neck. "As you grow, you will use a larger and heavier weapon," he continued. "By then, you will have strengthened the muscles of your arms, shoulders, and back. For now, you will practice with this every day."

With a strange sort of contentment, Catrin settled back to watch the teacher and his pupil silhouetted in the glow of the firelight.

"You make a blow from the shoulder with your arm straight." Bran positioned Richard's body and adjusted his outstretched arm. "The sword is a rigid, yet responsive and flexible extension of your arm."

Bran moved Richard's arm downward as he spoke. "You'll slash like this and this. Keep your eyes on your opponent. Never let your defenses down. Now practice." He stepped out of the way.

For long minutes, Richards slashed with his child's sword, eventually learning the knack of it. Catrin saw that he grew weary, but she said nothing. Neither did Richard. The boy would die before admitting any weakness in front of his instructor.

Finally, Bran raised his hand. Richard lowered his arm, staring up at him wide-eyed. "Now, I will show you how to use a shield."

Bran picked up his shield from near the hearth, carrying it on his left arm. In his right hand, he grasped his newly burnished war sword. Standing there, in battle dress, all but his helm, he presented the perfect picture of a warrior knight.

"You use the shield to parry your opponent's blow," he told Richard. "You must be quick on your feet. If you cannot parry with the shield, you must duck or leap out of the way.

One favorite blow is at your knees. To avoid the sweeping slash, you must jump over it."

Bran demonstrated every move. He was a good swordsman, nimble on his feet with lightning quick reactions. He put on his display, twisting sideways from the hips, bending sideways, and jumping as if he leaped over a slashing sword. Catrin could not help but admire him. Bran was magnificent at the art of war.

She shuddered, reality slamming hard against her chest. How had she let herself forget? This knight may have killed Father and Gilbert.

Bran paused and faced Richard. "Now, come at me."

Catrin recognized her brother's sudden fear.

"I'll not hurt you," Bran said good-naturedly. The boy hesitated still. "Come or are you a coward?"

Richard charged in, swinging. Bran parried his first and second strokes, not fighting back. He nimbly avoided the strikes. He twisted away from the third blow. Still, Richard pressed forward.

As Catrin watched, the two of them began laughing, so caught up were they in the game of cat and mouse. She recognized Bran's purpose with Richard, that of practice. Her woman's heart rebelled, understanding that war games were a necessary function that prepared men for real war. Yet did they have to enjoy the game so much?

"Enough!" Bran called, dropping to the hearthstone near Catrin's feet. "Rest easy, Lord Rothmore."

The lad lowered his arm, panting, but giggling all the same. "What, my lord? You tire of practice?" He and Bran exchanged jovial glances.

"Nay, 'tis time we devote our attention to your lovely cousin," Bran answered. His searching gaze caught Catrin's.

She stared into his intent black eyes until the lower part of her body began to throb with unholy yearning. Avoiding him, she turned her head away in time to see Richard drop his sword. It clattered to the rush-strewn stones.

Alarmed, Catrin pushed herself up from the chair as her brother suddenly uttered a strangled cry.

Catrin's own scream echoed throughout the hall. "Richard!"

The boy crumbled to the floor, writhing, his muscles jerking and his breathing shallow. His eyelids blinked rapidly and his eyes rolled back in his head, showing the whites. Both Catrin and Bran rushed toward him.

"*Mon Dieu*! What is wrong?"

"Give him room!" she ordered and held Bran's arm when he would go down on his knees to restrain him.

Catrin analyzed her brother's condition, noting there was nothing nearby that could harm him. His arms and legs twitched, but he appeared to be breathing well enough. She glanced over her shoulder to see servants crowding around. "Make them stand back," she begged Bran.

"Go back to your work!" The new lord of Northbridge's tone permitted no defiance.

All but Meg faded away. Catrin swallowed her fear, dropping down now on one knee to place a shaking hand on Richard's forehead. He was calmer now. The spasms, thankfully, lasted for only a few minutes.

"Catrin?"

"Shh," she warned, hoping she covered his use of her name.

"Where am I?" He was confused. "What happened?"

"You had a fit." Catrin crossed herself. "You were overly tired."

Tears of defeat seeped from the corners of both his eyes. He shut them tightly as if facing the world were too much. "Oh," he moaned.

Catrin soothed his brow, much as she'd done on other occasions when the fits had lasted longer. "Hush, little one. All will be well," she crooned.

Yet would it? What would Bran do now that he knew the horrible truth?

Richard held a brain sickness. He was possessed by demons, some said. Some would put him away, lock him in chains, or isolate him in a dudgeon. Fearful of this, Isadora had been careful to keep the fact of his illness from those at court. She protected her son, just as Catrin guarded him now.

Slowly, she lifted her gaze. Bran towered above her, the firelight casting him in dark, menacing shadows. She blinked once to bring him into focus, only to find his forbidding eyes staring back at her with vicious anger.

CHAPTER TWENTY-FOUR

Did Olwen believe he would harm the young earl?

Scowling, his anger rising, Bran stared down at his wife's upturned face filled with fear. Did she not yet trust him?

Granted, his first reaction had been surprise. He thought he'd somehow harmed the boy, but then he recognized Richard was having a brain attack. Had no one thought well enough of him to confide the truth?

He knew about such attacks. His foster brother, Waryn de Grey, had been plagued with seizures as a lad. By the time Bran left the care of Waryn's family, the boy's body seemed to cure itself with age.

"Stand aside, my lady." Bran failed to keep the anger from his voice. When she made no move to rise, he reached down and grasped her by the arm, pulling her up. She started to say something. "Peace! I'll not harm the lad," he said, resenting the fact he needed to say the words.

Kneeling, he placed a hand on Richard's shoulder.

The boy's lip quivered and he looked away. "I'm sorry, my lord."

"I once knew a lad much as you," Bran began, softening his voice. "He outgrew such fits, as I know you will too."

"Do you think I might?" Richard's gaze connected with his.

"I am sure of it." The relief in the young earl's eyes touched Bran's heart. "Yet you must not let those around you see your weakness. The convulsion is over. Stand now, hold your head high, and comport yourself as one of your rank."

Richard nodded. "Aye, my lord."

Bran grasped the boy by his upper arms and stood him on his feet, holding him a moment to let him gain his balance. "You have others to think about now, my lord, not just yourself." The weight of his new responsibilities seemed to tug on the lad. He raised his chin with a haughty look of someone older. Bran grinned at the change in attitude. "Now take yourself upstairs and rest before tonight's celebration."

With a glance toward his cousin, Richard darted away. Bran was left facing Olwen, her look of reproach an unspoken barrier between them.

"Thank you, my lord," she said in a halting voice.

Once more anger suffused him, making his jaw tighten. "For what? Not sending the earl to the dudgeon? What think you of me? That I'm an unruly barbarian?"

Her face paled, betraying her thoughts. "I oft know not what to think, my lord."

Bran looked down at her, aching to touch her as he'd done while she lay wounded. Once more a silver net crespine and an elaborate headdress banding her chin hid her flaxen hair. He longed to strip the coverings from her head and rake his fingers through her long silken tresses. Could she not see what she did to him?

Her sapphire eyes scowled at him, this time in what seemed more like confusion than hatred. Still, the fact she did not trust him swelled his impatience. "Will you sup with us tonight?" he asked formally as if he spoke to a distant acquaintance.

She dropped her gaze and took a long breath. "Nay, I am tired. I'll dine upstairs."

"So be it," he snapped. "Meg! Where are you? See to your mistress."

He turned from her then, seeking the warmth of the fire, pretending indifference. A moment passed, and then he heard the rustle of her skirts as she departed. After he was sure she had climbed the stairs, Bran let himself relax. He sought the lord's chair and flung himself into it. Calling for a flagon of ale, he allowed himself the pleasure of downing the dark, bitter liquid until there was not a drop left.

He thought land and property would solve his problems. Ha! A fool's philosophy! His troubles had magnified a hundred times over. Sometimes he wished for the freedom of travel and the comradeship of a few good men like Rhys. Sometimes he wished he had never done the king's bidding so well.

Bran frowned at the firelight. Why delude himself? His problem lay not with the castle and the folk of Northbridge, but with their mistress. And with his sudden, unexplainable devotion to a woman who cared naught for him.

THE NEXT DAY, Christmas day, Catrin prayed and attended Mass. For most of the day, on her knees in the castle's drafty chapel, she pleaded harder than she e'er prayed in her life. For the souls of her father, brother, and maid. For Richard, that he overcome his sickness. For herself, that she overcome her obsession with a man who bewildered her.

Was this man wickedly vile or deceptively noble? Had he done what she accused him of doing? Kill Father and Gilbert? Or was her assumption only another evil trick played upon her by a false specter?

Weary, she rocked back on her heels, her knees aching, and stared at the crucifix above her. Votive candles cast an eerie glow on the altar, their smoke curling heavenward just as she hoped her prayers were doing.

Was this why the real Olwen spent so much time with her beads and her prayers? Seeking answers for life's mysteries where no answers existed? Catrin had been always much more grounded in the world and worldly things. Now in the quiet coolness of the darkened chapel, she sought comfort in the spiritual.

After another moment, her shoulders sagged. Father Ellis was right. Her scheme was risky and ill advised. She had not yet discovered the answers she longed for, nor had she gained peace. For the most part, she uncovered only uncertainty and a newfound disregard for her own ability to reason. A practical person would never let emotion overwhelm her spirit.

Why couldn't she control her raw feelings of wanton desire that shamelessly oozed from every fiber of her being whenever Bran was near?

Catrin sighed. Recriminations ran rampant through her mind. She should do better. *Be* better. She arched her back and then straightened once more on her knees in the pose of the penitent. In front of the cross, in the sight of God, she returned to reciting the words of her beads.

Perchance tomorrow would be different. Today, the day of Christ's birth, she sought His help and longed for a certain, palpable peace.

BOREDOM BROUGHT her downstairs once more several days into the twelve-day feasting. She could think of no other reason to hide away, especially when she remembered Bran's admonition to Richard. "Comport yourself as one of your rank," he had said, and Catrin took the words to heart. She was a Fitzalan, after all. Why skulk away like a thief? Surely, the peace she sought could be attained if she faced her problems head on.

Again, she miscalculated. Catrin knew it as soon as she took a seat once more beside her "problem." From the head table, she gazed at the rows of lower tables filled with celebrating guests and castle folk and tried to ignore the man by her side.

"Your appetite has not returned," Bran commented, leaning nearer to her with an offering of boar meat.

The smell cramped her stomach, and she felt lightheaded. "I am able to eat only little bits at a time," she told him and accepted the juicy bite from his fingertips, chewing it slowly.

"You must regain your strength," he said simply. "Richard, bring your cousin something sweet to tempt her appetite."

Richard, who stood at Bran's left shoulder as befitting his position of page, nodded quickly, and dashed off.

Catrin watched him leave. His recovery seemed assured, yet she nonetheless feared for his safety. Her heart throbbed with the love she felt for the gallant boy. She longed to reach out, pull him nearer, and keep him protected forever.

"You must not fear letting him go," Bran said. Catrin turned to find his black eyes watching her. "The lad must fulfill his destiny, whatever it may be."

Had he read her mind? She stared at him, nonplused. "You're telling me what I have told myself many times, my lord."

"But you do not believe it." His regard searched her face, and Catrin felt another shimmer of fervor sweep her body.

She glanced away. "No, I have a hard time believing 'tis not in my power to protect him forever."

All that she loved died. She'd lost everyone, even Olwen whom she could never contact again. Why had she ever longed for love? It hurt too much.

"You have but the natural tendency of a woman." Bran picked up his cup and drank deeply. After he put it down, he placed a hand on her sleeve. "Do not vilify yourself for what is normal."

He meant well. Catrin could see it in his eyes when she looked at him. She had a hard time meeting those eyes, so soul-searching they seemed.

"Thank you, my lord, for your encouragement," she said, "and thank you for your kindness to Richard when..." She could not finish her sentence.

Bran removed his hand. "I accept your thanks. Yet I did nothing more than what someone with good breeding would do."

Catrin cocked her head and now readily surveyed his face. "You know full well many of the nobility would have treated him naught."

"Then shame on them," Bran stated, his eyes lighting with annoyance.

Catrin sank back in the chair with a sigh. "Aye. Shame on them."

Why did he scramble her head? In appearance, he remained the formidable black knight, but in action, he took on another character. One she could even like.

"My lady, Cook has sent up a mince pie for you," Richard interrupted her thoughts.

Catrin turned and smiled at him. "Thank you, my lord. Tell Cook this pleases me."

And it did, for the steaming oblong pastry smelled of spices—cinnamon, cloves, and nutmeg—tempting enough to whet the puniest appetite. She took a spoon and carefully dipped it into the pie, breaking the crust and letting the heavenly aroma escape with the steam.

As she ate, she felt Bran's gaze upon her flushed face. Ill-at-ease, she tried not to let his presence shake her. But it did. To the very core.

After a few bites, she stopped eating.

The noise around them grew, magnified by the vastness of the hall. Laughing, shouting, clapping, dancing, everyone seemed to be having a joyous time. Yet, the two of them, seated in a place of honor at the head table, were isolated from the boisterous crowd. Catrin focused on Bran. She licked her lips as she glanced once more into his eyes.

"I would like to dance with you," he said quietly.

His look spoke more than he must know. Catrin swallowed. She was vividly aware that he wanted to do more than dance.

"Yet, first I must speak to you of a serious matter."

"My lord?"

"You told me some time ago about a man named 'Harry' who might have knowledge of your cousin's death."

Catrin twisted in her chair so she could better see him. Earlier, he thought her foolish when she mentioned the serving man. Had he changed his mind? Guilt pricked her that she had not been able to tell him the truth.

"Have you found him?" she asked breathlessly.

"Perchance." He hesitated and then nodded. "I learned while you were ill that a stranger named Harry was skulking near the stables and around the castle outbuildings. He came with Lord Leighton but must have stayed when Leighton left."

"I knew it!" Elation thundered through her. "I knew Guy de Hastings had something to do with the murders!"

Bran turned from her and tapped the rim of his cup with a forefinger. "Nay, we do not know that. All we know is what I said."

"Certainly you cannot deny the implication?"

"Until I have proof, I will deny what seems too obvious." Bran pushed away from the table and stood. "That is why I sent word to Rhys about the matter." He smiled down at her. "Now come, my lady. Let us not dwell on the unpleasant. For once, let us make merry!"

A carol-dance was forming where the tables had been pushed aside. When he handed her down, everyone clapped and greeted them happily. Catrin smiled, her head buzzing with sudden excitement.

"May we?" Bran asked with a courteous bow.

A couple gave up their spot in the circle, so the lord and his wife could join the other four couples. Bran pulled her into position on his right, standing by her side and grasping her right hand with his right and her left hand with his left so that their arms crossed.

His nearness and the warmth of his hands sent shivers down her body. Catrin chanced a glance upward and found him looking down at her, his gaze bathing her with almost a worshipful light. She choked back her uneasiness and shifted hers away.

Guilt rose up once more, but she tamped it down. She would *not* think now. As Bran said, she would make merry for once. Turning off her consciousness, she let her body simply react to the music.

The leader began singing *acapella* the French carol *Angelus ad Virginem*, and the others joined in. *The angel, coming secretly to the Virgin calming the Virgin's fear, said: 'Hail! Hail, Queen of Virgins!*

The five couples circled clockwise eight steps and then opened out facing in, all ten dancers joining hands. With eight more steps, they converged on the center and then retired, facing their partners once more.

Catrin allowed the happy notes to pour over her. Her natural rhythm and her love of dance rinsed away all disappointment and fear. At the first clapping sequence, the strength of Bran's hands against hers and the cautious pleasure in his eyes magnified her delight.

And then they were parted chaining their way around the circle to finish with a new partner, ready to repeat the steps to the words of a new stanza. When the carol ended after five stanzas, Catrin was reunited with Bran. The rightness of the reunion saturated her whole being.

But it was *not* right. She had lied to him. She was not his wife. Their marriage was counterfeit. Suddenly overpowered by a profound sadness, Catrin stood in the circle, clapping and congratulating the other dancers, and trying to act as if she was the true Mistress Olwen.

"Another dance, my lady?"

Catrin gazed into Bran's face, the spell of his presence pulling her toward him. "Nay, I am tired," she begged off, unable to silence the ever-present upsurge of guilt.

Bran looked back at her blandly not giving away his feelings. He made a stylish bow and taking her by the elbow, led her toward the high table.

Suddenly, the hall erupted with an uproar. They paused, turning, to see a traveler striding toward them from the entrance door. Catrin smelled the winter outdoors on his clothing and sensed agitation in his manner.

"My lord!" The man nodded in greeting. "I have word from your sergeant-at-arms."

A smile lit Bran's face. "What news? Is Rhys well?"

"Aye, well enough, but he finds life at court full of intrigue," the messenger said with an uneasy laugh. Then his eyes became guarded.

"Go on, man. Lady Olwen can hear whatever you say. I keep no secrets from my wife."

"You may not want others to hear."

Catrin's stomach churned. What was wrong? Bran ushered them both toward the hearth where they could have privacy. Turning his back on them, the messenger briefly warmed his hands before the fire.

"Out with it," Bran ordered after a time, seeming as anxious as Catrin to hear the news.

The messenger turned around. "Rhys thanks you for

sending word of the spy at Northbridge." He glanced cautiously at Bran, as if reluctant to continue.

"Speak up!"

"Troubling rumors are rampant at court." The man lowered his voice, unable to meet Bran's eyes. "My lord, some say that you killed both of the earls of Rothmore."

"'Tis but an old rumor, one discounted by the king," Bran said, dismissing the news.

"But now they say you also killed Lady Catrin!"

"What!" Bran's sudden outcry turned a few heads.

"There is also talk of fear for your wife, Lady Olwen," the messenger went on, lowering his voice. "Some say her injury was no hunting accident as you claimed. Some say you tried to kill her too."

CHAPTER TWENTY-FIVE

"'Sdeath!" Bran fisted his hand and glanced quickly at Catrin, anger bright in his eyes. "What says the king?"

The messenger cleared his throat. "Rhys told me to tell you 'tis strange Edward has said nothing. No word of support. Nothing."

Alarm squeezed in Catrin's breast. She searched Bran's face. In the moments after the courier's reply, Bran drew himself up sharply, standing nobly erect, his eyes now shuttered.

"Thank you," he said to the messenger. "You have served me well. Go ease your hunger and see to your thirst."

"Thank you, my lord." The man quickly bowed and backed away, leaving them alone.

Ignoring the chill that touched her, Catrin sought to comfort Bran. She gently touched his sleeve and felt him tense. His gaze slanted down at hers.

"The king's silence means nothing."

A muscle flexed in his jaw. "It means everything." He

turned his head away and stared into the fire. "It means I have lost favor with the crown."

"How can that be?" Catrin inhaled quickly. "You are Edward's faithful servant. He gave you Northbridge!"

Edward had also given Bran a wife. That his confidence in the King's Raven could be so easily shaken was indeed troubling.

"I know not how this happened, Olwen," Bran said. "Being away from Edward has not helped my position. Your cousin Catrin must have planted seeds of doubt in the king's mind, and with her death and your wounding, he has come to question me."

Insight blasted through Catrin, heating her with sudden fury. Guy and her stepmother must be at court. It took more than her complaints of Bran to the queen the day after Gilbert's death to turn people against him. It took the concerted efforts of those bound to do him harm.

Her natural hatred of Isadora and distrust of Guy de Hastings added fuel to the fire of her anger. They must somehow be involved in spreading rumors. She knew it as surely as she knew her own name.

Yet what was her name?

Olwen or Catrin?

Her mouth ran dry as she fought to stop her crazy speculation. The truth was Catrin Fitzalan was *not* dead. She had switched places with her cousin in a mad scheme that fast spun out of control because of Catrin's own weakness, her growing devotion to the man who was not her husband. Once again Father Ellis' warning sounded in her head.

Sweet reason, what was she to do? Admit the truth? Accuse Lord Leighton and Isadora? Bran was right. She had no convincing evidence. Who would believe her stepmother or Guy were involved in any plot to murder the whole Fitzalan family, let alone to harm Bran?

Her fingers bit into the fabric of Bran's sleeve. She had suspected him. But now, as he pressed his calloused palm over her cold fingers and felt the warmth of his hand, Catrin knew she was wrong. No truly cruel man could so devotedly care for her and be so understanding of Richard and his illness.

"At the end of the twelfth night celebration, we shall travel to court," Bran said making up his mind. "You will accompany me so all can see you are unharmed. I must repair the damage and restore my good name."

Catrin longed to say words of comfort, but they would not come. As Olwen, she was his possession. He could do with her as he would.

His property. His good name. All meant more to him than she.

Silly goose. She chided herself. What right had she, an imposter, to expect something more? And what more did she want?

A headache gripped her. She tilted her chin up to look once more at his shuttered eyes. She wanted to be let into his confidences—to truly comfort him as he comforted her during those long nights of her convalescence. She wanted him to lose his heart to her as she had lost hers.

Her head pounded like a solitary drum. She had fought so hard against the harshness of reality, trying not to trust or invest her love. She had failed with this black knight. She had failed as miserably as she'd fallen short in finding Gilbert's murderer. The enormity of that failure oppressed her.

"I will be ready, my lord," she said with dispassion.

Slipping her fingers out of his grasp, Catrin turned toward the spiral stone steps that led to the solar. She could do nothing more but continue the charade. Bran was already in trouble with Edward. If the king found out she had married him under false pretenses, he'd suffer the consequences. And she did not want that.

She protected those she loved.

As the days progressed, Bran lost interest in the twelve-day festivity of Christ's birth. He was tired of feasting and drinking. He was tired of forcing himself to celebrate when, in truth, a dull ache of despair drummed within. The New Year had come and gone, bringing with it no joy for the future. Life had so often bestowed upon him trouble. Now, when his fortune had turned, when he'd become master of his own house and husband to his own wife, bad luck had once more befallen him.

Closing his fingers around his cup, Bran brought the silver vessel up to his lips and drank deeply. He knew he drank too much. Yet, it seemed the only way to ease the burden of the bad news Rhys sent. Beside him, Olwen chatted with the wife of a neighboring knight. Bran slanted his glance her way, heat rising in his groin.

There was one more way to ease his burden. He was tempted to take it and force himself once more upon his reluctant wife. He placed his cup back on the table, considering his options and trying to tamp down the growing need hiding itself well within the folds of his surcoat.

Having a wife such as Olwen should be balm for his lustiness. She should provide him with the physical comfort he needed when life played its vile tricks upon him. Instead, she teased him with her heated glances and tender touches, emasculating him with her compassion.

Taking up his cup again, Bran drank once more. His mood ran ugly. Enraged by what fate dealt, he was even more infuriated by his growing inaction where Olwen was concerned. As he stared at her over the rim of his cup, he vowed to do something soon about the desire that was fast driving him mad.

CATRIN SENSED the restlessness in Bran. She glanced at him from under lowered lashes, wondering about his unease. Why had he had not spoken about the news from court? He kept close counsel all week, and it chafed her as badly as an ill-fitting shoe.

Something had to happen. She felt it. Even a trip to court, where danger abounded for her, would be better than this perpetual inaction and disruption of her sanity.

"A dance, my lord?"

"Our thoughts run much alike," he lowered his voice to a whisper. "I would be happy to dance with you."

He stood abruptly, offering her his hand. She shifted in her seat, excusing herself to the lady on her left. Then drawing a deep breath, she rose. When she turned back to Bran, he captured her hand, lacing his fingers through hers. Heat blasted through her as tension popped between them. With their fingers clasped together, they were bound as surely as if a ghostly specter had blessed their union.

She sought out his eyes, black and glittering, full of promise. Her lips trembled with sudden excitement. She dared not glance away. His hair, so long and black, fell to his shoulders, reminding her once again of his heritage. This time she thrilled at the prospect of dancing with him, holding his hand for however briefly. She delighted at the chance to be with him. To touch him. Laugh with him. Sing with him.

Yet, there was no laughter on his lips or in his eyes, only an intense glare. He stood straight and motionless in front of her. Was he silently willing her compliance? Did he request her obedience? Wordlessly, they seemed to communicate. And Catrin knew what he wanted, for it was what she wanted. She throbbed with that wanting, feeling faint and energetic all at once.

Father Ellis burst into the crowded hall. "My lord! Make way, knave!" Shoving past dawdling servants and banqueting guests, the priest lumbered toward the high table.

Even from afar, Catrin discerned his urgency. Her fingers gripped Bran's hand tightly.

"What say you, Father?" Bran called down from the head table.

"My lord, a courier has come from the king!" Father Ellis cried out so everyone heard. He lifted a weathered envelope. "Look! The king's seal!"

Bran dropped her hand and reached for the royal missive. The loss of contact sliced through Catrin as keenly as the sudden fear that stabbed into her chest. In view of the latest news from Rhys and at this festive time of year, word from the king was especially ominous.

The whole of her predicament weighed upon Catrin with an all-encompassing sense of doom.

Bran tore open the envelope and unfolded the letter.

Scowling, he scanned its contents and then lifted his black-ened eyes. "Read this," he said, thrusting the letter toward her.

"As you wish, my lord." Catrin could hardly speak. With shaky hands, she took the message and squinted at the Latin phrases.

Horror struck her. She drew a quick breath and crossed herself.

Bran waved an impatient hand. "Read it!"

She glanced up, tears pricking the corners of her eyes.

"If it is bad news, be quick! Read it!"

As if haste would overcome the news, she thought with dismay.

"My lord." Her voice quivered. "Your liege lord, King Edward, sends word to you that your sergeant-at-arms, Rhys of Llangollen, was killed at court by a thief who stabbed him in the back with a knife and took his purse."

The moment following the telling of the ill news unfolded with marked slowness. She saw Bran's chest rise and fall. He briefly bowed his head. When he lifted it, his face was as expressionless as the stone façade of the castle. Yet, Catrin saw within his dark eyes the haunting shadow of anguish so fathomless and overpowering it frightened her.

"My lord," she breathed, reaching out toward him with her hand.

Without a word, he spun away from her and strode the length of the hall, his footsteps echoing in the sudden stunned silence. She watched him go. Immobile. Unable to stop him. Unable to do more than utter his given name in heartfelt sympathy so massive it threatened to take her breath away.

～

MOMENTS LATER, she motioned to draw her brother to her. "Richard, follow him, lest he hurt himself," she whispered when the boy came to kneel at her feet, "but do not let him know you are near."

"Aye, my lady."

"Be quick with you!"

Richard, in his role of page, jumped up and scampered away, leaving Catrin to face the forbidding scowl of Father Ellis. *I told you so.* His condemnation was written across his countenance and in his unyielding stance.

She turned from him, smiling faintly at the curious neighbor and retreated to the hearth and its scant privacy. Father Ellis followed, his harsh breathing resounding in her ears.

"No need to scold me, Father," she said to fend off his opening blow. "I have oft, of late, scolded myself."

"Rhys is dead." Father Ellis dropped his voice, his words hot on the back of her neck. "We will be next."

Catrin waved her hand impatiently as if shooing a fly. There was no need to point out the obvious. Yet Rhys had been killed miles away from them wherever Edward was keeping court at the time.

"Then you better attend to your prayers for fear of your soul," she snapped.

Her advice sounded harsh. Rude. She was suddenly sorry for it. Her hand rising to her lips, she turned. "Father, I did not mean it."

"I will see to *my* soul," he hissed with anger. "Be careful, my lady, you don't condemn innocents to the hell you face because of *your* actions."

Catrin's eyes narrowed. She had lost an ally. "I told you once I'm tired of having all of mine taken from me. Never fear. I will not doom those I love because of what I have done."

He bowed stiffly, backed away, and left Catrin alone by the roaring fire. Her back warmed nicely, but the front of her remained cold—as cold as her heart. Lifting her chin, she turned away from the curious stares of the castle folk. They had not heard what passed between them, but they had seen in Father's manner their disagreement.

Holding out her palms, she let heat bathe them. She stood motionless, silent, gazing at the flickering and dancing light and permitting her mind to wander. Chiding herself would prove useless now. She refused to grow morbid. There must be a way to help Bran overcome his understandable suffering because of Rhys death. Just as there must be a way to extricate herself from her predicament and discover the murderer—or murderers—of those she loved.

She hated inaction, but at the moment she embraced it, eventually allowing Meg to drag the master's chair nearer to the fire. Catrin sat silently while the guests said their goodbyes and the servants crept away to their duties or their families. The great hall was swept of the dinner makings and the trestle tables were taken down and removed.

While she pondered the imponderable, Catrin remained near the fire as if it were her salvation.

Sometime after Vespers, Richard came to her and brushed her sleeve. Catrin looked up at his gentle touch. "You have word?"

His cheeks were chafed from the cold, his nose bright red. He nodded his head, blowing on his fingertips. "Aye,

Catrin, I followed him to the stables where he saddled the destrier from Freesland, Taran."

"His war horse?"

Richard nodded again. "I didn't follow him, having no leave to take a horse, but he soon returned and gave the stallion up to Will to put away. He had ridden hard."

Catrin folded her hands in her lap, her fingernails biting into her palms. She was so filled with worry. "He came to no harm?"

"Nay, but his mood remains foul. The stable lads kept their distance. I was glad for your instructions not to be seen."

Catrin moistened her lips, considering. Bran had dealt with his initial sadness. What now? She glanced at her brother. "Where is he at present?"

"While he was gone, another messenger came from the king, bearing the body of my lord's sergeant. Father Ellis took the remains to the chapel and began to say prayers." The boy gulped a breath. "My lord refused to enter the chapel. He is now in the mews with his raven, talking to the bird as if the creature were human." There was awe in Richard's voice and a little fear.

Mon Dieu. Was he mad?

Catrin pushed herself to her feet. "You have done well, Richard. Now go tend to your needs. I will see to Lord Northbridge from here on."

She climbed the steps to the solar thinking she needed her fur-lined cloak if she were to venture forth in the cold. The sight of the master's bed sent her head into a violent spin. Her breath, already ragged from the climb, left her completely. As surely as the sun would rise on the morrow, she knew what she must do to ease Bran's suffering. The only thing she could do.

She would make love to him—willingly, for once—and bring him the physical comfort a husband expected from a wife.

CHAPTER TWENTY-SIX

The night air was brittle, her breath frosty. In the scant light, Catrin picked her way across the deserted and silent grounds of the bailey. A deep thrill of anticipation sliced through her, making all her senses come alive.

At the door to the mews, she stopped a moment, breathing in the sharp midnight air. Whatever befell her on this night, she knew she could not go back. For better or for worse, she'd act the part of wife and let destiny fall where it may.

Wrapping her cloak firmly about her, Catrin pushed open the door and entered the dark, spacious quarters of the mews. Surprised she could stand upright once inside, she inhaled the tart scent of sawdust and the smell of long ago bird droppings. Empty perches stood like ancient crosses in rows across the floor where once Olwen's father had kept his collection of proud and temperamental peregrines, gyrfalcons, and sparrow hawks.

Now only one bird remained. Bran's raven was barely visible in the darkness. Catrin saw its beady black eyes were focused directly on her, following her every movement with curious intent. She crossed herself. What did this malevolent harbinger of impending doom know? As some believed, could it see into the future?

Trreeck!

Startled, Catrin jumped back a pace, her hand flying to her lips to keep from crying out.

"She will not hurt you."

Turning toward the sound of Bran's hushed voice, Catrin was keenly aware he watched her in the dark. "So you say." She proudly lifted her chin.

"My lady, I never lie to you."

She heard the rustle of fabric as he materialized from out of the shadows and walked toward her, tall and foreboding. Enough light filtered through the open door allowing Catrin to see his dark hair tumbled loose, tangling on his shoulders. She could not see his face clearly, only its angles and shadows, yet she sensed the power of his presence. An ache of sudden desire swelled full-blown within her.

The King's Raven, so like his ominous namesake, cloaked in midnight and mystery, enthralled her with his dark, seductive promise.

He halted a few steps away from her with his legs braced in a wide stance and his arms crossed as if challenging her not to come nearer, but at the same time, almost defying her to do so. The gap between them seemed insurmountable.

Catrin drew a breath, searching his dark eyes, half-hidden by black lashes. "Your bird symbolizes death," she said in measured tone.

Bran stared at her face, unmoving. "Ravens are intelligent, inquisitive creatures, my lady."

Catrin looked toward the black bird. "They frighten me."

"They need not," he said, closing the space between them, staring down at her just inches away. "In Wales, they are believed to bring prosperity to the houses where they perch."

She let go of a jagged breath and lifted her gaze to his. Through the heaviness of her cape, she felt the warmth of his body. "Has this bird brought prosperity to you?"

His own breath came roughly. "In a way."

Catrin fought to hold his gaze, running her tongue over her upper lip. "How so?"

"You can say Mair has brought me you."

His breath skimmed her forehead. She held herself stiffly, refusing to yield to her impulse to go to him. "I thought the king bestowed Northbridge upon you." Her forced laugh was short and husky.

"Northbridge—and its mistress, *cariad*." He used the Welsh term of endearment, his voice low and filled with hunger.

She felt hungry herself, but could not stop her dangerous banter. "What the king gives, he can take away."

"The king will never take you from me." He made a growling sound and placed his hands against the side of her face, devouring her with a poignant look filled with yearning.

"Why?" she gasped, relishing the feel of his calloused hands upon her cheeks. "Because I am your possession?"

"No, because Holy Church has made us man and wife together. No king can deny that claim."

She trembled at the very nearness of him and at his words, however false she knew them to be. "A king can do his will. You cannot stop him."

A tremor shook him. "Then I will take what is mine and

flee to the mountains of Wales. I will live like an outlaw and defy royal command."

His assertion was wild and rash, yet somehow the words thrilled Catrin. Her breast rose and fell. "As did Llewellyn, the Prince of Wales?" she whispered, unable to resist the sting of truth.

"Why did you come here? To taunt me?"

His sad eyes stabbed her soul, causing an attack of compassion and more than a little shame. "To tell you I'm sorry for your loss," she said softly, letting her lashes drift down over her eyes. "I know you cared for Rhys."

"Aye, Rhys was a good man."

She heard his voice break. Not looking at him, she sensed his perplexity. "I hoped to bring you comfort."

He dropped his hands from her face and turned away. "There is no one who can comfort me."

Her cheeks felt flushed against the sudden chill where his hands had been. Catrin lifted her fingertips to touch the side of her face and raised her head, staring at his broad back, half-hidden in the shadows. "I too have lost those I love," she said to him, unable to keep the bitterness and anger from her voice. "I understand your sorrow, for I'm afraid to love another. The risk is much too great."

He faced her, his expression unreadable. "Then we have more in common than we know."

She pressed her lips together, gazing up at him, her nerves alive with longing. Finally, she murmured, "I would be your wife."

He stood stock-still, almost as if he did not believe her words. Yet he knew full well the meaning of them. She was offering him her body. Her duty as a wife. No matter she was a fraud. But he didn't know, and for a reason she declined to explore, she needed to be his wife tonight. She wanted to give of herself. To ease what suffering he had.

A suffering her actions may very well have fashioned.

With a low sound, Bran released a breath. For once, he allowed her to see his eyes, revealing a poignancy that took her breath away. Silently, he lifted her left hand and kissed the back of it, his lips brushing over the engraved wedding ring that gleamed in the faint light. Her body shuddered at his touch.

"I cannot accept your gift here in the cold, *cariad*, but I will accept it where it is fitting. Upstairs. Where it is warm. In the master's bed."

"Aye, my lord."

Her words of surrender propelled him into action. In a swift move, he scooped her into his arms, ducked under the door, and marched across the bailey. They did not speak. His countenance mirrored that of a Crusading warrior, intent with purpose.

Catrin pressed her face into the folds of his surcoat, smelling his musky man smell and the faint scent of woodruff clinging to his clothes. She felt his muscles rippling beneath.

Wickedly, she took pleasure at being the cause of his forceful action. Could she tame the wild raven again? Waves of alarming delight pulsed through her, wiping away all reason. Once she had straddled him, nicking his skin with the blade of a knife. That she now wanted to torment him in this feminine way defied all logic.

Her face against the rough fabric, Catrin smiled. She had nothing to lose. Fate held her in its grip. She would play out her destiny now with wondering abandon.

~

BRAN COULD NOT BELIEVE his good fortune, nor hope to understand it. He didn't want to try. He accepted Olwen, for once, at face value. His body needed what she was offering. He would take it, her generous offering, as was his right as her husband. Later he would probe the puzzle that was this woman in his arms. Later he would wonder why her mood changed toward him.

He pulled her to his chest, holding her with a mixture of tenderness and a feeling of ownership. Fighting the surge of excitement that raced through him, he strode as quickly as he could through the great hall and climbed the spiral stairs.

The firelight flickered faintly in the solar. The serving woman Meg was dozing by the fire. When he kicked open the door with his foot, she startled and then jumped to her feet.

"Place another log on the fire and get out!"

"Aye, my lord."

Although she scurried to do his biding, he saw the blatant look of alarm that crossed her eyes. But she obeyed, bobbing a curtsy and fleeing the room. He shoved the door shut and with his wife still in his arms, turned toward the symbol of his authority—the marital bed.

Yet when he dropped Olwen to her feet, his mood changed. Softened. She was his, but she was also an intelligent, caring woman. Her bravery in the face of all that had befallen her rubbed his heart raw with emotion.

"I will make you warm," he said, lowering the ermine-lined cape from her shoulders and dropping it to the floor.

He stared into her eyes, seeming so innocent. He didn't

want to question their authenticity. He wanted only to feel and react. To let his fingers and lips speak for him.

Anxious, he stripped from her head the flat-topped cap and confining barbette that banded her chin. "How I hate to see your beauty hidden by these things."

"'Tis the fashion, my lord."

"Then, I hate fashion!"

Skillfully, he removed the silver crespine, revealing the mass of her flaxen hair, bundled at the nape of her neck. He made quick work with the hairpins, tossing them aside as if he'd done this many times before. The loosened bulk of hair fell heavily onto her shoulders and down her back. Bran caught the silken strands, gently brushing them away from her eyes, and smoothing them so they made their own head-dress around her face.

He had only faint awareness of disrobing her, and then she was standing before him, naked, her perfect female body taut in the buttocks and legs from riding, her breasts—half-hidden by her hair—full and enticing.

That's when Bran remembered to breathe—to inhale the sweet scent of her, lavender and roses, delicate, yet hauntingly sensual. She shivered in the cold.

Seeing this, Bran ripped his surcoat and tunic over his head and bent to pull off his boots. He hated the restrictions of clothing and the awkwardness of removing them. Finally, standing in only his braies, he ventured a glance at her, briefly speculating about his good fortune.

Olwen stared up at him, as if she too felt the wonder of the moment. He fumbled to untie the strings at his waist.

"Let me help you."

He trembled at her touch. At last unclothed, he reached for her, but she stepped back a pace.

"No," she whispered. "I will comfort you."

Without his consent, she laid her palms on his chest. Shyly, like the maiden she was once, she began to tickle him with her fingertips. He shook under her gentle stroking. Her hands were like soft threads, thrilling his skin in the places where she touched. And then she lifted up on her tiptoes and touched her tongue to a nipple.

"*Cariad*," he moaned, as if dreaming.

He rocked back on his heels, waves of hot sensation coursing through him. She put her hands on his waist, as if to steady him. The touch only magnified the way his body thundered with anticipation. He fought himself for control so he could allow her to have her way with him.

When she knelt and took his hips between her hands and touched him there with her tongue, he groaned like one dying. "I fear I cannot stand much longer, *cariad*. Let me put you into bed."

"No, this is mine," she gasped, caressing his man part.

"I will let you," he promised, raising her up and capturing her in his arms in a swift motion that took more strength than slaying an enemy in battle.

He tossed back the fur coverlets and placed her gently on the bed as if she were a precious jewel. She looked so lovely lying there amid the white linen sheets. He wanted to cry. Making a little whimpering sound in his throat, he lowered himself beside her, resting on his side so he could lovingly search every inch of her womanly body.

She did not remain inactive but pushed herself up on an elbow and traced the ragged red scar on his arm, letting her hair drape over his shoulder. Its sweet scent filled his nostrils. "I will comfort you," she said again in a husky whisper.

With surprising force, she pushed his shoulder until he understood what she wanted and fell on his back, staring up at her and her mass of tangled hair. And then she straddled his waist with her strong thighs. Lowering her head, she kissed him greedily. He slid his fingers down her back and into the curve at the top of her buttocks.

His body arched, and he returned her kisses, his tongue taking her mouth with fierce possession. He touched her buttocks with his erection, craving release, throbbing, near to explosion. Yet she played with him by not covering him with her moistness. He felt her on his abdomen, but she would not accommodate his needs, only tempting him with the promise of her wet heat. Her tongue now licked down his throat to once again flick over his nipples.

"Myn Duw!"

Still she would not relent, but scorched his skin with her fingers, her tongue, and the movement of her thighs against his hipbones. His muscles quivered from her onslaught. She was torturing him with a pleasure so profound it pained him.

All the while, he was able to watch her with half closed eyes. She dropped her head to let her hair surround them. Then she threw her head back, breathing hard herself, a wicked, wanton smile spreading faintly on her lips. By pleasuring him, she was pleasuring herself, and at the same time driving him mad with her deliberate seduction.

"Cariad, please." He made a hoarse sound, raising his hips up, touching her buttocks, begging.

She answered him with a whimper and pushed herself up on her knees briefly. When she lowered herself, she was sitting full on his hard length.

"Myn Duw!"

She was so wet. He burned for her. He reached up to her breasts and cupped them, teasing her nipples until they peaked, and she tossed back her head, her mouth falling open as she panted hard.

Finally, she began to move, rubbing up and down so she drove him beyond madness. He writhed beneath her and clutched her arms. His fingers bit into her flesh. She rose up again and came down gently on the tip of his shaft, hovering there so he felt her slick and throbbing.

She ran her tongue over her lips and gazed down at him with a taunting look. He was hers to control. He closed his eyes and moaned his need. Again she settled around the full length of him, surrounding him with pure delight, letting him fill her. She dropped her hands beside his head for support as she drove against him, pushing him to the brink of despair.

"*Cariad*," he cried out. "I love you!"

He exploded, thrusting upward, every muscle in his body recoiling and then bursting forth with waves of sweet, dazzling sensation.

Closely after his climax, she shuddered and cried out. "*Mon Dieu!*"

He opened his eyes to see sweet torture contort upon her face. Her body shook, out of control, and then she collapsed full length upon him, breathing roughly in his ear.

CHAPTER TWENTY-SEVEN

Sated and relaxed, Catrin sprawled across Bran's warrior body. Her face nestled close to his ear within the tangled mass of his black hair that spread like a blanket over the sheets. Smiling to herself, she inhaled the scent of sex and felt the warmth of his body beneath hers.

She closed her eyes and rode gently upon the rise and fall of his chest. He remained hard within her. Wiggling, she savored his fullness and the groan he uttered as if pleasured by her movement. What had made the difference this time? Why now had their coupling so fulfilled and completed her?

In his passion, Bran had cried out his love. "*Cariad, I love you!*" Then he came, and she had burst forth soon after, trembling with the joy of her release.

Did he truly love her? Or were these simply words of a man in the throes of passion? She had no experience other than with Bran, so she didn't know how men behaved. Surely, they didn't declare their love so readily. Bran had not. Not at first. Not until that moment when he cried out the words she ne'er expected to hear.

That her sworn enemy had said the words was indeed a cruel complication.

Bran's fingertips lightly brushed a strand of her damp hair away from her face. He stoked her cheek. Was he watching her? Catrin was afraid to sneak a look for fear of what she would find in his eyes.

If Bran ap Madog, the lord of Northbridge Castle, was in love with her, 'twas because he thought her his wife Olwen. No matter, he did not love Catrin Fitzalan. Now more than ever, the warning of Father Ellis haunted her.

"I must leave you tomorrow, *cariad*," he whispered against her cheek.

Catrin squeezed her eyes even more tightly shut. "Why?"

"I must take Rhys home to the Dee River Valley, home to Llangollen."

She clutched a strand of his black hair as if that would keep him with her. "I do not want you to leave."

"I must. I promised him years ago to see him buried in the valley." He kissed her cheek. "When I return, we will go to court. Together. I'll not leave you again."

A sweet promise, like the one he made to Rhys. But Catrin knew Bran could not keep it. Someday, he would leave her, especially if he found out the truth. Then he would hate her too. She deserved her fate, and she whimpered aloud.

"Do not cry," he said, touching her lashes with his lips.

She didn't realize there were tears at the corners of her eyes. A wave of emotion engulfed her. She loved this man, who thought her another woman. She couldn't tell him the truth for fear of losing him. In all fairness, she couldn't even proclaim her love. Yet she could show him how she felt.

In a quick move, she opened her eyes and pushed

upright, balancing with her hands on each side of his head. Looking down at his battle-scared face, she smiled a teasing smile. And then she began to ride him again. Slowly, up and down, griping him with her thighs. His shaft, that had begun to soften inside her, sprang forth to full attention.

"Ah, Olwen," he muttered. "You will send me away tired but happy."

"I do not send you away, my lord," she replied, drawing in a deep breath and throwing back her head to concentrate on the fire beneath her, "but I do plan to make you happy."

'TWAS VERY STRANGE with Bran gone. She moped about the solar and poked around the mews, feeding the frightful raven and speaking to the stable boy Will. Her concentration was gone, and she delegated her chores, putting Meg in charge as if her servant was the true mistress of North-bridge. The castle folk did not think it odd for the real Lady Olwen oft drew apart from them, tending her herb garden or reading alone in the solar. No, their mistress' behavior didn't bother them. She was newly married and her husband gone. Rumors ran rampant about the lord carrying his wife up the solar steps. Perchance an heir soon would be born, they whispered.

Only Catrin and her two accomplices knew the truth. Meg accepted her situation at face value, doing as she was bid and busying herself with her duties. Not so Father Ellis. He also moped around the castle, muttering under his breath and drinking too much. That he spent as much time with his wine cup as he did in his prayers set tongues in the castle wagging.

The twelve-day celebration for Christmas had been over for two days when chaos erupted in the bailey. From inside her sanctuary in the mews, Catrin gathered from the sudden noise that a party of travelers had arrived. The day was sunny, but chill. She drew her hood over her head and clutched her fur-lined mantle closely. Her curiosity aroused, she peered outside.

The bailey was filled with yeomen, squires, a page, and one knight escorting two cloaked ladies upon stout palfreys. Northbridge grooms hurried hither and yon, catching hold of bridles and attending the winded horses.

Catrin's chest grew tight. She recognized the coat of arms blazoned upon the surcoats of the men-at-arms. *Gules, a lion rampant or.* The same symbol she and Olwen had embroidered on Gilbert's tourney scarf.

Isadora had come to the keep of Northbridge.

Panic struck Catrin. She lifted her fingertips to her lips and stepped back a pace from the door into the gloomy shadows. What did Isadora want? Would she recognize her? Of course, she would. Catrin had grown up under the watchful eyes of her stepmother. There was no way to escape detection.

Yet, she might be able to avoid her stepmother. Without any more thought, Catrin lifted the hem of her skirt and scurried from the mews, blending into the hustle and bustle. At one point, she was near Isadora's horse when her step-mother dismounted, but she quickly turned her back and fled up the castle steps.

In the hall she spoke to Meg. "My stepmother has come," she whispered. "Stall her. Tell her Olwen is ill and cannot receive her."

She reached the first turn of the spiral steps when she

heard the familiar high-pitched voice echoing through the hall calling for her son. Painful memories flooded her. Clutching her skirt even more tightly, Catrin took the stairs two at a time, much as she had as a child when escaping from Isadora.

Reaching the solar, she shut and bolted the door. She retreated to the window seat, sitting down to catch her breath, pulling her legs up under her, and hugging her knees with her arms.

Why did she behave like a child? Granted, there was more at stake now than just her hatred of Isadora. Olwen's safety, for one. Richard's welfare. And Bran. How could she forget the man she had married falsely? How could she forget the man who fulfilled her and cried out his love?

When she began this scheme, Catrin was impetuous, not giving serious thought further than the moment. She hadn't thought to see Isadora again. She hadn't thought to fall in love. Waves of nausea swept her. Clutching her knees, Catrin swayed back and forth and stared blankly at the empty bed that filled the room so silently.

Once more she lacked control over her life. Her destiny. Trading places with Olwen had been a risky attempt to gain some power. Instead, she had failed to win any control as surely as she had failed in her quest to find Gilbert's murderer.

For a moment, she wallowed in a spate of regret, feeling sorry for herself and wishing things were different.

But they couldn't be, she knew. She had started this chain of events, and she'd see them through.

Sucking in a cleansing breath, Catrin uncurled her legs and stood. Perchance with Isadora so near, she could test her theory that her stepmother and the feckless Guy were in league together.

To do this, she must arm herself as any woman might. Stripping off her old clothing, she redressed herself in Olwen's wedding finery—the blue gown made of silk and the surcoat fashioned in a deeper shade of blue, decorated by images of golden hounds and harts embroidered into the fabric.

Wearing the fine wedding dress might help her play the part of the mistress of Northbridge with convincing authority. Perchance, her cap and barbette would hide her identity enough to trick Isadora. The headdress had fooled Bran into believing she was another woman.

Why delude herself? 'Twould not work. Still, doing something gave her a measure of control, and because of that, she was glad.

For the final touch, Catrin attached the silver-encrusted pin made from red jasper at the neck of her surcoat. The stone symbolized Bran's love. No matter what happened, she would keep the jewel as her talisman and cherish his recent words of devotion in her heart.

CATRIN STOOD before the fire in the solar, warming her chilled hands. Her stomach growled with hunger. The midday meal was near. Now dressed in the wedding garb, she lacked the courage to go downstairs, avoiding the inevitable confrontation.

"Catrin!" Richard called.

Her brother's frightened voice and the sharp rap on the door drew her up smartly. She crossed the floor, her breathing hard, and placed her hand on the latch, pausing a moment to collect herself.

"Catrin, I need to talk to you! I am alone."

"Come in." She swung open the door, and the boy hurried through. Shutting the door, Catrin turned to face him.

They gazed at each other in silence. Richard's face was pale, and she suddenly feared for his health. Yet, what could she expect? His mother had arrived.

"My mother has come." His words were barely audible.

She glanced at him. "Aye, I know," she said, feigning a calm she did not feel.

"I have news, Catrin." Richard lifted his chin as if to bolster his courage. "Bad news."

"What else could it be with your mother surprising us?" She moved away from him, giving him space, and returned to the fire. As if she had no care in the world, she extended her hands to the heat once more. Her knuckles were red from the cold.

Richard followed and plopped down on the stool, now behaving like a young lad, not the proper page and rightful earl of Rothmore. "She will know you, Catrin," he gave sharp voice to his fears.

Catrin glanced down, longing to smooth his tousled hair and remove the worry from his eyes. "Aye." She nodded. "I expect she will not think me Olwen."

"I want to ask you what you will do, but first I must tell you her plans."

Catrin found a second stool and sat across from him. "You have already spoken to her?"

"As soon as she found me, she drew me aside and gave me her news."

"Where is she now?" Catrin tried to put off hearing Richard's report.

"I let her use my solar room so she can clean up before the noon meal. She says she wants to be away soon after, and she will thank you for a fresh change of horses."

'Twas common courtesy, surely. Catrin shrugged, thereby giving her consent. By chance, her luck might hold. If Isadora left quickly, Catrin could avoid going below. Avoid giving herself away.

The boy squirmed nervously. "Catrin, she means to take me with her!"

"What?"

"She says Lord Northbridge is under suspicion at court. She doesn't trust him."

Shaking her head, Catrin frowned. "This makes little sense. She cannot simply remove you from Northbridge Castle. You are the lord's ward."

Richard leaned toward her. "It makes no difference to her, she says. She is going to marry Guy de Hastings, Lord Leighton, and she says King Edward will then give the wardship to him!"

Disbelief rushed through her. Isadora possessed a brazen courage. Reckless even. "But those rumors about Bran aren't true," Catrin said, her voice uneven.

"I know that. I tried to tell her," he insisted. "She wouldn't listen. She never listens."

Catrin folded her hands. "I know. Isadora pursues her own wishes, oft to the detriment of others."

"I don't want to go, Catrin. I like it here." His eyes clouded. "I forget I'm sick here, and Bran is teaching me what I need to know when I grow up."

Breathing fast, Catrin shut her eyes and lifted her fingertips to her temples, massaging them slowly. If Isadora removed Richard, and if, as was said, Bran's reputation had been sullied, then Edward might take away the wardship. The blow to Bran's esteem would be immense, not to mention the impact it would have on his wealth and his ability to hold Northbridge.

Her suspicions of Isadora and Lord Leighton seemed doubly founded. Isadora, through Richard, stood to gain much with the death of her father and brother. She had never trusted Guy de Hastings. For one, no one confirmed his account of her father's death. Now with marriage to Isadora, he could control her wealth, her dower lands, and the Lord of Rothmore himself.

Anxiety overwhelmed her, and she opened her eyes to gaze at the youthful face of her half-brother. Was his life at stake now? As long as his mother and Guy controlled the Fitzalan holdings through Richard, he had reason to live. After he came of age, what then?

Now more than ever she must overcome her fear and face Isadora. She must persuade her stepmother the folly of her marriage and make her understand the harm that might come to her son.

Resigned, Catrin climbed to her feet. "I must speak with Isadora."

"Catrin, you can't! What if she recognizes you?"

"I will take that chance, and if she does, perchance she will listen to me. More importantly, she will know Catrin Fitzalan is not dead. That Lord Northbridge didn't harm her and that Olwen is safe at White Ladies. Perchance she will leave you here when she returns to Clun."

"But she goes to find Edward at his court, not home to Clun Castle."

Catrin forced a smile and stretched out her hand to tousle Richard's hair. "All the more reason for me to try to stop her."

Catrin did not tell Richard there was not a chance in hell Isadora Mortimer Fitzalan would fail to recognize her. And, if as she feared, Isadora were behind the murders, then revealing herself would do more harm than good.

Nevertheless, she must try.

CHAPTER TWENTY-EIGHT

Catrin paused at the foot of the solar steps. A dull ache lodged beneath her breastbone. If only Bran were here. She needed the support of his arms, not to mention his vast diplomatic experience. In a strange way, she longed to tell him the truth. Yet she knew, full well, fear of his rejection would always keep her lips tightly sealed.

Sighing faintly, Catrin stepped into the normal turmoil that was the great hall at mealtime. The tables were erected and places set. She nodded her head to the steward, who called everyone to dinner. Isadora and her female companion stood near the fire with their heads together as if gossiping. Her stomach in knots, Catrin approached the two of them.

"Welcome, my ladies," she said. "I bring you greetings from my husband Lord Northbridge, who is away at the moment. Welcome to our home."

Isadora turned, her eyes slowly widening in surprise. This was the woman who had made Catrin's childhood miserable. She felt justified in harboring hatred and suspicion for Isadora had oft played high-and-mighty, never giving due respect to those she considered beneath her.

"Thank you, Lady Northbridge." Isadora tipped her head in polite greeting. "You may remember Lady Chase, my mother's cousin and my companion?"

"Aye, indeed," Catrin nodded, acknowledging the second guest.

"We had word of your recent accident," Isadora continued. "All court has been concerned for your welfare."

Catrin met Isadora's knowing look full on. Her breath caught. That her stepmother knew the truth, she was certain.

"My husband tended me well." Catrin maintained the friendliness of the charade. "As you can see, I'm completely mended."

"Aye, I can see many things." Isadora's lips twisted into a sly smile. "I have been concerned for my son and his welfare here at Northbridge. Now I see that I have many reasons for my anxiety."

Richard intervened at that moment in his role of page, ushering the guests to their places at the head table. Catrin began to breathe normally again and followed them. The lad pulled out the chair for his mother, seating her and then her traveling companion. Next he attended Catrin, who took Bran's place in the lord's seat.

The noonday meal was interminable, as was the incessant chatter of Isadora's cousin. Waryn de Grey's mother despaired of finding a wife for her fussy son. A child in Shrewsbury had survived a light case of the pox. Lady Chase had purchased fine silk and baldekin from a merchant lately come from the Holy Lands.

Would the woman's chitchat ever stop?

Catrin picked at her food, remembering how Bran oft prompted her to eat by feeding her tasty tidbits. She remembered much more. The feel of his hands upon her breasts, the way he shouted out his love. Her face warmed when she thought about last night and how she'd come away fully satisfied and wanting more.

"You do not eat, my lady." Isadora pointed toward Catrin's full trencher. The golden Rothmore ring gleamed in the torchlight.

Catrin slanted her stepmother a quick look. "I'm not hungry."

"In the family way, perchance?"

Why did Isadora's every word, every spiteful nuance, make her so angry? "I doubt it," she replied, her nose in the air.

"Or could it be that my arrival has ruined your appetite?"

Catrin hid her hands beneath the table and squeezed her fingers into hard fists. "That and the news you wish to defy the king's command and remove your son from my husband's safekeeping."

Isadora's eyes sharpened, and she leaned nearer. "And what, my lady, do you know of ignoring the king's command?" Her words hissed like that of a snake.

"I know more than you might think, *my lady*." Catrin's mouth ran dry. She placed her palms flat on the table. "And much of murder and foul play."

"Then we both have need for private conversation." Isadora squared her shoulders and sat back, her gaze challenging.

"That talk, I welcome, and soon." Catrin's eyebrows knitted together. "For I fear I cannot allow you to remove Richard from this household."

"That remains to be seen, does it not?" Isadora turned away and dipped her spoon into a dish of blancmange.

Truly, Isadora was insufferable. With cold fingers, Catrin gripped her goblet of wine, bringing it to her lips for a sip. The liquid seemed strangely bitter on this morn. She choked as it went down and turned her head away, coughing.

Much later, amidst the turmoil of after-dinner clean up, Catrin faced Isadora near the relative privacy of the great stone hearth. Richard, pallid and drawn, stood a short distance away with his back toward them to chase away anyone who approached.

"You can stop the pretense and tell me why you claim to be Olwen de Belleme," snapped Isadora. "I know you are Catrin Fitzalan. Yet I know not why you have played me false and let those at court believe you to be dead. Have you and the King's Raven killed your cousin?"

Catrin was no longer the resentful child who had confronted Isadora in the Rothmore tent at the time of Gilbert's death. She was a woman, fully bedded, and she had righteousness on her side. She need not take censure from her stepmother.

She straightened her spine. "Olwen is safe in a nunnery, as she wished."

Isadora's intense gaze seemed to see into Catrin's soul. "That doesn't explain your presence here in the guise of your cousin. That doesn't explain why *you* claim to be married to Bran ap Madog."

"When I escaped from those who would murder me and did murder my maid, just as they also killed my father and brother, I came to Northbridge and Olwen." Swallowing hard, Catrin continued, "I learned of Olwen's upcoming marriage and her desire to take holy vows. Switching places with her seemed to be a way of insuring her safety and a way for me to discover the truth about Bran ap Madog."

Isadora cocked her head, her eyes brimming with speculation. "And what did you learn?"

"I learned he could not have murdered Father and Gilbert." Catrin felt the assurance of her conviction.

"Your evidence?"

What *was* her evidence? The kind and just way he treated the castle folk? The way he instructed Richard. His deep concern when he cared for her during her illness? The way he cried out his love? Catrin couldn't say these things to Isadora. She would give too much of herself away. These reasons were only reasons of the heart, nothing more. She had no true proof. For once, her confidence lagged.

"I just know," she said stubbornly.

"And what does your husband know?"

"He doesn't know the truth about me." Catrin paused, once more the weight of the priest's misgivings ringing like warning bells in her ears. "He thinks me Olwen."

Sudden triumph lit Isadora's eyes. "Then you're not truly married. You have committed unholy sacrilege, making your marriage a sham. Bran ap Madog is not wed to the de Belleme heir. Therefore, he is not lord of Northbridge."

"'Tis not the way you make it sound!" Catrin raised her hands, palms facing out as if she could ward off Isadora's blow of words.

"Oh? Then how is it? You are not Olwen de Belleme, you admit. In that case, Sir Bran has no rights to this castle, its land, *or* my son."

Catrin hated the sound of Isadora's infuriating voice. She hated her own folly. Still, she had to salvage something of this meeting—for Bran's sake, if nothing else.

She lowered her hands to her sides. "King Edward gave Richard, Earl Rothmore, into Sir Bran's safekeeping because of his faithful service to the crown. The king trusts Bran and knows that he will do his best for Richard."

"Trusts him?" Isadora laughed. "When all of court is a-buzz with rumors about his role in the deaths of the Fitzalans?"

"Those rumors are false! I am not dead. Another villain threatens our family."

"You might say," Isadora reasoned, her eyes narrowing, "that Sir Bran murdered John and Gilbert and tried to murder you so he could gain control of Rothmore and all its lands and people."

"That is disgusting." Catrin's nose flared, anger tightened her chest. "How can he gain control of Rothmore with Richard as heir?"

"Olwen has claim to Rothmore through her mother. That he married you instead, after thinking you dead, is amusing." Isadora smiled again, sweetly and triumphantly.

Catrin fisted her hand and fought the urge to strike her stepmother in the face. Isadora, ever a reader of her adversary's emotion, pressed her point. "The king unwittingly placed my son in the hands of the enemy of our family. That is why I have come for Richard. We'll go to court and plead our case. I'll not leave my son in the clutches of a wicked murderer and a woman who clearly has been deceived by a man's prowess in bed."

"You know not what has moved me," Catrin retorted. "Besides, how do I know you're innocent in all that has occurred? Through your son, you serve to gain by the deaths of my father and all his heirs!"

"My motives are simple," Isadora said with obvious

disdain. "I protect my son no matter what. You have no more evidence for your threats than you have proof of the innocence of your so-called husband. I always thought you contentious, Catrin. Now I consider you merely naïve."

The words stung as Isadora had meant them too. "What about the motives of your lover de Hastings?" Catrin posed, any pretense of civility now gone.

"Lord Leighton is not under suspicion here." Isadora waved her hand to dismiss Catrin's question. "'Tis your behavior and that of Bran ap Madog that the king will find damning. I now have proof the King's Raven is no fit guardian for my son. You'll live to regret this day."

With that parting threat, Isadora made an elaborate curtsy and swept away, calling for her lady companion and her armed escort. They would ride hard, she told them all, hoping to make Shrewsbury before nightfall and then set forth on the morrow to Rhuddlan Castle and the king's court.

Richard protested, but to no avail. His mother, who only spared him a tearful glance back at Catrin, pulled him out of the hall.

Catrin stood by the hearth, her knees week and her mind blank. What would she do now? How could she explain this to Bran? When he knew the truth, he would hate her.

Folding her arms across her breast, she turned from the fire and climbed the gray stone steps. Somehow she had to make all of this come out for the better. Her purpose had been honorable. Surely, God would not rebuke her for simply loving her family and trying to protect them.

As she reached the darkened solar, Catrin's mind blazoned bright with a white light of awareness. God had already punished her for her folly.

Falling in love with Bran was a curse she would carry with her forever.

~

BRAN RODE hard from the Dee Valley, reaching Northbridge Castle long after the gates had closed for the night. He awoke the guards and gave his lathered horse to a sleepy Will. Delight at being home churned through him, causing his pace to quicken as he mounted the steps to the solar.

He had missed Olwen sorely. All the time he was doing his duty for his friend and companion, Bran longed to be with his wife. No matter what happened when they went to the king, he would still have the comfort of his marriage to Olwen. No king could shake holy vows.

Armed with this assurance, he was eager to speak to Edward. They had a grudging respect between them. His liege would not believe false rumors once he could defend himself in person.

The solar was dark and chilly. Bran shut the heavy door and turned to face the marriage bed, illuminated only by a faint glow from the sputtering fire. Olwen was there, under the fur coverlet, sleeping soundly. Tenderness overcame him. Quickly he stripped off his clothing, and naked, crawled under the covers.

Bran eased himself into the center of the bed, drawing Olwen into his gentle embrace. She sighed in her sleep, snuggling closer, her sweet breath soft upon his face. Content, he relaxed, and as he drifted off to sleep, he realized the only thing important to him was his wife.

If he could hold onto this woman forever, he would gladly become a poor knight again.

CHAPTER TWENTY-NINE

Catrin awakened slowly, feeling safe and snug as if wrapped inside a mother's womb. She knew morning had come and stirred within the welcome warmth, turning toward it, reluctant to face the raw cold of the new day.

A soft, sighing breath tickled her nose and touched her lips. Her eyes fluttered open. Bran! Love and bitter sadness welled within her. His bare arm lay like a heavy weight across her waist. He was big and hard with wide, powerful shoulders and the muscular forearms of a trained knight. Thinking him asleep, she gently caressed his temple and traced a fingertip down to his beard-roughened jaw.

"*Bore da*," he said, surprising her.

"Good morning." Her voice was thin and wispy, full of emotion.

He opened his eyes, and a hint of a smile crossed his lips. "I am glad to be home."

He wants me. She was awed by the reverent way his eyes skimmed over her as if she were a precious jewel.

Her hand lingered against his cheek. Catrin dared not

speak, for an icy sense of doom froze her heart. What would he do if he discovered the truth? All she could do was cup his jaw with her palm, feeling the solid bone beneath his unshaven skin.

"I have missed you," he growled, seeming impatient.

Catching her hand in his grip, he rolled on top of her, his body taut over hers, his eyes glinting in the faint light of dawn.

Moments later, when he filled her, his breath ragged against her ear, she accepted him inside with a willingness she found hard to comprehend. And when she joined him in the lovemaking, 'twas like he had never parted from her.

CATRIN COULD NOT SHAKE the cold. Wailing winds blowing from the mountains of Wales promised snow or at least a chilling rain. A strong draft swept the great hall, and smoke coughed from the fire. She shivered. All around, castle folk were astir while family hounds scurried out of the way or snuffled for scraps on the floor.

A kitchen boy offered her a crust of bread, a chunk of yellow cheese, and a tankard of ale, and she broke her fast seated on a stool in front of the hearth.

On this chilly day, Catrin wore a cotte of blue English wool. With heavy folds and tight sleeves buttoned from her elbow to her wrist, the garment was serviceable for such a blustery day. A pelican, an over-tunic also made of good wool in a brighter shade of blue, and her fur-lined cape draped over her knees brought her even more protection from the cold.

She ate in silence, watching the morning routine in the

hall. How many memories had she made here at North-bridge? Memories she would carry with her the rest of her days.

The boy came back, now carrying a laver. She nodded absently. "Thank you, lad."

He waited patiently while she dipped her fingers into the warm water to rid them of grease. Then she wiped her hands on a linen cloth. If only she could as easily wash away her feeling of despair.

Once more she nodded her thanks to the lad who scur-ried away. Bran crossed the hall, coming toward her as she'd seen him do so many times. He stopped to speak to one person after another, his magnificent presence filling the room with energy. He carried himself like a prince.

Shaking herself, Catrin rubbed her hands together and tucked them into the folds of her pelican. Isadora was right. They were not truly wed. Their marriage was a sham. She had the love she had always wanted within her grasp, yet 'twas not meant to be.

She drew her lips together into a thin line and stared into the fire. Her dreams of love had smoldered into ashes with the fires of hatred that engulfed her after the king's tourna-ment and the death of Gilbert. That she could have once hated Bran so much and now love him so deeply must be a cruel quirk of fate.

Bran pulled up the lord's chair up and sat across from her. "What is this about Lady Rothmore taking Richard?"

His tone was conversational. Still, Catrin's head light-ened with alarm. She turned her head to gaze upon his eyes that were alert, but bore no ill trust.

She gathered her courage. "Isadora heard rumors about

you and fears for her son's welfare. Against my protests, she took Richard to court."

Her gaze skittered downward, away from the eyes that looked at her with trust. She had left out one crucial part—Isadora knew the truth about her identity. She was not Olwen, his true wife.

"The sooner I speak to Edward, the better my position will be." Bran stood and warmed his hands by the fire. "The king heard those rumors, but I've not been able to defend myself."

"Now Lady Rothmore will carry more tales," Catrin pointed out. "She means to marry Guy de Hastings and obtain Richard's guardianship from the king for her new husband."

The import of the events was not lost on her husband. Bran faced her, his eyes shuttered, his countenance dark. "Are you ready for a rough and dangerous journey through the mountains of Wales?"

Catrin cocked her head. "Why so, my lord?"

"*My lady*," he said, teasing, picking up on her use of the formal form of address. "'Tis the only way we can reach Edward before the determined Isadora."

Love swelled within her heart. As troubled as he was, he remained playful with her. That spoke much to their changed relationship.

Catrin held Bran's gaze, her mind a-clutter with all that could be, but wouldn't. She owed it to him to explain her actions to King Edward. 'Twas her only chance to save Bran and salvage something of her life with him.

But by saving Bran from Edward's wrath, she took the chance of alienating her husband when he discovered the truth.

That was a risk she must now take.

"Aye, I'm ready to do what I must," she answered softly, overcoming a tight ache in her chest

Bran smiled, seemingly satisfied. "Then we make ready to leave."

He took her hand, helping her to rise. His look bathed her with so much love and longing that Catrin caught her breath. She lowered her eyes a moment, her senses alive with guilt.

And then a shout rang out. Bran's grip tightened around her fingers.

"They've come for us!" Father Ellis cried, charging into the hall, his long robes a kilter, and his arms flapping wildly. "Officers of the king! They've come for us!"

Bran cursed under his breath. "The man has gone mad."

Had the stress of the lie she'd forced him to tell addled the poor priest's thinking? Catrin lifted her free hand to her lips. Father Ellis stumbled to a halt before them.

"Prepare yourself," he said to Catrin in a harsh whisper.

She crossed herself. "Father, all will be made right. But *you* must pray for me." She touched his sleeve. "And light a candle…in the chapel."

"In the chapel?" he glanced around, rubbing his hands together.

"'Tis best to light one there." She nodded, urging him to go.

"Aye. That I will do." He whirled and fled the hall just as several armed yeomen entered the hall followed by a knight.

Fear gripped her. The heraldic leopards of England. King Edward's men. The coat of arms spoke to the veracity of Father Ellis.

"Sir Otto, welcome to my new home!" Bran departed her

side and strode forward. He extended his hand seemingly pleased by the arrival of the king's men. "Olwen, come meet my friend." He glanced back at her. "When I entered the king's service, Sir Otto guided me well."

Catrin now recognized Sir Otto Grandison, the king's closest friend. He had accompanied the then Prince Edward on his crusade, serving at the siege of Acre like Bran. Surely, his presence did not bode well.

"'Tis not a pleasure visit, Sir Bran," the older knight said, refusing to take the proffered hand.

Bran dropped it by his side and surveyed his friend. "Why is that?"

"In the name of Edward, King of England, Lord of Ireland, and Duke of Aquitaine, I arrest you for the murders of Sir John and Sir Gilbert Fitzalan, the Earls of Rothmore, and of Lady Catrin Fitzalan, the earl's daughter."

Bran's hand went to his hip, but he wore no sword. "That is outrageous!"

The yeomen startled at his action, their own hands finding their sword hilts. Sir Otto signaled his men to remain calm. "I don't want to restrain you, but I will," he warned Bran.

Defiant, his stance erect and his shoulders squared, Bran glared at the men as if daring them to take him. "I have not done what you charge me of doing."

"You'll have your day of judgment before the king."

"I welcome that." Bran relaxed a bit. "I planned to ride to court today, in fact."

Sir Otto frowned. "Edward is at Rhuddlan Castle. He has ordered me to take you to the Tower. There to wait for him until he returns to London after the birth of his child."

Catrin gasped. Queen Eleanor was not due yet for several more months.

Bran glanced her way and then turned back to the king's man. "I demand to see Edward now."

"You are in no position to make demands," Sir Otto reminded him calmly.

Her heart thundered with denial. If Bran were locked away in the horrible dudgeon, he would be forgotten. Many a man had perished in that wicked prison.

"Why do you not take my husband to Rhuddlan, my lord?" Catrin spoke for the first time.

She stepped forward, seeing Sir Otto's questioning assessment of her. Catrin prayed he didn't know her or Olwen well enough to be suspicious.

"The king's orders, my lady," he said with a slight bow.

Catrin captured Bran's arm, clinging to him as a shy, loving wife might. "Then you must grant me a boon, my lord. Consider it the wish of a newly wedded woman," she said dipping her head and letting a small smile touch her lips. "Let me have one more night alone with my husband before you take him away. Stay with us and let your men rest."

Bran cocked an eyebrow. She felt him stiffen, but he gave nothing away.

Sir Otto eyed them, stroking his chin with his gloved hand and finally, after what seemed like an eternity nodded his head. "I suppose it would be best to start fresh on the morrow."

"Thank you, my lord." Catrin dipped a curtsy, coyly smiling up at him.

The seasoned warrior snorted, not impressed by her woman's wiles. "Men, see to your horses. We stay the night."

Always one to manage his affairs, Sir Otto stationed a yeoman at the hall door before he followed his troop outside.

With the men gone, Bran jerked her toward the privacy of the hearth. "What is this, my lady?" This time there was no teasing in his voice, only anger.

"You saved my life," she whispered, moistening her lips. "I have a plan to save yours."

He scowled at her in disbelief. "How so?"

Catrin lifted her chin. "'Tis time for you to merely watch and wait," she murmured, "and to put your trust in me."

As CATRIN SUSPECTED, waiting was hard for Bran. They dined at noon, and Catrin made sure the food and the entertainment kept their guests occupied and well fed. She sent for Will, instructing him to come to her in the guise of a kitchen boy. Bran had flashed a questioning look when he spotted them talking, but he had held his tongue. He would not openly challenge her in front of the king's men.

Throughout the meal, Catrin made great play at being the fervent wife. She wanted no one to mistake her reason for wanting her husband to remain with her another night or be surprised when they climbed the steps to their chamber early.

They left the company with the setting of the winter sun.

Bran bolted the door and whirled to confront her. "What is this game, Olwen?"

"'Tis no game," Catrin was able to say before he grabbed her shoulders and pulled her into his arms.

He kissed her, plunging his tongue deep into her mouth,

forcing her head back. She closed her eyes. He acted like a madman now, wanting to possess her. Catrin caught his frenzy, his haste. In her woman's place deep within, she began to yearn. *Brand me,* she screamed silently, opening to him, allowing him to scorch the tender skin of her throat with his tongue and lips. *Mark me as your own!*

She knew this might be their last time together.

"Myn Duw," he released the words against her neck. He grasped her pelican, ready to strip it from her shoulders.

"No," she groaned. "Now."

She clutched at him, letting waves of sensation wash through her aching core. The cadence of her yearning increased. Catrin circled his neck with her arms, and lifted one leg around his waist. Bran gripped her hips. Moaning, she brought up the other leg, holding on. Her skirts draped around them.

Breathing hard, he plunged his tongue again and again into her mouth as he held her and staggered forward. Reaching the great bed, he rested her on its edge. She was hot and ready.

"Please," she begged as he pushed up her skirts around her exposed body.

With one thrust, he slipped inside her and like a magnificent and powerful stallion mounting a mare, drove his seed deeply into her.

CHAPTER THIRTY

Her pulse slowed. Her eyes drifted shut. Catrin felt deliciously warm in Bran's embrace. Now the fur coverlet surrounded them, tickling her nose. How she wanted to stay this way forever. How she wanted to forget what must be done.

But it could not be.

Catrin opened her eyes. Bran's face swam before them and the musky odor of his body mingled with the faint smell of the lavender scented sheets beneath the fur. She stroked his face with a gentle finger. He kissed her once on the cheek, a simple action that tore her heart in two.

"We must go," she murmured, still dreamy.

"How do you propose we slip away from the king's guards below in the hall?" A touch of humor lightened his voice.

"Through the secret passage."

Bran sat up. He searched her face in the gloom. "You speak the truth?"

Catrin almost said she always spoke the truth, but that lie refused to leave her lips. She nodded instead. "My cousin and I played in the passageway as children."

"It leads outside the castle?"

She nodded again. "The stable boy, Will, has Merch and Taran and provisions for travel hiding in the woods across the Severn from lower town."

"*Cariad*, you *have* saved me!" Bran kissed her full on the lips and leapt from the bed. "Quick. We must be away from here so that we can put distance between us and Sir Otto."

Once more Catrin caught his urgency. She scuttled from the bed while he started riffling through the large chest in the corner of the room.

Bran stood and looked at her. "I must arm myself. I need your help."

She caught a quick breath. This task had belonged to Rhys. Now it fell to her.

Without a word, she laced the back of Bran's quilted aketon, the long-sleeved undergarment that reached to his knees. Over that he put on his mail hauberk. He pulled on padded hose. Before she knew it, he stood before her, his mail covered by his plain black surcoat, a sword belt knotted at his waist holding his arming sword. He wore a thick padded arming cap over his mail coif, completely covering his long hair.

When he picked up his shield, emblazoned with a blood-red raven, Catrin saw the vision of the black knight—the same knight who'd ridden against Gilbert in the king's tourney.

She wavered slightly, thinking of Gilbert and Father and how she had once hated Bran. He must have seen hesitation in her eyes. Believing her to be Olwen, he came toward her quietly and framed her face with his big hands.

"I know not the reason for this change of sentiment," he said, "but I am thankful for it."

She couldn't speak. Couldn't voice the love she felt. Moreover, she couldn't tell him the truth. Mesmerized by his beautifully rugged face and the sincerity in his eyes, Catrin simply gazed back at him. Precious moments were lost as they stood together, each absorbed in thought, linked by a fine thread of something akin to love. Finally Bran broke the spell, kissing her hastily and turning from her.

"Dress warmly," he ordered. "Our journey will be cold and dangerous."

He didn't question whether she would go with him. He assumed her loyalty. Guilt once more gnawed at her stomach as she donned an old pair of men's braes under her woolen gown and surcoat.

Bran had sheathed his long sword, put on his leather gloves, and gathered his great helm under his arm. He stood by the fire watching her. Catrin drew her fur-lined cape over her shoulders and went to her own coffer. She needed one more thing before she left this place that had been her home for such a short time.

"Will you help me?" she asked softly and handed him the silver-encrusted brooch made from red jasper that he had given her.

Setting down his helm and shield, Bran held the brooch in his gloved hand. Was he thinking about what it symbolized? *Did* he love her as he had cried out in passion? These were questions she was too afraid to ask because she had no right, not being his true wife.

He tugged the cape snuggly around her neck and pinned the brooch there. "Now, what must we do?"

Catrin breathed deeply, gazing at him, longing for what could not be. Then she sighed and stepped back. She crossed to the hearth and opened the squint, looking down on the great hall below. All was dark. The castle slept.

When she turned, he laughed at her, knowing how she had spied upon him. "We all have our secrets, I see," he said with a sly grin.

Catrin drew herself up like a queen, lifting her chin. "My cousin and I played with the peep hole," she said and shouldered past him.

Still laughing, he followed her to the wall hanging that secreted the door. "You surprise me all the time, *cariad*."

Ignoring him, Catrin tripped the mechanism that opened the door. It yawned before them, cavernous and dark. A draft of cold air filled the room. Somber now, Bran gathered his arms, slinging the shield over his back. He then lifted a torch from the wall and lit it in the fireplace. Holding the light high over his head, he returned to her.

"Lead on, Olwen," he said. "I trust you with my life."

Whatever qualms Catrin had, she suppressed them. Having set this drama into motion, she would act out her part. She would follow what fate had laid out for her and hope only for the best.

TRUE TO HIS WORD, Will had brought the two horses to the hiding place in the woods. He stood at their heads, searching the darkness and stamping his feet because of the cold.

"Well done, lad," Bran said as he quickly checked the

packs of provisions tied across the rumps of the horses. He fastened his long sword to the front of his saddle.

"Thank you, my lord. Meg helped me," Will answered, eager to give credit where credit was due.

"Aye, but you took the risk of being seen leading the horses out of the castle." Bran came to Taran's head, patting the black's neck. "Take care of my raven while we're gone," he ordered, glancing down at the boy, "and keep yourself safe."

"I will do that, my lord. God be with you."

After the boy darted away into the darkness, Catrin stood gazing at the castle gleaming in the moonlight high above the Severn. Her thoughts tumbled in disarray, her nerves aflutter. Their escape had been easy. Much too easy. No one had stopped them on the cartway once they had extinguished the torch and slipped out of the cave. In fact, they'd seen no one on their journey into town and across the bridge. Could God truly be on their side?

Bran came up behind her and circled her in his arms, hugging her tight. He kissed her head, giving her an extra squeeze and pulling her against him. She wore no restricting headdress tonight. Just her net crespine bound her hair out of the way. She had pulled up the hood of her cape, but even it did not give much protection from the cold.

"We will win this, my lady."

She leaned back against his chest, feeling the metal of his mail bite into her shoulders. How could she have dreamed she would be standing like this with him? From the first day on the tourney field, she and Bran had been at odds. Sadly, they still were. Even though they seemed as one in this, she knew the truth, and it hurt her sorely.

"I hope you're right," she murmured.

"I won't lose you." He hugged her again. "That much I know."

Bran gave her a leg up and then mounted Taran. Together, they reined their horses away from the Severn and Northbridge Castle, and without a backward glance, headed northwest toward the Welsh foothills.

O'er the next few days, Bran's knowledge of the land and language stood them well. More oft than not, they rested in the modest cottage of a sheep farmer or made camp in a cave protected from the wind. They traversed obscure pine forest tracks or rutted paths made only for wild creatures, keeping far away from the much-traveled roads.

During the second day's journey, they crossed the dyke said to be built by the Mercian King Offa. A linear earthwork consisting of a ditch and rampart, the barrier roughly followed the Welsh and English boundary and gave them an open view into Wales. Catrin felt easier, but every loud noise caused her head to jerk for fear Sir Otto and his men had caught up with them.

"We are safe enough now," Bran told her, riding beside her on the trail when he could.

He reasoned aloud that the king's close friend would not discover them missing until late the following morning and then only after breaking down the door. By that time they would have gained a good start. In truth, Sir Otto didn't know their destination or the direction they'd taken. Any move he made would be a guess. And Sir Otto didn't like to guess.

So it was with confidence that Bran guided them from Northbridge directly toward Rhuddlan, heading through his home terrain in the Dee River valley.

"Isadora went to Shrewsbury," he said, explaining his way

of thinking. "She would journey to Rhuddlan by first going to Chester and then traveling along the coast road. With Richard along, she'd not push her retinue hard."

"She told me she thinks of Richard's safety at all times," Catrin said, reflecting on her stepmother's denial when she had accused Isadora of murder.

"Then I think all will be well."

But would it? In silence, Catrin rode the sturdy palfrey, concern clogging her throat. Oft she ignored the beauty of the countryside, the spectacular limestone cliffs rising from the woodland or a lone hawk silhouetted against the bright blue winter sky. She couldn't forget what had taken place or stop worrying about what was to come.

"You will live to regret this day," Isadora had told her.

Yet what Catrin regretted most was lying to Bran.

What would she do once they arrived at the castle? Could she gain a personal audience with the king? Or would it be better to see Eleanor? She knew the queen liked and trusted her.

Several days after their escape, they stood beside their horses' heads atop a small mountain in the Clwydian range. For much of the way, they had walked, forced to lead their mounts. The blisters on Catrin's feet made her wince with each step, yet for the first time, the magnificent view of the snow-capped mountain Bran called Eryri drew her breath away. The high peak, several days' ride, gleamed in the morning light. To the east, sunlight glittered off the Irish Sea.

'Twas a shame she had been unable to enjoy her first trip into the glorious land that had given birth to her mother and husband.

Their journey wasn't yet over. They must ascend and

descend a series of small mountains, but Rhuddlan Castle and the king were near. As Catrin, leading her mare, followed Bran down the next steep path, she knew her destiny was finally at hand.

CHAPTER THIRTY-ONE

Catrin awoke slowly to the feeble light of a cloudy dawn and the luscious smell of stewing meat that wafted up the ladder to the cold loft where she had spent a restless night. Bran had promised her a good night's rest at the humble cottage of a farrier who'd once been in service to the king, and he had kept that promise. Drowsy still, she hung onto the dregs of sleep, reluctant to face the day and what it held. Her heart drummed to a dull thud of fear that never seemed to leave her now. 'Twas a wonder she'd slept at all.

Her stomach growled, and Catrin placed her palm against the thin blanket covering her fully clothed body. She had not undressed, except for removing her crespine. For one, 'twas too cold in the small, single-room cottage, and for another, she had been so tired she could barely stand let alone climb into the loft. But climb she did at Bran's behest, her thoughts a-jumble from weariness so great she selfishly failed to think about where he would sleep.

Now she missed him, her body aching not only from the cold but also from the loss of his warmth she'd grown accustomed to sharing. Catrin shut her eyes, overwhelmed once more by regret and by a rising sense of guilt that threatened the very air she breathed.

How could she save him? Once so quick to devise a plan to find Gilbert's murderer and plan their escape from Northbridge, she was now at a loss.

In the room beneath her, Bran and their host Alun of Rhuddlan, a maker of fine sword blades as well as sturdy horseshoes, murmured together. They were speaking in Welsh and Catrin could not make out a single word.

Opening her eyes, she pulled back the skimpy blanket and sat up. No matter how hard, she must face the day. Shaking her hair to loosen the tangles, she clawed her fingers through the long blond strands. Then gulping a breath, she faced the ladder and descended to the room below.

Behind her back, the rushes rustled. Bran's hands circled her waist, guiding her down the remaining two rungs. He turned her around to face him.

"Thank you, my lord," she said in a voice much too subdued and unfamiliar even to herself.

"How fared you last night?" Bran grinned at her, brushing back a pesky strand of hair from her eyes.

"Very well, thank you." She glanced away like a blushing maiden. Her knees felt week.

"I like your hair down," he whispered so that their host could not hear. "Without a net covering."

"I need to braid it to keep it out of my way." Her body pulsed with excitement. He did this to her by a mere look. By a simple touch. Desire shook her, and she fought the tight ache in her throat.

"I will be glad to help you braid it," he said and kissed her full on the lips.

She leaned into his kiss, willing him to continue, begging for more, and fearing this would truly be their last.

"Harrumph!" Alun cleared his throat, chuckling. "I'd best be at the forge, else I'll draw suspicion to this house. 'Sides, you need privacy, my lord."

Catrin heard the man shuffle toward the door, but her senses concentrated only on her husband, his hands upon her breast and his demanding tongue inside her mouth. Her head swirled with delight as she opened to him, devouring him, and at the same time pressing against his black surcoat. She throbbed with wanting, with love, with the knowledge that this man was hers. Her husband. Now and forever.

But Bran ap Madog, the King's Raven, the supposed Lord of Northbridge, was none of these things.

Shame stopped her. Catrin struggled to control her lust. She placed her hands against Bran's chest, feeling the ripple of the mail beneath the surcoat and gently pushed against him.

Finally, she knew what she must do.

"Bran," she said, fighting dizziness. "As much as I want you to make love to me now as a husband makes love to a wife, we must talk."

He shook himself, as if remembering where they were and what they were about on this momentous day that would decide their futures. He pulled back from her. He framed her face with his strong hands. "You're right, Olwen. I'll feed you, and while you eat, I'll tell you what I have learned."

She laid her cheek against the warmth of his hand and thought she'd die from sadness.

Bran made her sit in the only stool in the room. As she braided her hair, he dished up a bowl of good, thick soup laced with chunks of vegetables, and placed it before her on the bare, wooden table. Catrin forced herself to eat, knowing she needed the nourishment.

Watching her, Bran rested against the doorjamb, his arms folded across his chest. "Alun tells me Sir Otto was not far behind us. He arrived last night."

She held her spoon in mid-air, glancing up at him, and then shoved it into her mouth, swallowing with difficulty.

"Isadora arrived yesterday. Richard is with her." Bran gave her the grim news. "The Rothmore pavilion is pitched outside the curtain walls where others of the king's vassals have camped. Edward is rebuilding the castle. There is not enough room inside to accommodate all the members of his royal party, let alone camp followers and honest petitioners."

"'Tis always so for those traveling with the king and queen," Catrin said, as if she were merely making small talk at a midday meal.

He pushed away from the door to stand beside her, a tall, foreboding presence clad in black. Catrin did not fear him now. She only feared the secret she harbored.

"I'm in danger if I step out of this door," he said, squatting down beside her and taking her hand. "Yet, I'll face my accusers. I'll go to the Rothmore tent and take Richard with me to see the king."

Catrin shoved the bowl away. "'Tis dangerous."

"I don't shirk from danger." He smiled, squeezing her hand. "The reward will be worth the risk."

She was his reward. Or Olwen was. Catrin knew what had motivated him from the start. Power and land. What was his motive now? Looking into his dark eyes, she saw the light of unspoken love. A light she must dim if she wanted him to go into battle forewarned. Panic shot through her veins.

"I must tell you something," she said quickly else her courage falter. "In some ways, 'tis good news."

Bran lifted a questioning eyebrow. Catrin looked straight at him, trying not to think, only act. She drew on all the courage she could muster, straightening her shoulders as if that would help. "I am not Olwen de Belleme. I am Catrin Fitzalan. I was not murdered when outlaws set upon my party. They killed my maid Gwendolyn." She drew a breath and turned her gaze away from his now bemused expression.

He dropped her hand. "Where is Olwen de Belleme?"

"In a convent."

"Yet you said vows with me."

Catrin forced herself to look at him. "Yes," she said letting out her breath slowly.

"Why?"

"Because Olwen couldn't marry you. She was too grief-stricken. We thought you had killed Gilbert. She always wanted to go to a convent." He stared at her, all emotion draining from his face while her words of explanation tumbled out. "Olwen was too fragile, don't you understand? She couldn't physically have withstood marriage to you, not with your demands upon her body." Catrin looked away. "All that I loved had died. I wanted Olwen to be safe. To live the life she wanted. I thought if we changed places, I could make her safe, and then I could get you to admit you killed my father and brother."

Her reasoning seemed so inane now. As if she'd had the power to control destiny. Instead, she'd set into motion events she had little power to comprehend and no power to direct.

"Why tell me now?"

Catrin faced him once more. "Isadora knows." Her voice was raw with anguish. "I don't want you to meet the king without knowing the truth."

"How noble of you."

The sarcasm of his voice was like a slap. He was angry. She'd expected it.

Bran rose to his feet and lifted his cloak from a peg, draping it over his shoulders. Catrin stood too, feeling faint and winded. He came back to her, tilted up her chin, and unlike the first time that day, held her face hard in his grip. In an odd way, she welcomed his wrath and the pain of his fingers biting into her flesh.

'Twas somehow fitting.

His gaze bore into her. Was he trying to read her mind?

"You must know what harm you have caused," he said with evident restraint. "I can forgive you for the charade. What I cannot forgive is that you lied to me."

His hand fell. Turning away, he sheathed his sword and picked up his helm, cradling it under his arm. Then without a backward glance, he opened the cottage door. Icy wind from the nearby seacoast whooshed inside. With a sweep of his cloak, he was gone. Catrin ran to the door and stood there. The wind caught her skirt and tangled it about her legs.

Holding the door, she shut her eyes to the biting force of the wind and sucked its coldness into her lungs. She swayed, the door her only support, Catrin felt the overpowering misery she had anticipated. It swept over her like a crushing sea wave.

All she loved she lost.

Loving Bran ap Madog, the King's Raven, was no exception.

BRAN'S fingers fumbled with the girth as he saddled Taran. The horse had rested well and was eager for a run. Bran thought to oblige the animal. Collecting his reins, he inserted one foot into the left stirrup and swung atop the saddle, allowing the stallion his head as soon as he was settled in the leather seat. Somehow these very mundane tasks were comforting.

Ha! Why hoodwink himself? Nothing calmed him now. The act of tacking the horse simply bought time, permitting his mind to go numb from the anger that threatened to spill forth in violence. Best to channel that aggression for now while he let himself come to terms with the news his wife had revealed to him.

Why did he call her his wife?

Olwen was not his wife. The woman he had wed, had bedded, and cared for was not Olwen, but an imposter. She had duped him. Lied to him. She had admitted it in a tranquil, uncaring voice, as if she did not realize its impact on him or those in his care.

The harsh truth twisted in his gut. He, Bran ap Madog, knight of the royal household, king's champion, was no longer responsible for anyone.

Only himself.

As it had always been. Himself and Rhys, but Rhys was dead and gone. He had loved Rhys. That was the sorrow of it.

He had also given his love to this woman. What was her real name? Catrin? Lady Fitzalan. He remembered now. *The woman in the apple green gown from the king's tourney.*

The irony was not lost on him.

Alun's cottage stood apart from the old town of Rhudd-lan, hugging the road to the coast. Bran traveled that road now, galloping hard, welcoming the wind that whipped his cloak back from his shoulders and stung his eyes through the sights of his great helm. He cared not for the travelers that passed him nor for their strange looks. His mind was deadened. Frozen by disbelief, betrayal, and by an anger that welled deep within.

She had played him for a fool. Wiled him with her womanly ways. Depended on him so he had felt tenderness toward her. So he had grown to love her. He had used her body freely to pleasure himself. *And her.* Never forget that. She liked it too, their lovemaking. She had cried out for him, just as he had shouted her name. *Olwen. Cariad. Sweet charlatan.*

How could he not know? Why had the servants not alerted him? Father Ellis? The maid?

Bran sat back on the horse, slowing to a canter. Father Ellis knew. That is why he took to his cups. The maid knew too. Olwen had not done this deed alone.

His fingers closed tightly on the reins, causing Taran to jerk up his head. Bran sat deeper in the saddle, relaxing, and bringing the horse down to a walk. She was not Olwen, but Catrin. He must think of her that way now. *Catrin Fitzalan.* Wedded to him under false pretenses. He had been deceived. He'd been made to look the fool. The Church would annul their marriage.

What bothered him the most was the way she had lied to him.

And yet he had let himself love her.

Bran ap Madog, bastard, was no longer a great lord with land and people to command. So be it. He had longed for a son to carry on his name and give him a sense of belonging. What had that impossible dream gotten him?

He held nothing but his good name, now tarnished by rumor and false accusation. He had done nothing wrong. That angered him too. Just as Catrin had played him false so had someone else, the real culprit in this whole filthy matter —the true murderer of noble father and son.

The smells of the sea drifted on the chilled breeze long before Bran came to the end of the road. He topped a small rising, the sand beneath the horse's hooves giving way. Stretched out before him, vast and gray, was the Irish Sea. White capped waves crashed against the sandy beach of the Welsh coastline, reminding Bran of his supposed wife. Full of power and passion, like a wave breaking and tumbling to the beach. One minute she could be fiery. The next minute, like the wave unrolling peacefully along the sand, she was calm and loving.

Nay! He would not think of her like that. He would not think of her at all. She didn't love him. Else, how could she have deceived him so?

He must think only on how to remedy his troubles. For all he had now was his life. And his name. As it had always been and always would be.

Bran reined the horse around and set out at a canter for Rhuddlan and the king. If nothing else, when he cleared his name, he would find out who had actually killed John and Gilbert Fitzalan, the Lords Rothmore.

CHAPTER THIRTY-TWO

"Catrin!"

Oblivious to everything, her mind in a stupor, Catrin heard her name shouted in alarm, and jerked her head up from staring at the muddy road she traveled on foot. A troop of the king's men galloped toward her. She froze. Sir Otto!

Before the first rider reached her, someone grabbed her arm and yanked her out of the path. She hit the ground with a hard *thwack*. The mounted knights and yeoman dashed past, not even sparing them a glance.

"Are you hurt?" a high-pitched boy's voice asked.

Catrin fumbled to right herself amid the jumble of skirts and her long, concealing cape. She managed to sit upright and found herself staring straight into the worried eyes of her half-brother.

"Richard! What are you doing here?"

"I'm going to see the king," he said, scrambling to his feet. "What are you doing here?"

"I'm going to see the queen."

"You can't." Richard shook his head no, his manner grave. "She is in confinement in Caernarfon Castle."

Catrin's stomach sank. Queen Eleanor awaited the birth of her baby away from the rigors of court life. Relaxing back on the heels of her hands, her arms supporting her, Catrin gazed up at Richard. What was she to do now? Eleanor liked her. She would have listened and understood.

Foreshadowing the gentlemanly knight he was to become, Richard extended his hand. Catrin grasped it and let him pull her to her feet. She dusted off her skirts, giving herself time to think.

"How did you get here? We heard Sir Otto went to arrest Bran."

"That was Sir Otto who passed," Catrin told him. "I helped Bran escape. He, too, means to go to the king. And Sir Otto means to find him."

Catrin fought hard to mask her ever-increasing fear. This time, she was sure Sir Otto would bind Bran with chains so he couldn't escape.

In a daze still, she turned and started toward the castle.

"This way!" Richard grabbed her hand and tugged her off the road. "'Tis safer to go through the fields and the back ways. You'll be found out if you travel the main road."

He was right, of course. Catrin let Richard lead her, content for the moment to relinquish control and let someone else be in charge.

As they walked, she thought back to this morning when Bran's eyes had gone blank. She shuddered at the memory. Did he hate her now? Of course he did.

When Bran had departed, the walls of the tiny cottage had quickly closed in on her as if they moved by a force of evil. Catrin had fought her rising panic, knowing she could no longer abide there. Collecting her cloak from a wooden peg, she had flung the garment over her shoulders and lifted the hood to provide protection against the wind and hide her identity.

Having seen Bran ride toward the coast, she set out in the opposite direction, mindlessly picking her way along the rutted road toward Rhuddlan oblivious to the few passersby.

That was, until Richard miraculously saved her life. She blinked, clearing her vision, and looked down at the serious, would-be warrior who marched along with her in tow.

What had moved Richard to be so bold?

"Why do you go to the king?" she asked.

"Because Mother and Lord Leighton mean to have an audience with Edward about me. They want to take me from Sir Bran. I'll have no say in the matter." He looked at her, a defiant glint in his eye. "I am Lord Rothmore now. I should be able to choose where I live, no matter what they say Sir Bran has done." He dropped his gaze. "I dislike this man my mother plans to marry."

"I dislike him too," Catrin acknowledged, glancing up at the opaque sky. "Since he brought father's body home, I've thought Guy de Hastings, Lord Leighton, to be a conniving knave."

Richard stopped. "You told Mother that, but she did not believe you, did she?"

Anger seized Catrin once more. "I think Leighton is behind Gilbert's death, and I don't trust his word about how Father died." She let out a sigh and glanced away. "Yet I have no proof."

"I don't like the way he controls my mother," Richard said with a frown. "She's so foolish about him that she does whatever he says. That is why she came for me at North-bridge. Lord Leighton told her to do so."

Catrin bit her tongue. In her mind, Isadora was just as culpable as Guy. They were in this together. Old enmity died hard, especially one born of childhood fear and sadness. Yet she didn't tell her thoughts to Richard. After all, Isadora was his mother. Catrin had never known hers but understood how a child loved his own mother—even a malicious, spite-ful, domineering woman such as Isadora.

"Leighton made one of his servants travel with us from Shrewsbury," Richard revealed. "A lackey called Harry with an ugly scar upon his cheek. He didn't like me much. I had seen him in Northbridge, and he remembered me."

Harry! Harry was the name she'd heard from her hiding place in the underbrush after the ambush. Was it true this particular Harry, Lord Leighton's man, was at the castle and disappeared after she'd been wounded? Catrin breathed deeply, trying to tamp down her elation. She only knew the voice she had heard when in hiding. How would she ever prove this was the same man?

She turned to Richard. "How did you escape?"

He shrugged. "Lord Leighton arrived and started arguing with Mother. I simply left the tent. No one noticed."

"Can you take me close enough to this lackey of Lord Leighton's without us being seen?" she asked. "Someone named Harry murdered Gwendolyn. If I heard his voice once more, I would know him."

Richard grinned, enjoying the challenge. "Follow me!"

He led her behind cottages, along fencerows, and through fields. They crossed the river above the castle and came back toward the tent city that had been erected nearby. For all his bookish ways and frail appearance,

Richard was more resourceful than Catrin had ever
guessed.

Nearing the pavilion that flew the red and gold pennants
of the Rothmore earldom, Richard suggested they crouch
low. They dashed from tree to tree, bush to bush, much as
children playing games. He lifted an index finger to his lips,
urging her to be quiet.

Catrin couldn't help the smile that tweaked the corners
of her mouth. Her brother was so full of self-importance at
the moment. But this wasn't a game. She nodded, drawing
her eyebrows together, and silently followed the young earl
to a stack of chopped wood behind the tent.

They waited, smelling wood smoke and listening to the
guttural banter of the men huddled by a campfire. Catrin's
nerves tingled with fear and anticipation. Finally her legs
began to cramp from squatting. Just when she thought she
could endure no more, Catrin heard a man curse and shout
"Harry!"

Two men approached their hiding place. Catrin ducked
lower, thoughts of the pain in her legs vanishing. Could they
hear her thudding heartbeat?

"You bastard!" A hand slapped flesh. "You told me the
Fitzalan wench was dead!"

"My lord, I thought she was."

Was that Harry's voice? On pins and needles now, Catrin
strained to hear.

"Lady Rothmore tells me she lives and is posing as
Olwen de Belleme, wife to Bran ap Madog," Guy barked.
"You lied to me, Harry."

"Those men you hired told me she was dead."

Catrin heard the frantic breathlessness in the second
man's voice.

"You lie. Didn't you tell me you'd seen her body?"

Catrin and Richard exchanged meaningful looks. She clenched her hand in triumph. 'Twas validation to learn Guy had been behind the attack on the road to Clun. If he tried to kill her, then it stood to reason he had slain her brother after the tourney, throwing suspicion on the King's Raven by starting false rumors.

Why? What had possessed him to do murder so foul? She frowned, knowing his misguided motives were of little matter.

"Find Bran," Catrin mouthed the words to her brother. "Tell him what we've heard."

Richard nodded, eagerness burning bright in his wide eyes. He stole backward and then turned and slipped away. Catrin watched until he disappeared behind another tent. After a moment, she looked back, hoping to hear what more was being said.

Suddenly, gritty-tasting fingers closed around her mouth and a sinewy arm clamped around her chest. She was jerked to her feet. Her hood fell back. Hot breath, reeking of rotting teeth and the stench of onions, hit her face.

"What do we have here?" her captor guffawed in her ear.

Catrin struggled against him. Searing, all-encompassing fear engulfed her. She had fought like this once. That night so long ago, she'd resisted her attacker, thrashing in the same way, fighting against him.

But that black-cloaked man had been Bran. Something had happened that night. A mighty force was unleashed between them, connecting them, binding them. At that time, she could never envision what was to come.

This was different. Her attacker was one of Guy's

minions. She didn't need any fortunetelling gifts to know the outcome of this fight would be much, much different.

"My lord!" Holding her around the waist, the man lifted her up. Her legs kicked in the air, and Guy's man dropped her. Lifting her again and again, he lugged her around the side of the tent. "I caught a spy!"

When the man's hand slipped from Catrin's mouth, she let out a bloodcurdling scream.

Two men ran toward them. One was Lord Leighton, his eyes flashing. He backhanded Catrin across the mouth. "Shut up, you troublesome bitch!"

Her head wrenched sideways. She tasted blood. *Bastard.* She was the daughter of the Earl of Rothmore. He couldn't do this to her.

Shaking her head to clear it, Catrin righted herself and glared up at Guy de Hastings, Lord Leighton...her enemy.

"Murderer," she said softly, making the word sound like a curse.

He laughed in her face. "Ah, you *have* been spying on us." Guy turned to the other man. "Harry, this is the woman you were supposed to kill."

"Why did you kill my brother," Catrin cried. "And my father?"

"You assume much, my lady." Guy gloated giving her a mocking bow.

"I have no use for liars and murderers," she spat.

Guy brought his hand up to his chin, making play at studying her. "I don't know why I failed to discover your true identity at Northbridge," he mused. "How could I miss the common Fitzalan resemblance, the sharp chin and the beady eyes?"

Catrin lifted that sharp chin. "Because you thought me dead," she replied through gritted teeth.

Harry shifted from foot to foot, glancing around uneasily. "What do we do with her now, my lord?"

Guy cocked his head and took his time to study the situation. Then he turned to the much-maligned servant. "Harry, I expect you now must kill her." He grinned evilly but with a pointed stare at the man. "This time, for good, if you value your life."

"My pleasure, my lord."

'Twas like a dream at night, full of wild imaginings and horrible scenes where one twisted and turned in sleep. Harry's triumphant face reeled before Catrin's eyes. She felt faint and sick.

At that moment, Isadora rushed from the tent, wringing her hands like a comic version of a frantic mother. "Guy, Richard has disappeared! I heard a scream, and when I looked for him, he was missing!"

Her stepmother faltered when she saw Catrin restrained by one of Guy's men. She turned a questioning gaze to her lover. "What is she doing here?"

Catrin squared her shoulders, still proud and defiant. "I'm looking for Gilbert's murderer." Guy signaled his man to cover her mouth once more. The filthy hand made her gag, and she strained against its confinement.

"Lady Fitzalan is the reason your son has run away, my sweet," Guy declared, oozing smugness as if to gain favor. "Why else would she be here, ready to play tricks upon you as she did upon the king?"

Isadora marched up to Catrin and wagged a finger. "What have you done with Richard?"

Catrin glared at her stepmother. Why couldn't she see

the evil in this man? Did she not know about his crimes? Why did Isadora adhere to his greedy and evil plans?

"Let her speak," Isadora ordered, glancing back at Guy.

Guy put his arm around Isadora. "My lady, I think it best Harry and Miles find out what we want to know."

"Shouldn't we take her when we see the king?" Isadora asked. "She'll give us proof Bran ap Madog is a murderer."

If only they would take her to Edward! Catrin would offer proof and much more.

"My men will bring her later after we have had a chance to talk to the king first. Now go back inside, my dear, and finish your toilette. I'll be along shortly." Guy urged Isadora back inside her tent. Once she was out of sight, he jerked his head at the two men holding Catrin. "Take her away! And this time, finish your task."

Guy would not let her live long enough to talk to the king. Or anyone else. Catrin had no hope now of saving Bran from his ill fate, a fate made unavoidable when her good intentions had gone so terribly awry.

CHAPTER THIRTY-THREE

The powerful hooves of the black stallion pounded the road toward Rhuddlan. Bran felt the strong equine muscles move between his legs as he urged the horse faster and faster. He was hardly aware of Richard riding pillion behind him. The boy's thin arms encircled Bran's waist and his cheek pressed against his surcoat and mail hauberk.

Catrin awaited them at the Rothmore pavilion with evidence of his innocence. How strange. He could scarce think of the woman he had wed as Catrin. Richard openly called her by her real name now, although at Northbridge he had called her 'Olwen.' Even then the boy had known her identity. She was his half-sister, after all.

"You must forgive her," Richard had pleaded, running a hand over his close-cropped hair. "She only wanted to help Olwen and find Gilbert's murderer."

Bran reserved judgment. He had already heard Catrin's story and was not sure he had it in him to forgive her.

The rocking movement of the horse jarred Bran's body and blurred his vision. Seen through the sights of his visor, the road ahead was oddly straight. 'Twas as if there was only one path to take—no deviation from his purpose to vindicate himself and bring Guy de Hastings to justice.

Yet he wore no blinders. He knew the victories in life were not so easily won. Life was full of starts and stops, twists and turns, mountains and valleys. One must make the best of what life dealt.

With Catrin's testimony, Bran now had the power to clear his name. The irony was not lost on him. Catrin Fitzalan, in part, created his trouble when she falsely married him.

Thinking her Olwen, he had been prepared to accept her as his wife. How did he know he would grow to love her?

As Taran's hooves ate up the ground, Bran pictured her face contorted in agony from the arrow wound and later pale from infection. He saw her head thrown back in laughter and heard her soothing voice as she read to Richard. Once more, he felt her hair clutched between his fingers and her legs wrapped around his hips. He heard her cry out when he held her in his arms and then shudder with satisfaction.

Catrin had risked her life to help him escape from Sir Otto. *'Tis time for you to merely watch and wait and to put your trust in me*, she had said to him. He had believed in her then, and she had not let him down.

Perchance she still was not letting him down. She had told him the truth, hadn't she? She loved him enough to risk his hatred and to forewarn him so he would not walk into a trap.

Did she have any idea how valiant she was?

"There's the tent!" Richard yelled in his ear.

Bran slowed the horse, and they approached the Rothmore pavilion at a brisk walk. Taran blew hard and bobbed his head, prancing and begging for another run. The servants recognized Richard riding behind the black knight. Drawing together and chattering among themselves, they stared as Bran guided the horse through them and around the back of the tent.

"Catrin!" Bran called out, tasting her true name for the first time upon his lips.

"She was there." Richard pointed toward the woodpile. "Now she's gone."

The first inkling of fear crept through Bran. He returned to the front of the pavilion, and a groom came to stand at the horse's head.

"I'll find my mother." Richard slid from the saddle and dashed inside the tent.

Trying to curb his impatience, Bran forced himself to relax in the saddle. He felt like Taran, who was champing at his bit.

"Sir Bran, they're gone!" Richard rushed out of the tent. "My mother's maid Kate was huddling in the corner. She said my mother and Lord Leighton have gone to see the king."

Bran looked down, resting his forearm on the high-peaked pommel of the saddle. "What happened to Catrin?"

"Kate was going to the latrine when she saw Harry, the one I told you about, and another Leighton man drag Catrin toward the forest. Yonder." Richard turned and pointed.

Bran's apprehension grew. "Catrin did not go willingly?"

Richard flushed white from his own fear. "The maid said the men held her captive." He gulped a breath. "Sir, Kate would not lie. She hates Lord Leighton too. She's very scared."

"Stay here." Bran's stomach clenched and his grip tightened on the reins. "I'll go after her." He jerked the horse's head around. The groom jumped sideways just as Bran dug his spurs into Taran's sides. The big black leaped forward into a full gallop.

How dare Leighton harm his wife? The man was more bastard than he, for all his fine upbringing and lineage. Since that time in France when Bran had bested him at a tourney, Guy de Hastings had loathed him. If that were his motive, then the man surely was a spineless fool.

As Bran rode, something inside him altered. Fear now mixed with fury. Catrin was in danger. Clearing his name no longer held any import. All he thought about was Catrin, the woman he had claimed as his. He would get her back.

Or he'd die trying.

THE TWO MEN stopped long enough to bind Catrin's hands behind her back and gag her mouth with a foul rag. Harry stole the jasper brooch and hid it in his clothes, and then he stripped Catrin of her fine fur cloak and concealed it under a log.

"I'll return for that later," he told the other man.

"Let's pleasure ourselves." Harry's companion smirked and ran his grubby hand roughly up and down Catrin's arm, licking his chops like the cur he was.

"Nay, we must kill her quickly."

"Stab her here and leave her body for the wolves."

Harry's eyes narrowed as he studied Catrin. She shot back an irate glare, vainly kicking out at him with her riding boot.

"Stabbing is too good for the likes of her. She's evaded me twice." Harry rubbed his chin. "I have always been partial to drowning."

Both men chuckled, sending chills down Catrin's spine. Harry's fingers bit into her arm. She winced. They laughed again and jerked her forward, forcing her to walk between them along a rocky path.

If only Bran would come. Sadly, if Richard found him, he might not want to save her. She had shattered his hard-won trust, betraying him in the worst way by denying him his dream of land and power. Glancing at the gray sky threatening snow, she felt death near.

Yet there were worse things than death. Loss of loved ones. Loss of honor. She was not afraid to die for what she believed. She knew full well if given the chance, she would again switch places with Olwen. She would marry the King's Raven once more to save her cousin.

Nevertheless, regret filled her soul. She would die without wiping away the look of empty disappointment from Bran's eyes and without telling him of her love.

The first flake of snow touched her nose. She lowered her head, and the tiny bits of cold hit her lashes. Bran. She loved him with all her heart. Silently, she told him of her love. Silently, she willed him to find her and make everything right. Her mind swirled with a longing so deep and poignant it threatened to overcome her ability to concentrate. She stumbled.

"Bitch!" Harry wrenched her arm, and pain knifed through her.

They kept walking. Her wrists grew numb. Her mind grew blank except for the words *Bran, I need you* that she repeated over and over silently.

When they broke the cover of the oak and ash, they headed directly toward the riverbank. The walls of the Edward's towers stood in the distance, but they were alone in this clearing. No one stirred. 'Twas a secluded place for murder. Her body would wash down the river and sweep into the cold, churning waters of the sea. Catrin shivered, but not from the cold.

Suddenly, the ground shook with the thunder of galloping hooves approaching fast from the direction of the castle. Catrin heard the chink of armor and the heavy breathing of a straining destrier. She jerked up her head.

Bran! She fought to cry his name, but the gag prevented it. Hope and horror filled her. The black knight in full battle charge was a terrible sight.

Both of her captors were common lackeys in the employ of Lord Leighton. Catrin knew without horses or proper mail and carrying only short swords, they were at a great disadvantage against a mounted knight. The men knew it too. The second man dropped her arm and bolted for the cover of the trees.

Bran veered from his course and bore down on the fleeing man. He was virtually standing in his stirrups. With his mighty war sword raised high above his head, its blade burnished like a mirror, Bran swung from his hips with a great sweeping motion and sheared off the villain's arm with one powerful stroke. Blood spewed from the wound. The man screamed in death agony and fell to his knees.

The shock of the blow didn't unseat Bran. He yanked Taran around in full stride and spurred the horse once more toward them, descending upon Catrin and her captor like an avenging angel.

Harry was wiser. He stepped behind Catrin, pulling her

hard against his chest with one arm and held the blade of his sword to her throat.

"Frightened, my lady?"

Catrin squirmed in his grasp. Surely, he could feel her fear. She bent her knee and kicked back at his leg with her heel. She found her mark.

"Bitch," he growled, jerking her against his chest and knocking breath from her lungs.

Kill me, she wanted to cry out. *Go ahead. Then Bran will certainly kill you.*

Taran, his sides heaving and his nostrils flaring, skidded to a stop in front of them. Bran sat immobile on the stallion's back. Watching. Waiting. The silence was profound.

"I will kill her," Harry swore, his grip on Catrin growing tighter.

"You hide behind a woman's skirts?"

Harry answered the quiet taunt with an insult of his own. "If I had my longbow, you'd be dead where you sit in the saddle."

"I have seen your marksmanship," Bran snarled, his voice sounding far away behind the visor of his great helm. "Your aim is not true. You seem to prefer a knife in the back to honorable combat."

"Spoken like a true bastard."

Catrin swallowed when she heard Harry's slur. She remembered full well how important Bran's name was to him.

Keeping his body rigid and controlled, Bran pointed his bloody sword at them. "Let my wife go, and I'll let you live."

Catrin stared at Bran in disbelief. He had called her his wife. She longed to see behind the obscuring visor of his great helm. To read what was in his eyes. Did he really consider her his wife? Or was that a slip of the tongue?

"You dare not fight me fair," Harry goaded. "You, who call me coward are no better, Welshman."

Deliberately, Bran sheathed the huge war sword in the scabbard tied to his saddle. "You deserve no respect, Saxon, for you stab men in the back and shoot women from afar. Yet I will fight you any way you want."

In one swift movement, Bran swung his leg over the pommel of the saddle and dropped to the ground. Even wearing mail, he was agile and quick. Stepping away from Taran, he drew from his belt his shorter arming sword. "Now fight me on the ground, if you dare."

Harry cursed under his breath. He gave Catrin a rough shove, sending her sprawling toward Bran, who lowered his guard to keep her from falling. He caught her in his arms. At that moment, Harry struck, springing forward with his sword high over his head.

Bran shoved Catrin aside. She fell like a sack of grain. When she looked up from the frozen ground, she realized Harry's first blow could have split her skull in two. Instead, Bran was nimble and swift enough to counter his attacker's move. Now the two men were locked in a deadly battle. Their grunts and the sounds of their clashing swords spoiled the pristine winter tranquility.

Catrin rolled over on her side, her hands still bound behind her back, and propped herself up on an elbow. Breath rushed through her lungs. Fear clouded her vision. Watching the man she loved in deadly combat, she fought back tears and sent a quick prayer skyward, promising penance if he won.

In a quick move, Bran leapt aside, turned and slashed

downward with his flat-bladed sword. Harry deflected the blow with his weapon and whipped around to strike again. Bran ducked out of the way, regaining his stance, and turned to confront his opponent. Harry rushed forward. Bran raised his sword. Swinging from the shoulder, his arm and weapon straight, Bran hacked his blade downward.

The blow caught Harry above the collarbone. The man screamed as he fell forward, blood gushing from the death wound in his neck.

Catrin jerked her eyes away from the grisly scene. Silence returned. Except for Bran's heavy breathing, all was quiet.

"That's for killing Rhys," Bran said softly. "And for wounding Catrin."

He called her by her real name! She turned to look at him, and her heart did a gradual roll, disbelief flooding her. Bran slowly walked to where she lay. He stood over her much as he had stood over the dead man, his surcoat marked with blood, his arming sword now pointing down by his side. His visor masked his face and eyes. He remained fearsome, tall and majestic.

Bending down on one knee beside her, he placed his sword flat on the ground. Then he reached toward her and gently lowered the gag from her mouth.

"Thank you." She gazed upon his visor. "You saved my life."

Wordlessly, he leaned across her and untied her hands bound behind her back. Catrin shook them free, feeling the tingle of blood rushing once more through her fingers. He stood and offered his hand. She accepted it, and he gingerly pulled her to her feet.

They faced each other in silence. What was Bran thinking? He had battled for her, much like one of King Arthur's legendary knights. Had he also forgiven her? She cried out silently for answers. Would he not raise his visor so she could at least discern something from the look in his eyes?

Suddenly the hush was broken by the deep, throaty *kraa* of ravens circling overhead. *Scavengers. Birds of death.* Catrin's skin crawled, and she turned her face away from Bran, sickened with sadness and despair.

"They will not hurt you, my lady." His words of assurance were muffled behind his visor.

"Only those you love have the power to hurt you," she murmured, unable to look at him.

"I had once thought the only thing important to me was a land and property. A son to carry on my name, mayhap."

Catrin dared glance at him. Bran had removed his helm and stood with it under his arm. He had also pushed back his mail coif and padded cap so that she could see his black hair plastered to his scalp. His face was smeared with grit. Yet his eyes were bright and fierce with passion.

"I am sorry I have ruined your dream for you."

"I am like the raven." Bran turned his gaze to the black birds silhouetted against the gray sky.

Catrin held her breath. What did he mean?

"When ravens choose their mates," he said tenderly, now taking a step toward her, "they do so for life."

Catrin swallowed, mesmerized by the idea. Bran placed his helm on the ground beside his sword. Then, lifting a gloved hand to her cheek, he stroked it tenderly.

"*Cariad*," he whispered. "When we said our vows, I chose you as my wife, my helpmate. I would gladly become a poor knight again if you will remain my wife now and forever."

She pressed her cheek against his hand, feeling its warmth and strength. "My lord, are you serious?"

"Aye, Catrin. I have never been more serious in my life."

Suspended in the moment, she accepted the love vibrating between them. "Oh, Bran," she said, sighing. "You *are* my white knight."

He threw back his head and laughed. "You fill your head with too much romance, *cariad*."

Did he know her so well? She smiled up at him, suddenly shy. "You would do well to learn more of courtly love."

"Why? I have all the love I want here. I need go nowhere else."

He kissed her then, full on the lips, his hands on her waist, pulling her close to him as if he would never let her go.

Catrin took his beard-roughened cheeks between her hands, forcing him to look at her. "I will be with you," she promised, "through the good times and the bad. Forever."

"I can ask for nothing more, my dear wife. I love you."

"And I you."

Suddenly, the clank of mail, the shouts of men, and the thud of horses' hooves reverberated down the valley. Catrin caught her breath.

"Sir Otto," Bran muttered without glancing over his shoulder.

"Run!" she urged, knowing he would not.

He shook his head. "'Tis time for justice to be served."

Together, they turned to face the oncoming troop. Bran's hand closed around hers, and Catrin knew his love would always protect her.

CHAPTER THIRTY-FOUR

Icy tendrils of fear wound around Catrin's heart. She breathed deeply and paused, looking up to Bran, who stood by her side at the entrance to the great hall. He took her hand in his gloved one, holding hers fast, offering his support. But no matter. The cold leather of Bran's glove provided little comfort.

"Go, sirrah!" Sir Otto prodded Bran with the tip of his sword. "Your king awaits."

And your judgment. Catrin knew what faced them. King Edward would not be happy. But would he understand? She feared her guilt was assured with no witness to testify to Guy's treachery. Bran had slain the hapless Harry. Perchance he had made a grave mistake, for there was no one to speak for them.

Bran squeezed her hand for reassurance before he dropped it then stepped forward into the crowded hall. Catrin kept pace beside him, joined together in whatever transpired.

Curiosity and hostility hung heavily in the air. The

bejeweled and well-dressed noblemen and women, parting in front of them, murmured in recognition and then fell silent. Heads held high, Bran and Catrin walked the straight path toward the dais and throne where Edward, King of England, Lord of Ireland, and Duke of Aquitaine sat waiting.

"I see reports of your death were highly exaggerated, Lady Catrin," Edward spoke as she and Bran knelt before his presence.

Catrin kept her gaze direct, ne'er flinching, longing for the smile and friendly face of Queen Eleanor. Instead, she faced the forbidding stare of her monarch. "Aye, your grace. I am very much alive. The outlaws killed my dear maid when my company was attacked on the road to Clun. Because of her quick thinking, I escaped and found my way to Northbridge Castle."

Edward motioned with his hand, and Catrin rose. Lady Rothmore, her stepmother, and Lord Leighton stood by the side of the dais. Catrin sensed their fear, but also Guy's audacity as if his nefarious plans were nearing a satisfying conclusion. Nay! Not if she could help it. Not while there was breath in her body.

"And where is Olwen de Belleme, the lady of Northbridge?"

"At the nunnery of the White Ladies, if it so please your grace."

"It does not please me. None of this knavery pleases me." Edward stood, peering down from the dais. "Rise, Sir Bran, and acquit yourself."

Bran climbed to his feet, lifting his chin valiantly like the brave knight he was. "Sire, I have done my duty to you and yours, as requested. I have married, as you graciously gave me leave, and tended to the people and lands of Northbridge."

"Yet it appears you took holy vows with the wrong cousin."

A murmur of disbelief rumbled through those in attendance. Tension seethed throughout the great hall. Catrin felt the pressure of it, the stress of condemnation and conviction.

"Your grace, Sir Bran is not at fault." Catrin swallowed hard her dread, raising her voice high to speak for the man she loved. "'Twas my idea to dupe your humble servant. He knew nothing of my charade."

"You say he believed you to be Olwen de Belleme?"

"Aye, sire." For once, Catrin lowered her eyes, hoping to humble herself before her king.

"For what purpose did you play me false, my lady?"

"I chose this manner to seek out those who murdered my father and brother."

"Your father was killed in combat."

"So says Lord Leighton." Catrin turned her eyes toward her stepmother's lover. "I had no reason to believe the sole word of our neighbor. He has oft coveted Rothmore lands."

Edward's eyes narrowed. "Hearsay at best. What proof have you?"

"None, your grace. Yet today I overheard Lord Leighton admit to sending cutthroats to murder me."

Guy de Hastings stepped forward. "Lie!"

Edward inclined his head at the nobleman to silence him. "Once again, your word against one of my trusted lords," he said to Catrin.

Her head spun. Isadora knew nothing of the truth. Richard had heard the same conversation, but he was not here. She was loath to single out her brother, for his life might be in jeopardy if this audience with the king did not go well. She could not trust her stepmother to protect her son from Leighton.

"The two men who attacked me on the road to Clun are dead." Catrin was forced to admit.

"Slain by Bran ap Madog," Lord Leighton charged, his voice high-pitched.

Bran stepped forward as if to attack his accuser. Catrin's hand stayed him, then she squared her shoulders and spoke proudly, "My husband saved my life."

The assembled noble men and ladies whispered their shock when they heard Catrin claim to be Bran's wife.

"And so we return to the problem at hand," Edward said. "Your treachery to the crown."

In a quiet, penitent voice, Catrin explained her reasoning for sending Olwen away and taking her place to gain the confidence of the man she considered the murderer of her brother and father. She was careful to leave out Olwen's shyness, for no one need know her cousin's fear of bedding the King's Raven. Catrin was careful to lay full blame upon herself.

"I thought, at first, Sir Bran had plotted to destroy my family. Married to him, I soon saw a different side of the king's knight. Bran was kind, but firm, generous to those at Northbridge. He could not have murdered my family." Catrin turned toward Isadora and her lover. "It was Lord Leighton, your grace. He plans to wed my stepmother. You see, with all of us gone, and Lady Rothmore under his thumb, he controls the Rothmore lands until my brother Richard is of age. And now I fear even more for his life."

Hearing her words, Isadora gasped. "You lie! A vicious lie! My stepdaughter has always hated me!"

"Enough!" King Edward's cry silenced them. He turned to Bran. "What say you, Bran ap Madog? You have served me faithfully, as many here. Tell me why I should not punish you and this woman?"

Bran straightened his stance. He was a proud man, Catrin knew. She had put him in this place when all he had wanted was a family of his own, when all he'd given her was his love and trust. Aching for him, she stood quietly. What more could she do for the man she loved?

"You must punish me, your grace," Bran said. "I have failed you. Yet you must not rebuke Lady Catrin. What she has done comes from a good heart and from devotion and loyalty to her family. She is the woman I love. I will gladly become a poor knight again, if you will spare my wife and reprimand me."

King Edward took his seat, gripping the arms of his throne. "You have presented me with a difficult problem, Sir Raven. I am not wont to let perfidy go unpunished."

"Then punish the one who has truly betrayed you!" A small voice resounded through the hushed crowd. "Make way! Let me by! I will speak to the king."

The crowd parted opening a tiny path for a slight, frail boy. Richard, the current Lord Rothmore, strode through the throng, his flowing black robes flapping with each stride.

"Richard!" His mother took a step toward him, but Lord Leighton was faster. He drew a blade and rushed the approaching child.

Bran sprang into action, catching the schemer's wrist and shaking the knife free. Sir Otto's men joined in the fight.

In a blink of an eye, they had captured both men, bound them, and brought them to stand before the king.

Edward's expression did not change. It remained hard, unforgiving. "I grow tired of this drama," he said. "Guy de Hastings, your actions have proven your guilt. Sir Otto, take him away to await his trial." He waved his hand, and the hapless Lord Leighton was paraded from the great hall to the jeers of the crowd.

Catrin moved forward to stand beside her husband. Together they awaited the king's pleasure.

Seeing her overture of support, Edward's eyes soften. "For the rest of you, the crown will decide your fate," he said, hiding a smile. "If I can untangle this scandalous web you've woven."

EPILOGUE

Bran entered the solar of his own castle to find his wife asleep. The new babe Richard was swaddled and slept as soundly as his mother in a cradle near the lord of the manor's bed.

How oddly things had turned out. Leighton had been tried for murder, found guilty, and executed. Ironically, Edward had given Bran the Leighton lands in reparation for de Hasting's offenses against him. Moreover, in his wisdom, Edward had pardoned Catrin. Hearing the news, Catrin, already with child, had insisted they remarry, so they would be truly wed in the eyes of the Church. The king had gladly blessed their true union.

As for Isadora, Edward had banished her to a convent for the sin of lust. Catrin had expressed the belief it was more likely her stepmother's failing had been that of naiveté. The silly woman had trusted Guy de Hastings, falling in love with him as well as into his evil trap. Although Isadora claimed she'd no knowledge of her lover's crimes, she had plotted with Leighton to take her son from Bran's care.

Richard, Lord Rothmore, was once more in Bran's protection and guardianship until he came of age. He thrived with them, taking on his early military training as eagerly as he embraced his studies.

Standing inside the solar door, Bran offered a silent prayer of thanks. Everything he wanted was right here—his wife, his child, and a sense of belonging, because of the woman who now stirred in bed and glanced up at him. Bran strode to her side, bursting with love. He smiled as he took her hand.

"*Cariad,*" she whispered.

He brought her fingers up to his lips to kiss, aware of the irony of her endearment. "I have news," he said softly with a backward glance at the sleeping babe.

Catrin propped herself up on an elbow. "Sit. Tell me."

Bran joined her, sitting on the side of the lord's great bed. She was so lovely, as beautiful as the first day he laid eyes upon her in the pathway. "Waryn de Grey soon returns from duty in Gascony."

Catrin scooted to prop herself against the headboard. "Then my cousin's fate is at hand."

"Seems so," Bran acknowledged. Olwen de Belleme had not been spared the king's directives. At that moment, she remained closeted at the nunnery but was to be wed as soon as her betrothed collected her from her sanctuary.

"I hope she will be as happy as we." Catrin touched his shaven face.

"Aye, for we are happy."

Catrin smiled her response and gave him a small nod as an obedient wife. "If it pleases you, my lord."

He laughed, feeling his throat grow thick with adoration.

"You know full well it pleases me. I am content with you, *Cariad*. You and our child. Forever."

THE END

ABOUT THE AUTHOR

,Whether it is the Bluegrass of Kentucky, the mountains of Montana, or Medieval England, Jan Scarbrough brings you home with romances from the heart.

Jan Scarbrough is the author of two popular Bluegrass series, writing heartwarming contemporary romances about home and family, single moms and children. Living in the horse country of Kentucky makes it easy for Jan to add small town, Southern charm to her books and the excitement of a Bluegrass horse race or a competitive horse show.

Leaving her contemporary voice behind, Jan has written paranormal gothic romances: Tangled Memories, a Romance Writers of America (RWA) Golden Heart finalist, and Timeless. Her medieval romance, My Lord Raven is a story of honor and betrayal.

A member of Novelist, Inc., Jan self-publishes her books with the help of her husband. She has published 26 romances.

Jan lives in Louisville, Kentucky, with one rescued dog, two rescued cats, and a husband she rescued 24 years ago.

When she isn't writing, she loves to ride American Saddlebred horses, drive grandchildren to activities, and volunteer with Alley Cat Advocates. There is nothing she enjoys more than curling up with a good book.

Subscribe to Jan's monthly newsletter and receive a free eBook.https://janscarbrough.com

READ AN EXCERPT OF TANGLED MEMORIES

Present Day

His eyes were gray. I had never noticed before. They weren't the color of slate but smoky and mysterious.

Swallowing a hard knot of dread that surfaced in my throat, I walked down the silent aisle toward him. Chin held high, very lady-like in posture and demeanor, a trace of smile upon my lips—I was the picture of confidence.

Inside, I trembled.

I stopped in front of the altar. A cloying scent of gardenias assaulted my senses. How curious the delicate white flowers in my bouquet should be so overpowering. Just like the man beside me. Just like the deep, heady gray of his eyes.

I extended my hand. He took it, and I drew a breath and held it. The firmness of his fingers surprised me.

"Friends." The minister glanced up at us and smiled. "We are gathered together in the sight of God to witness and bless the joining together of Mary and Alexander in Christian marriage."

Alex was tall, so tall I had to look up to connect with those mesmerizing eyes. I was aware of my breathing, erratic and shallow. I'd married for the second time in my life and, once again, my reasons were more practical than romantic.

How even more ironic was the Methodist minister's white stole, a symbol of purity and love. I felt neither pure nor in love. His black robes better matched my somber mood.

"I ask you now," Reverend Watts continued, "in the presence of God and these people, to declare your intention to enter into a union with one another."

To enter into a union.

Heaven help me. Would it be a union? How could it be? Our union was a business arrangement, plain and simple. I understood that. For some reason though, sadness settled around my heart.

Reverend Watts looked at me. "Mary, will you have Alexander to be your husband to live together in holy marriage? Will you love him, comfort him, honor and keep him, in sickness and in health, and forsaking all others, be faithful to him as long as you both shall live?"

Alex's penetrating gaze burned upon my upturned face. "I will," I said at last.

"Alexander, will you have Mary to be your wife?"

From underneath my lashes, I watched him. He wore his black hair swept back and long, curling at his neck. A stray lock touched his forehead and set off his eyes. His high cheekbones and jawline gave him a classic look. His lips were full and inviting. Enigmatic in his formal black tuxedo, crisp white shirt, and bow tie, he seemed a brooding Byronic hero. Handsome, though austere, his masculine good looks belonged to another century or, at least, on the cover of a romantic novel.

How different would my life have been if I hadn't become pregnant my freshman year in college...if I hadn't married Bill...if I hadn't miscarried? What if I had met Alexander Dominican under different circumstances, before life touched me so cruelly?

"I will." His deep voice resonated throughout the empty chapel.

Turning from the minister to me, Alex's eyes brightened as his gaze captured mine. Out of habit, I licked my lips, but nothing eased my tension. The strain I felt surely communicated to the self-assured man who held my hand. Did he feel the hypocrisy of our oath? Or was he simply satisfied with a marriage of convenience?

Daring him with my stare, I narrowed my own eyes in challenge to his casual acceptance of our deceit before God. His black brow lifted to meet my taunt. He cocked his head as if to tell me I could yet back out. I could walk away a single woman. Poor, but single.

I shifted my gaze, unable to continue our silent joust. He

knew full well I couldn't back out. Bill's death had made my current situation untenable.

"Let us pray. Eternal God, creator and preserver of all life."

I bowed my head but couldn't shut my eyes. My dilemma didn't seem right. Nothing seemed right these last few weeks. Not since the dark-clad police officer had come to my door telling me my husband of eight years had been killed in a car accident.

Bill and I hadn't been lovers in the end. Or even in love. Oddly, ours had been a pragmatic marriage because of the baby...the baby who died. Yet, we had made a compact and married before God. I had honored our agreement, much as I planned to honor my new one with this man by my side.

When the prayer ended, the minister motioned us to face each other and join both our hands. I gave my bouquet to Gail, my maid of honor. She hesitated as if to object, then took it. I was able to accept Alex's free hand. The grip of his fingers transmitted tingling warmth through my arms. Trite as it sounds, I felt my heart skip a beat.

What was this reaction? It had been a long time since I'd felt sexual attraction, and I certainly did not expect to feel ardor toward this man with whom I had signed a contract. What good would my feelings do? Although married, we had an arrangement. Ours would be a platonic relationship. Because his wife Allison had died so suddenly, I would be a mother to his infant daughter. He would pay my debts.

Why had I agreed to such a stark and precise agreement? It left no room for this unexpected play of emotion.

"I, Alexander, take you, Mary, to be my wife."

To be my wife.

My throat constricted. I had met Dr. Alexander

Dominican the night I lost my baby. The partner of my regular OB-GYN, Dr. Hilliard, Alex had been on call. Still regretting my teen years, I knew I had been such a fool to let myself get pregnant.

Straightening my shoulders at the thought, I caught the slight narrowing of Alex's eyes, and turned self-consciously from his scrutiny. What did he really think about me? Did he remember that scared eighteen-year-old-patient of eight years ago? I had changed. Did he know I'd changed? Did he care?

The minister nodded. Summoning all my willpower, I repeated in a hushed voice the same vows. My hands were damp when Alex released them to turn to his best man, Dr. Hilliard. At the same time, Gail handed me a wide gold band. Unable to meet Alex's gaze, I took his left hand and slid the band across his third finger.

A strange feeling of familiarity enveloped me. In a different time, I believed he would have bowed and kissed the back of my hand. Today, he held onto it and gently slipped the new wedding band into place on my finger. I glanced up to find his eyes appraising me. As I tightened my lips, my returning gaze did not falter. The weight of the ornate, gold ring nudged into my flesh and created a symbolic link between us.

"Bless, O Lord, the giving of these rings, that they who wear them may live in your peace and continue in your favor all the days of their lives."

Alex smiled a slow, half smile, as if he understood something I had failed to discern. The smile softened his stern features, bringing back my recollection of the gentle doctor who had once comforted and cared for me. I offered a smile in reply and was gratified to see his eyes lighten in response.

The minister joined our hands together again and wrapped his white stole around them. He cleared his throat and raised his voice to include all the guests in his pronouncement.

"Now that Alexander and Mary have given themselves to each other by solemn vows with the joining of hands and the giving and receiving of rings, I announce to you that they are husband and wife; in the name of the Father, and of the Son, and of the Holy Spirit. Those whom God has joined together, let no one put asunder."

A surprising disquiet pricked my scalp and traced down the back of my neck. What was wrong? I swallowed once, to ease the dryness in my mouth and then looked up from our joined hands. We were husband and wife. It seemed so appropriate, so right. As if it was meant to be. But how could it under the strained circumstances?

"Are you going to kiss the bride?" I heard amusement in the minister's voice.

Alex released my hands. I felt oddly bereft. He stared at me, his eyes shadowed by coal-colored lashes. I read the speculation in them. He lifted his hands, and I fixed my gaze upon them, charmed by the beauty of his tapered fingers. His hands lingered in the air briefly, and then Alex raised the thin veil from my face. My gaze now held spellbound by his, I watched as he gently elevated my chin with a fingertip and caressed my cheek with a thumb.

For an instant, my heart hung suspended in my chest, then dropped into a relentless beat. Why did I welcome the touch of his hand upon my skin?

He stood so very close. His warm breath touched my face. I saw the flecks of dark in the lighter gray of his eyes. My own eyes widened in dismay as Alex lowered his lips to mine, tenderly touching them with a kiss so poignant it pierced my soul.

The kiss startled us both. I could tell by the way he hesitated, seeming to gasp for breath. With his left hand, he caressed my face, connecting us to each other in an untold way. I found it hard to breathe. I found it hard to move. In the recesses of my mind, warning bells clamored.

I straightened my shoulders and shifted my chin away from his touch. We may be married, but his kiss was not appropriate for two people with a business arrangement. Awkwardly separating, we held each other's gazes an instant. I felt dazed, swaying from side to side. Alex set his jaw and glanced away.

"Congratulations." Reverend Watts pumped Alex's hand.

Gail gave me my bouquet and offered me a swift hug. Her face was strained, her lips pursed. "I hope you'll be happy, Mary."

"Thank you."

Holding on to Gail's hug longer than necessary, I then stepped back, embarrassed. I knew she was upset with me for marrying Alex. My friend had tried to talk me out of it, especially so soon after Bill's death. My reasons were wrong she told me. I was being purchased like a broodmare for the price of my late husband's gambling debt. A significant gambling debt, I tried to remind her. Bill had owed more than three hundred thousand dollars that became my debt after his death. I had no other way out. Gail and I had argued. It was no surprise we now had so little to say to each other. We treated each other uneasily.

Nearby, Dr. Hilliard congratulated Alex, slapping him on his back.

"How do you capture the pretty ones, my man?" Dr.

Hilliard asked. "How do you do it? You've got a beauty here for a wife. I ought to know…." He finished his sentence with a meaningful wink.

I thought his remark crude. He was my gynecologist, after all, and, of course, *knew* me in a medical sense. But I overlooked it and allowed him to congratulate me with what I thought was to be the obligatory kiss for the bride.

It was more like a lover's kiss. His tongue invaded my mouth. He held me tightly with too much familiarity.

Tasting bourbon, I abruptly ended the kiss, tossing my head as if to fling the flush of outrage from my heated face.

"Why, Dr. Hilliard," I snapped. "You certainly have a knack for exploratory surgery. Did they teach you that in medical school?"

He laughed. "Yes, Alex, I love a woman with spunk."

"Or is it just *my* women you love, John?" My husband's tone was slick ice.

I tried to assess the undercurrents swirling around me, only to find Alex's stony demeanor unreadable.

Thankfully, Reverend Watts interrupted our conversation. "Please step into my office to sign the marriage certificate." He stepped back to allow us to precede him out of the quiet sanctuary.

Alex took me possessively by the hand and tucked it under his arm. He kept hold of my fingers, his own hand warm and sure. I had no trouble keeping up with his deliberate pace. There was something strangely comfortable about the way our strides matched.

"He's been my doctor for eight years," I murmured, "but I never realized Dr. Hilliard could be so insufferable."

"You've only seen him on his best behavior at the office.

My esteemed partner usually doesn't come to work under the influence of Maker's Mark."

"He's not an alcoholic, is he?" I asked, thinking about my late husband.

Alex paused and looked down at me. "Let's just say he's walking a fine line where I'm concerned. I've been monitoring his behavior. Oddly, it has worsened in the months since Allison's death."

I gave Alex a slight smile, grateful for his explanation.

"They are waiting," he remarked. "Let's go in."

The minister's office was hot. Summer sunshine streamed through open drapes. We crowded inside while Reverend Watts went to a window air conditioner unit and turned it on. A blast of cool air erupted into the room. Returning to his desk, the minister shuffled papers for what seemed an eternity, finally producing a formal-looking document. When he nodded at us, Alex released me and stepped forward. Standing slightly away from him, I watched my new husband bend over the minister's desk and put his signature on the paper.

My situation seemed so unreal. Gail was angry with me. My trusted doctor had a drinking problem, and I was married…again…to a man who mystified but also intrigued me.

Suddenly, a high-pitched, ringing sound shrilled loudly in my ears, growing in intensity until it blocked out other sounds. Was something wrong with the air-conditioning unit? Alex turned toward me, offering me the pen. His mouth moved, but I couldn't hear him speak. The stuffy little office grew fuzzy. Sweat beaded on my upper lip. I felt weightless—as if I was floating.

Like Fourth of July fireworks, pulsating lights of

exploding colors shot before my eyes. I closed them. In the distance behind my eyes, I saw a young girl dressed in a strange yellow gown. The room vibrated....

Go to my website for more information about **Tangled Memories**.

THANK YOU!

For purchasing this book from
Saddle Horse Press, LLC